Goosebumps®

FRIGHT LIGHT™ EDITION

Look for more Goosebumps books
by R.L. Stine:

Goosebumps®

FRIGHT LIGHT™ EDITION

R.L. STINE

Three scary Goosebumps novels in one!

#9 Welcome to Camp Nightmare
#33 The Horror at Camp Jellyjam
#45 Ghost Camp

SCHOLASTIC INC.
New York

Pop-up light designed and produced by becker & mayer!

A PARACHUTE PRESS BOOK

ISBN 0-590-34119-7

12 11 10 9 8 7 6 5 4 3 2 1   7 8 9/9 0 1 2/0

Printed in China   10

First Scholastic printing, August 1997

CONTENTS

Welcome to Camp Nightmare

GOOSEBUMPS #9

1

I stared out the dusty window as the camp bus bounced over the narrow, winding road. I could see sloping red hills in the distance beneath a bright yellow sky.

Stumpy white trees lined the road like fence posts. We were way out in the wilderness. We hadn't passed a house or a farm for nearly an hour.

The bus seats were made of hard blue plastic. When the bus hit a bump, we all bounced up off our seats. Everyone laughed and shouted. The driver kept growling at us, yelling for us to pipe down.

There were twenty-two kids going to camp on the bus. I was sitting in the back row on the aisle, so I could count them all.

There were eighteen boys and only four girls. I guessed that the boys were all going to Camp Nightmoon, which is where I was going. The girls were going to a girls' camp nearby.

The girls sat together in the front rows and

talked quietly to each other. Every once in a while, they'd glance back quickly to check out the boys.

The boys were a lot louder than the girls, cracking jokes, laughing, making funny noises, shouting out dumb things. It was a long bus ride, but we were having a good time.

The boy next to me was named Mike. He had the window seat. Mike looked a little like a bulldog. He was kind of chubby, with a round face and pudgy arms and legs. He had short, spiky black hair, which he scratched a lot. He was wearing baggy brown shorts and a sleeveless green T-shirt.

We had been sitting together the whole trip, but Mike didn't say much. I figured he was shy, or maybe very nervous. He told me this was his first time at sleepaway camp.

It was my first time, too. And I have to admit that, as the bus took me farther and farther from my home, I was already starting to miss my mom and dad just a little.

I'm twelve, but I've never really stayed away from home before. Even though the long bus ride was fun, I had this sad kind of feeling. And I think Mike was feeling the same way.

He pressed his chubby face against the window glass and stared out at the red hills rolling by in the distance.

"Are you okay, Mike?" I asked.

"Yeah. Sure, Billy," he replied quickly without turning around.

I thought about my mom and dad. Back at the bus station, they had seemed so serious. I guess they were nervous, too, about me going off to camp for the first time.

"We'll write every day," Dad said.

"Do your best," Mom said, hugging me harder than usual.

What a weird thing to say. Why didn't she say, "Have a good time"? Why did she say, "Do your best"?

As you can tell, I'm a bit of a worrier.

The only other boys I'd met so far were the two in the seat in front of us. One was named Colin. He had long brown hair down to his collar, and he wore silver sunglasses so you couldn't see his eyes. He acted kind of tough, and he wore a red bandanna on his forehead. He kept tying and untying the bandanna.

Sitting next to him in the seat on the aisle was a big, loud kid named Jay. Jay talked a lot about sports and kept bragging about what a good athlete he was. He liked showing off his big, muscular arms, especially when one of the girls turned around to check us out.

Jay teased Colin a lot and kept wrestling with him, gripping Colin's head in a headlock and messing up Colin's bandanna. You know. Just kidding around.

Jay had wild, bushy red hair that looked as if it had never been brushed. He had big blue eyes. He never stopped grinning and horsing around. He spent the whole trip telling gross jokes and shouting things at the girls.

"Hey — what's your name?" Jay called to a blonde-haired girl who sat at the front by the window.

She ignored him for a long time. But the fourth time Jay called out the question, she turned around, her green eyes flashing. "Dawn," she replied. Then she pointed to the red-haired girl next to her. "And this is my friend Dori."

"Hey — that's amazing! My name is Dawn, too!" Jay joked.

A lot of the guys laughed, but Dawn didn't crack a smile. "Nice to meet you, Dawn," she called back to him. Then she turned back to the front.

The bus bounced over a hole in the road, and we all bounced with it.

"Hey, look, Billy," Mike said suddenly, pointing out the window.

Mike hadn't said anything for a long time. I leaned toward the window, trying to see what he was pointing at.

"I think I saw a prairie cat," he said, still staring hard.

"Huh? Really?" I saw a clump of low, white trees and a lot of jagged, red rocks. But I couldn't see any prairie cats.

"It went behind those rocks," Mike said, still pointing. Then he turned toward me. "Have you seen any towns or anything?"

I shook my head. "Just desert."

"But isn't the camp supposed to be near a town?" Mike looked worried.

"I don't think so," I told him. "My dad told me that Camp Nightmoon is past the desert, way out in the woods."

Mike thought about this for a while, frowning. "Well, what if we want to call home or something?" he asked.

"They probably have phones at the camp," I told him.

I glanced up in time to see Jay toss something up toward the girls at the front. It looked like a green ball. It hit Dawn on the back of the head and stuck in her blonde hair.

"Hey!" Dawn cried out angrily. She pulled the sticky, green ball from her hair. "What *is* this?" She turned to glare at Jay.

Jay giggled his high-pitched giggle. "I don't know. I found it stuck under the seat!" he called to her.

Dawn scowled at him and heaved the green ball back. It missed Jay and hit the rear window, where it stuck with a loud *plop*.

Everyone laughed. Dawn and her friend Dori made faces at Jay.

Colin fiddled with his red bandanna. Jay

slumped down low and raised his knees against the seat in front of him.

A few rows ahead of me, two grinning boys were singing a song we all knew, but with really gross words replacing the original words.

A few other kids began to sing along.

Suddenly, without warning, the bus squealed to a stop, the tires skidding loudly over the road.

We all cried out in surprise. I bounced off my seat, and my chest hit the seat in front of me.

"Ugh!" That hurt.

As I slid back in the seat, my heart still pounding, the bus driver stood up and turned to us, leaning heavily into the aisle.

"Ohh!" Several loud gasps filled the small bus as we saw the driver's face.

His head was enormous and pink, topped with a mop of wild, bright blue hair that stood straight up. He had long, pointed ears. His huge red eyeballs bulged out from their dark sockets, bouncing in front of his snoutlike nose. Sharp white fangs drooped from his gaping mouth. A green liquid oozed over his heavy black lips.

As we goggled in silent horror, the driver tilted back his monstrous head and uttered an animal roar.

2

The driver roared so loud, the bus windows rattled.

Several kids shrieked in fright.

Mike and I both ducked down low, hiding behind the seat in front of us.

"He's turned into a *monster*!" Mike whispered, his eyes wide with fear.

Then we heard laughter at the front of the bus.

I raised myself up in time to see the bus driver reach one hand up to his bright blue hair. He tugged — and his face slid right off!

"Ohhh!" Several kids shrieked in horror.

But we quickly realized that the face dangling from the driver's hand was a mask. He had been wearing a rubber monster mask.

His real face was perfectly normal, I saw with relief. He had pale skin, short, thinning black hair, and tiny blue eyes. He laughed, shaking his head, enjoying his joke.

"This fools 'em every time!" he declared, holding up the ugly mask.

A few kids laughed along with him. But most of us were too surprised and confused to think it was funny.

Suddenly, his expression changed. "Everybody out!" he ordered gruffly.

He pulled a lever and the door slid open with a *whoosh*.

"Where are we?" someone called out.

But the driver ignored the question. He tossed the mask onto the driver's seat. Then, lowering his head so he wouldn't bump the roof, he quickly made his way out the door.

I leaned across Mike and stared out the window, but I couldn't see much. Just mile after mile of flat, yellow ground, broken occasionally by clumps of red rock. It looked like a desert.

"Why are we getting out here?" Mike asked, turning to me. I could see he was really worried.

"Maybe this is the camp," I joked. Mike didn't think that was funny.

We were all confused as we pushed and shoved our way off the bus. Mike and I were the last ones off since we were sitting in the back.

As I stepped onto the hard ground, I shielded my eyes against the bright sunlight, high in the afternoon sky. We were in a flat, open area. The bus was parked beside a concrete platform, about the size of a tennis court.

"It must be some kind of bus station or something," I told Mike. "You know. A drop-off point."

He had his hands shoved into the pockets of his shorts. He kicked at the dirt, but didn't say anything.

On the other side of the platform, Jay was in a shoving match with a boy I hadn't met yet. Colin was leaning against the side of the bus, being cool. The four girls were standing in a circle near the front of the platform, talking quietly about something.

I watched the driver walk over to the side of the bus and pull open the luggage compartment. He began pulling out bags and camp trunks and carrying them to the concrete platform.

A couple of guys had sat down on the edge of the platform to watch the driver work. On the other side of the platform, Jay and some other guys were having a contest, tossing little red pebbles as far as they could.

Mike, his hands still buried in his pockets, stepped up behind the sweating bus driver. "Hey, where are we? Why are we stopping here?" Mike asked him nervously.

The driver slid a heavy black trunk from the back of the luggage compartment. He completely ignored Mike's questions. Mike asked them again. And again the driver pretended Mike wasn't there.

Mike made his way back to where I was standing, walking slowly, dragging his shoes across the hard ground. He looked really worried.

I was confused, but I wasn't worried. I mean, the bus driver was calmly going about his business, unloading the bus. He knew what he was doing.

"Why won't he answer me? Why won't he tell us anything?" Mike demanded.

I felt bad that Mike was so nervous. But I didn't want to hear any more of his questions. He was starting to make me nervous, too.

I wandered away from him, making my way along the side of the platform to where the four girls were standing. Across the platform, Jay and his buddies were still having their stone-throwing contest.

Dawn smiled at me as I came closer. Then she glanced quickly away. She's really pretty, I thought. Her blonde hair gleamed in the bright sunlight.

"Are you from Center City?" her friend Dori asked, squinting at me, her freckled face twisted against the sun.

"No," I told her. "I'm from Midlands. It's north of Center City. Near Outreach Bay."

"I *know* where Midlands is!" Dori snapped snottily. The other three girls laughed.

I could feel myself blushing.

"What's your name?" Dawn asked, staring at me with her green eyes.

"Billy," I told her.

"My bird's name is Billy!" she exclaimed, and the girls all laughed again.

"Where are you girls going?" I asked quickly, eager to change the subject. "I mean, what camp?"

"Camp Nightmoon. There's one for boys and one for girls," Dori answered. "This is an all-Camp Nightmoon bus."

"Is your camp near ours?" I asked. I didn't even know there was a Camp Nightmoon for girls.

Dori shrugged. "We don't know," Dawn replied. "This is our first year."

"All of us," Dori added.

"Me, too," I told them. "I wonder why we stopped here."

The girls all shrugged.

I saw that Mike was lingering behind me, looking even more scared. I turned and made my way back to him.

"Look. The driver is finished carrying out our stuff," he said, pointing.

I turned in time to see the driver slam the luggage compartment door shut.

"What's happening?" Mike cried. "Is someone picking us up here? Why did he unload all our stuff?"

"I'll go find out," I said quietly. I started to jog over to the driver. He was standing in front of the open bus door, mopping his perspiring forehead with the short sleeve of his tan driver's uniform.

He saw me coming — and quickly climbed into the bus. He slid into the driver's seat, pulling a green sun visor down over his forehead as I stepped up to the door.

"Is someone coming for us?" I called in to him.

To my surprise, he pulled the lever, and the bus door slammed shut in my face.

The engine started up with a roar and a burst of gray exhaust fumes.

"Hey — !" I screamed and pounded angrily on the glass door.

I had to leap back as the bus squealed away, its tires spinning noisily on the hard dirt. "Hey!" I shouted. "You don't have to run me over!"

I stared angrily as the bus bounced onto the road and roared away. Then I turned back to Mike. He was standing beside the four girls. They were all looking upset now.

"He — he left," Mike stammered as I approached them. "He just *left* us here in the middle of nowhere."

We gazed down the road at the bus until it disappeared over the darkening horizon. We all grew very quiet.

A few seconds later, we heard the frightening animal cries.

Very close. And getting closer.

3

"Wh-what's that?" Mike stammered.

We turned in the direction of the shrill cries.

They seemed to be coming from across the platform. At first, I thought that Jay and Colin and their friends were playing a joke on us, making the animal cries to frighten us.

But then I saw the scared, wide-eyed expressions on their faces. Jay, Colin, and the others had frozen in place. They weren't making the noises.

The cries grew louder. Closer.

Shrill warnings.

And, then, staring into the distance beyond the platform, I saw them. Small, dark creatures, keeping low, rolling rapidly along the flat ground, tossing their heads back and uttering excited shrieks as they came toward us.

"What are they?" Mike cried, moving close to me.

"Are they prairie wolves?" Dori asked in a trembling voice.

"I hope not!" one of the other girls called out.

We all climbed onto the concrete platform and were huddled behind our trunks and bags.

The animal cries grew louder as the creatures drew near. I could see dozens of them. They scurried toward us over the flat ground as if being blown by the wind.

"Help! Somebody *help* us!" I heard Mike scream.

Next to me, Jay still had two of the red rocks from his rock-throwing competition in his hand. "Pick up rocks!" he was shouting frantically. "Maybe we can scare them away!"

The creatures stopped a few yards from the concrete platform and raised themselves up menacingly on their hind feet.

Huddled between Mike and Jay, I could see them clearly now. They were wolves or wildcats of some sort. Standing upright, they were nearly three feet tall.

They had slender, almost scrawny bodies, covered with spotty red-brown fur. Their paws had long, silvery nails growing out of them. Their heads were nearly as slender as their bodies. Tiny red weasel eyes stared hungrily at us. Their long mouths snapped open and shut, revealing double rows of silvery, daggerlike teeth.

"No! No! Help!" Mike dropped to his knees. His

entire body convulsed in a shudder of terror.

Some of the kids were crying. Others gaped at the advancing creatures in stunned silence.

I was too scared to cry out or move or do *anything*.

I stared at the row of creatures, my heart thudding, my mouth as dry as cotton.

The creatures grew silent. Standing a few feet from the platform, they eyed us, snapping their jaws loudly, hungrily. White froth began to drip from their mouths.

"They — they're going to attack!" a boy yelled.

"They look hungry!" I heard one of the girls say.

The white froth poured thickly over their pointed teeth. They continued to snap their jaws. It sounded like a dozen steel traps being snapped shut.

Suddenly, one of them leapt onto the edge of the platform.

"No!" several kids cried out in unison.

We huddled closer together, trying to stay behind the pile of trunks and bags.

Another creature climbed onto the platform. Then three more.

I took a step back.

I saw Jay pull back his arm and heave a red rock at one of the frothing creatures. The rock hit the platform with a *crack* and bounced away.

The creatures were not frightened. They arched their backs, preparing to attack.

They began to make a high-pitched chattering sound.

And moved nearer. Nearer.

Jay threw another rock.

This one hit one of the advancing creatures on the side. It uttered a shrill *eek* of surprise. But it kept moving steadily forward, its red eyes trained on Jay, its jaws snapping hungrily.

"Go away!" Dori cried in a trembling voice. "Go home! Go away! Go *away*!"

But her shouts had no effect.

The creatures advanced.

"Run!" I urged "Run!"

"We can't outrun them!" someone shouted.

The shrill chittering grew louder. Deafening. Until it seemed as if we were surrounded by a wall of sound.

The ugly creatures lowered themselves to pounce.

"Run!" I repeated. "Come on — run!"

My legs wouldn't cooperate. Thev felt rubbery and weak.

Trying to back away from the attacking creatures, I toppled over backwards off the platform.

I saw flashing stars as the back of my head hit the hard ground.

They're going to get me, I realized.

I can't get away.

I heard the sirenlike attack cry.

I heard the scrape of the creatures' long toenails over the concrete platform.

I heard the screams and cries of the frightened campers.

Then, as I struggled frantically to pull myself up, I heard the deafening roar.

At first I thought it was an explosion.

I thought the platform had blown up.

But then I turned and saw the rifle.

Another explosion of gunfire. White smoke filled the air.

The creatures spun around and darted away, silent now, their scraggly fur scraping the ground as they kept low, their tails between their furry legs.

"Ha-ha! Look at 'em run!" The man kept the rifle poised on his shoulder as he watched the creatures retreat.

Behind him stood a long green bus.

I pulled myself up and brushed myself off.

Everyone was laughing now, jumping up and down joyfully, celebrating the narrow escape.

I was still too shaken up to celebrate.

"They're running like jackrabbits!" the man declared in a booming voice. He lowered the rifle.

It took me a while to realize he had come out of the camp bus to rescue us. We didn't hear or see the bus pull up because of the attack cries of the animals.

"Are you okay, Mike?" I asked, walking over to my frightened-looking new friend.

"I guess," he replied uncertainly. "I guess I'm okay now."

Dawn slapped me on the back, grinning. "We're okay!" she cried. "We're all okay!"

We gathered in front of the man with the rifle.

He was big and red-faced, mostly bald except for a fringe of curly yellow hair around his head. He had a blond mustache under an enormous beak of a nose, and tiny black bird eyes beneath bushy blond eyebrows.

"Hi, guys! I'm Uncle Al. I'm your friendly camp director. I hope you enjoyed that welcome to Camp Nightmoon!" he boomed in a deep voice.

I heard muttered replies.

He leaned the rifle against the bus and took a few steps toward us, studying our faces. He was wearing white shorts and a bright green camp T-shirt that stretched over his big belly. Two young guys, also in green and white, stepped out of the bus, serious expressions on their faces.

"Let's load up," Uncle Al instructed them in his deep voice.

He didn't apologize for being late.

He didn't explain about the weird animals. And he didn't ask if we were okay after that scare.

The two counselors began dragging the camp trunks and shoving them into the luggage compartment on the bus.

"Looks like a good group this year," Uncle Al shouted. "We'll drop you girls off first across the river. Then we'll get you boys settled in."

"What *were* those awful animals?" Dori called to Uncle Al.

He didn't seem to hear her.

We began climbing onto the bus. I looked for Mike and found him near the end of the line. His face was pale, and he still looked really shaken. "I — I was really scared," he admitted.

"But we're okay," I reassured him. "Now we can relax and have fun."

"I'm so hungry," Mike complained. "I haven't eaten all day."

One of the counselors overheard him. "You won't be hungry when you taste the camp food," he told Mike.

We piled into the bus. I sat next to Mike. I could hear the poor guy's stomach growling. I suddenly realized I was starving, too. And I was really eager to see what Camp Nightmoon looked like. I hoped it wouldn't be a long bus ride to get there.

"How far away is our camp?" I called to Uncle Al, who had slid into the driver's seat.

He didn't seem to hear me.

"Hey, Mike, we're on our way!" I said happily as the bus pulled onto the road.

Mike forced a smile. "I'm so glad to get *away* from there!"

To my surprise, the bus ride took less than five minutes.

We all muttered our shock at what a short trip it was. Why hadn't the first bus taken us all the way?

A big wooden sign proclaiming CAMP NIGHT-MOON came into view, and Uncle Al turned the bus onto a gravel road that led through a patch of short trees into the camp.

We followed the narrow, winding road across a small, brown river. Several small cabins came into view. "Girls' camp," Uncle Al announced. The bus stopped to let the four girls off. Dawn waved to me as she climbed down.

A few minutes later, we pulled into the boys' camp. Through the bus window I could see a row of small, white cabins. On top of a gently sloping hill stood a large, white-shingled building, probably a meeting lodge or mess hall.

At the edge of a field, three counselors, all dressed in white shorts and green T-shirts, were working to start a fire in a large stone barbecue pit.

"Hey, we're going to have a cookout!" I exclaimed to Mike. I was starting to feel really excited.

Mike smiled, too. He was practically drooling at the thought of food!

The bus came to an abrupt stop at the end of the row of small bunks. Uncle Al pulled himself up quickly from the driver's seat and turned to us. "Welcome to beautiful Camp Nightmoon!" he bellowed. "Step down and line up for your bunk assignments. Once you get unpacked and have dinner, I'll see you at the campfire."

We pushed our way noisily out of the bus. I saw Jay enthusiastically slapping another boy on the back. I think we were all feeling a lot better, forgetting about our close call.

I stepped down and took a deep breath. The cool air smelled really sweet and fresh. I saw a long row of short evergreen trees behind the white lodge on the hill.

As I took my place in line, I searched for the waterfront. I could hear the soft rush of the river behind a thick row of evergreens, but I couldn't see it.

Mike, Jay, Colin, and I were assigned to the

same bunk. It was Bunk 4. I thought the bunk should have a more interesting name. But it just had a number. Bunk 4.

It was really small, with a low ceiling and windows on two sides. It was just big enough for six campers. There were bunk beds against three walls and tall shelves on the fourth wall, with a little square of space in the middle.

There was no bathroom. I guessed it was in another building.

As the four of us entered the bunk, we saw that one of the beds had already been claimed. It had been carefully made, the green blanket tucked in neatly, some sports magazines and a tape player resting on top.

"That must belong to our counselor," Jay said, inspecting the tape player.

"Hope we don't have to wear those ugly green T-shirts," Colin said, grinning. He was still wearing his silver sunglasses, even though the sun was nearly down and it was just about as dark as night in the cabin.

Jay claimed a top bunk, and Colin took the bed beneath his.

"Can I have a lower one?" Mike asked me. "I roll around a lot at night. I'm afraid I might fall out of a top one."

"Yeah. Sure. No problem," I replied. I wanted the top bunk anyway. It would be a lot more fun.

"Hope you guys don't snore," Colin said.

"We're not going to sleep in here anyway," Jay said. "We're going to party all night!" He playfully slapped Mike on the back, so hard that Mike went sprawling into the dresser.

"Hey!" Mike whined. "That hurt!"

"Sorry. Guess I don't know my own strength," Jay replied, grinning at Colin.

The cabin door opened, and a red-headed guy with dark freckles all over his face walked in, carrying a big gray plastic bag. He was tall and very skinny and was wearing white shorts and a green camp T-shirt.

"Hey, guys," he said, and dropped the large bag on the cabin floor with a groan. He checked us out, then pointed to the bag. "There's your bed stuff," he said. "Make your beds. Try to make them as neat as mine." He pointed to the bunk against the window with the tape player on it.

"Are you our counselor?" I asked.

He nodded. "Yeah. I'm the lucky one." He turned and started to walk out.

"What's your name?" Jay called after him.

"Larry," he said, pushing open the cabin door. "Your trunks will be here in a few minutes," he told us. "You can fight it out over drawer space. Two of the drawers are stuck shut."

He started out the door, then turned back to us. "Keep away from my stuff." The door slammed hard behind him.

Peering out the window, I watched him lope

away, taking long, fast strides, bobbing his head as he walked.

"Great guy," Colin muttered sarcastically.

"Real friendly," Jay added, shaking his head.

Then we dived into the plastic bag and pulled out sheets and wool blankets. Jay and Colin got into a wrestling match over a blanket they claimed was softer than the others.

I tossed a sheet onto my mattress and started to climb up to tuck it in.

I was halfway up the ladder when I heard Mike scream.

5

Mike was right beneath me, making his bed. He screamed so loud, I cried out and nearly fell off the ladder.

I leapt off the ladder, my heart pounding, and stepped beside him.

Staring straight ahead, his mouth wide open in horror, Mike backed away from his bed.

"Mike — what's wrong?" I asked. "What *is* it?"

"S-snakes!" Mike stammered, staring straight ahead at his unmade bed as he backed away.

"Huh?" I followed his gaze. It was too dark to see anything.

Colin laughed. "Not *that* old joke!" he cried.

"Larry put rubber snakes in your bed," Jay said, grinning as he stepped up beside us.

"They're not rubber! They're real!" Mike insisted, his voice trembling.

Jay laughed and shook his head. "I can't believe you fell for that old gag." He took a few steps toward the bed — then stopped. "Hey — !"

I moved close, and the two snakes came into focus. Raising themselves from the shadows, they arched their slender heads, pulling back as if preparing to attack.

"They're real!" Jay cried, turning back to Colin. "Two of them!"

"Probably not poisonous," Colin said, venturing closer.

The two let out angry hisses, raising themselves high off the bed. They were very long and skinny. Their heads were wider than their bodies. Their tongues flicked from side to side as they arched themselves menacingly.

"I'm scared of snakes," Mike uttered in a soft voice.

"They're probably scared of you!" Jay joked, slapping Mike on the back.

Mike winced. He was in no mood for Jay's horseplay. "We've got to get Larry or somebody," Mike said.

"No way!" Jay insisted. "You can handle 'em, Mike. There's only two of them!"

Jay gave Mike a playful shove toward the bed. He only meant to give him a scare.

But Mike stumbled — and fell onto the bed.

The snakes darted in unison.

I saw one of them clamp its teeth into Mike's hand.

Mike raised himself to his feet. He didn't react

at first. Then he uttered a high-pitched shriek.

Two drops of blood appeared on the back of his right hand. He stared down at them, then grabbed the hand.

"It *bit* me!" he shrieked.

"Oh, no!" I cried.

"Did it puncture the skin?" Colin asked. "Is it bleeding?"

Jay rushed forward and grabbed Mike's shoulder. "Hey, man — I'm really sorry," he said. "I didn't mean to — "

Mike groaned in pain. "It — really hurts," he whispered. He was breathing really hard, his chest heaving, making weird noises as he breathed.

The snakes, coiled in the middle of his lower bunk, began to hiss again.

"You'd better hurry to the nurse," Jay said, his hand still on Mike's shoulder. "I'll come with you."

"N-no," Mike stammered. His face was as pale as a ghost. He held his hand tightly. "I'll go find her!" He burst out of the cabin, running at full speed. The door slammed behind him.

"Hey — I didn't mean to push him, you know," Jay explained to us. I could see he was really upset. "I was just joking, just trying to scare him a little. I didn't mean for him to fall or anything. . . ." His voice trailed off.

31

"What are we going to do about *them*?" I asked, pointing at the two coiled snakes.

"I'll get Larry," Colin offered. He started toward the door.

"No, wait." I called him back. "Look. They're sitting on Mike's sheet, right?"

Jay and Colin followed my gaze to the bed. The snakes arched themselves high, preparing to bite again.

"So?" Jay asked, scratching his disheveled hair.

"So we can wrap them up in the sheet and carry them outside," I said.

Jay stared at me. "Wish I'd thought of that. Let's do it, man!"

"You'll get bit," Colin warned.

I stared at the snakes. They seemed to be studying me, too. "They can't bite us through the sheet," I said.

"They can try!" Colin exclaimed, hanging back.

"If we're fast enough," I said, taking a cautious step toward the bed, "we can wrap them up before they know what's happening."

The snakes hissed out a warning, drawing themselves higher.

"How did they get in here, anyway?" Colin asked.

"Maybe the camp is *crawling* with snakes," Jay said, grinning. "Maybe you've got some in *your* bed, too, Colin!" He laughed.

"Let's get serious here," I said sternly, my eyes locked on the coiled snakes. "Are we going to try this or not?"

"Yeah. Let's do it," Jay answered. "I mean, I owe it to Mike."

Colin remained silent.

"I'll bet I could grab one by the tail and swing him out through the window," Jay said. "You could grab the tail end of the other one and — "

"Let's try my plan first," I suggested quietly.

We crept over to the snakes, sneaking up on them. It was kind of silly since they were staring right at us.

I pointed to one end of the sheet, which was folded up onto the bed. "Grab it there," I instructed Jay. "Then pull it up."

He hesitated. "What if I miss? Or you miss?"

"Then we're in trouble," I replied grimly. My eyes on the snakes, I reached my hand forward to the other corner of the sheet. "Ready? On three," I whispered.

My heart was in my mouth. I could barely choke out, "One, two, three."

At the count of three, we both grabbed for the ends of the sheet.

"Pull!" I cried in a shrill voice I couldn't believe was coming from me.

We pulled up the sheet and brought the ends together, making a bundle.

At the bottom of the bundle, the snakes wriggled frantically. I heard their jaws snap. They wriggled so hard, the bottom of the bundle swung back and forth.

"They don't like this," Jay said as we hurried to the door, carrying our wriggling, swaying bundle between us, trying to keep our bodies as far away from it as possible.

I pushed open the door with my shoulder, and we ran out onto the grass.

"Now what?" Jay asked.

"Keep going," I replied. I could see one of the snakes poking its head out. "Hurry!"

We ran past the cabins toward a small clump of shrubs. Beyond the shrubs stood a patch of low trees. When we reached the trees, we swung the bundle back, then heaved the whole sheet into the trees.

It opened as it fell to the ground. The two snakes slithered out instantly and pulled themselves to shelter under the trees.

Jay and I let out loud sighs of relief. We stood there for a moment, hunched over, hands on our knees, trying to catch our breath.

Crouching down, I looked for the snakes. But they had slithered deep into the safety of the evergreens.

I stood up. "I guess we should take back Mike's sheet," I said.

"He probably won't want to sleep on it," Jay

said. But he reached down and pulled it up from the grass. He balled it up and tossed it to me. "It's probably dripping with snake venom," he said, making a disgusted face.

When we got back to the cabin, Colin had made his bed and was busily unpacking the contents of his trunk, shoving everything into the top dresser drawer. He turned as we entered. "How'd it go?" he asked casually.

"Horrible," Jay replied quickly, his expression grim. "We both got bit. Twice."

"You're a terrible liar!" Colin told him, laughing. "You shouldn't even try."

Jay laughed, too.

Colin turned to me. "You're a hero," he said.

"Thanks for all your help," Jay told him sarcastically.

Colin started to reply. But the cabin door opened, and Larry poked his freckled face in. "How's it going?" he asked. "You're not finished yet?"

"We had a little problem," Jay told him.

"Where's the fourth guy? The chubby one?" Larry asked, lowering his head so he wouldn't bump it on the doorframe as he stepped inside.

"Mike got bit. By a snake," I told him.

"There were two snakes in his bed," Jay added.

Larry's expression didn't change. He didn't seem at all surprised. "So where did Mike go?" he asked casually, swatting a mosquito on his arm.

"His hand was bleeding. He went to the nurse to get it taken care of," I told him.

"Huh?" Larry's mouth dropped open.

"He went to find the nurse," I repeated.

Larry tossed back his head and started to laugh. "Nurse?" he cried, laughing hard. *"What* nurse?!"

6

The door opened and Mike returned, still holding his wounded hand. His face was pale, his expression frightened. "They said there was no nurse," he told me.

Then he saw Larry perched on top of his bunk. "Larry — my hand," Mike said. He held the hand up so the counselor could see it. It was stained with bright red blood.

Larry lowered himself to the floor. "I think I have some bandages," he told Mike. He pulled out a slender black case from beneath his bunk and began to search through it.

Mike stood beside him, holding up his hand. Drops of blood splashed on the cabin floor. "They said the camp doesn't have a nurse," Mike repeated.

Larry shook his head. "If you get hurt in *this* camp," he told Mike seriously, "you're on your own."

"I think my hand is swelling a little," Mike said.

Larry handed him a roll of bandages. "The washroom is at the end of this row of cabins," he told Mike, closing the case and shoving it back under the bed. "Go wash the hand and bandage it. Hurry. It's almost dinnertime."

Holding the bandages tightly in his good hand, Mike hurried off to follow Larry's instructions.

"By the way, how'd you guys get the snakes out of here?" Larry asked, glancing around the cabin.

"We carried them out in Mike's sheet," Jay told him. He pointed at me. "It was Billy's idea."

Larry stared hard at me. "Hey, I'm impressed, Billy," he said. "That was pretty brave, man."

"Maybe I inherited something from my parents," I told him. "They're scientists. Explorers, kind of. They go off for months at a time, exploring the wildest places."

"Well, Camp Nightmoon is pretty wild," Larry said. "And you guys had better be careful. I'm warning you." His expression turned serious. "There's no nurse at Camp Nightmoon. Uncle Al doesn't believe in coddling you guys."

The hot dogs were all charred black, but we were so hungry, we didn't care. I shoved three of them down in less than five minutes. I don't think I'd ever been so hungry in all my life.

The campfire was in a flat clearing surrounded by a circle of round, white stones. Behind us, the large, white-shingled lodge loomed over the sloping hill. Ahead of us a thick line of evergreen trees formed a fence that hid the river from view.

Through a small gap in the trees, I could see a flickering campfire in the distance on the other side of the river. I wondered if that was the campfire of the girls' camp.

I thought about Dawn and Dori. I wondered if the two camps ever got together, if I'd ever see them again.

Dinner around the big campfire seemed to put everyone in a good mood. Jay was the only one sitting near me who complained about the hot dogs being burned. But I think he put away four or five of them anyway!

Mike had trouble eating because of his bandaged hand. When he dropped his first hot dog, I thought he was going to burst into tears. By the end of dinner, he was in a much better mood. His wounded hand had swelled up just a little. But he said it didn't hurt as much as before.

The counselors were easy to spot. They all wore identical white shorts and green T-shirts. There were eight or ten of them, all young guys probably sixteen or seventeen. They ate together quietly, away from us campers. I kept looking at Larry, but he never once turned around to look at any of us.

I was thinking about Larry, trying to figure out if he was shy or if he just didn't like us campers very much. Suddenly, Uncle Al climbed to his feet and motioned with both hands for us all to be quiet.

"I want to welcome you boys to Camp Night-moon," he began. "I hope you're all unpacked and comfortable in your bunks. I know that most of you are first-time campers."

He was speaking quickly, without any pauses between sentences, as if he was running through this for the thousandth time and wanted to get it over with.

"I'd like to tell you some of our basic rules," he continued. "First, lights out is at nine sharp."

A lot of guys groaned.

"You might think you can ignore this rule," Uncle Al continued, paying no attention to their reaction. "You might think you can sneak out of your cabins to meet or take a walk by the river. But I'm warning you now that we don't allow it, and we have very good ways of making sure this rule is obeyed."

He paused to clear his throat.

Some boys were giggling about something. Across from me, Jay burped loudly, which caused more giggles.

Uncle Al didn't seem to hear any of this. "On the other side of the river is the girls' camp," he continued loudly, motioning to the trees. "You might be able to see their campfire. Well, I want to make it clear that swimming or rowing over to the girls' camp is strictly forbidden."

Several boys groaned loudly. This made everyone laugh. Even some of the counselors laughed. Uncle Al remained grim-faced.

"The woods around Camp Nightmoon are filled with grizzlies and tree bears," Uncle Al continued. "They come to the river to bathe and to drink. And they're usually hungry."

This caused another big reaction from all of us sitting around the fading campfire. Someone made a loud growling sound. Another kid screamed. Then everyone laughed.

"You won't be laughing if a bear claws your head off," Uncle Al said sternly.

He turned to the group of counselors outside our circle. "Larry, Kurt, come over here," he ordered.

The two counselors climbed obediently to their feet and made their way to the center of the circle beside Uncle Al.

"I want you two to demonstrate to the new campers the procedure to follow when — er, I mean, *if* you are attacked by a grizzly bear."

Immediately, the two counselors dropped to the ground on their stomachs. They lay flat and covered the backs of their heads with their hands.

"That's right. I hope you're all paying close attention," the camp director thundered at us.

"Cover your neck and head. Try your best not to move." He motioned to the two counselors. "Thanks, guys. You can get up."

"Have there ever been any bear attacks here?" I called out, cupping my hands so Uncle Al could hear me.

He turned in my direction. "Two last summer," he replied.

Several boys gasped.

"It wasn't pretty," Uncle Al continued. "It's hard to remain still when a huge bear is pawing you and drooling all over you. But if you move . . ." His voice trailed off, leaving the rest to our imaginations, I guess.

I felt a cold shiver run down my back. I didn't want to think about bears and bear attacks.

What kind of camp did Mom and Dad send me to? I found myself wondering. I couldn't wait to call them and tell them about all that had happened already.

Uncle Al waited for everyone to get silent, then pointed off to the side. "Do you see that cabin over there?" he asked.

In the dim evening light, I could make out a cabin standing halfway up the hill toward the lodge. It appeared a little larger than the other cabins. It seemed to be built on a slant, sort of tipping on its side, as if the wind had tried to blow it over.

"I want you to make sure you see that cabin,"

Uncle Al warned, his voice thundering out above the crackling of the purple fire. "That is known as the Forbidden Bunk. We don't talk about that bunk — and we don't go near it."

I felt another cold shiver as I stared through the gray evening light at the shadowy, tilted cabin. I felt a sharp sting on the back of my neck and slapped a mosquito, too late to keep it from biting me.

"I'm going to repeat what I just said," Uncle Al shouted, still pointing to the dark cabin on the hill. "That is known as the Forbidden Bunk. It has been closed and boarded up for many years. No one is to go near that cabin. *No one.*"

This started everyone talking and laughing. Nervous laughter, I think.

"Why is the Forbidden Bunk forbidden?" someone called out.

"We never talk about it," Uncle Al replied sharply.

Jay leaned over and whispered in my ear, "Let's go check it out."

I laughed. Then I turned back to Jay uncertainly. "You're kidding — right?"

He grinned in reply and didn't say anything.

I turned back toward the fire. Uncle Al was wishing us all a good stay and saying how much he was looking forward to camp this year. "And one more rule — " he called out. "You must write to your parents every day. Every day! We want them to know what a great time you're having at Camp Nightmoon."

I saw Mike holding his wounded hand gingerly. "It's starting to throb," he told me, sounding very frightened.

"Maybe Larry has something to put on it," I said. "Let's go ask him."

Uncle Al dismissed us. We all climbed to our feet, stretching and yawning, and started to make our way in small groups back to the bunks.

Mike and I lingered behind, hoping to talk to Larry. We saw him talking to the other counselors. He was at least a head taller than all of them.

"Hey, Larry — " Mike called.

But by the time we pushed our way through the groups of kids heading the other way, Larry had disappeared.

"Maybe he's going to our bunk to make sure we obey lights out," I suggested.

"Let's go see," Mike replied anxiously.

We walked quickly past the dying campfire. It had stopped crackling but still glowed a deep purple-red. Then we headed along the curve of the hill toward Bunk 4.

"My hand really hurts," Mike groaned, holding it tenderly in front of him. "I'm not just complaining. It's throbbing and it's swelling up. And I'm starting to have chills."

"Larry will know what to do," I replied, trying to sound reassuring.

"I hope so," Mike said shakily.

We both stopped when we heard the howls.

Hideous howls. Like an animal in pain. But too human to be from an animal.

Long, shrill howls that cut through the air and echoed down the hill.

Mike uttered a quiet gasp. He turned to me. Even in the darkness, I could see the fright on his face.

"Those cries," he whispered. "They're coming from . . . the Forbidden Bunk!"

7

A few minutes later, Mike and I trudged into the cabin. Jay and Colin were sitting tensely on their beds. "Where's Larry?" Mike asked, fear creeping into his voice.

"Not here," Colin replied.

"Where *is* he?" Mike demanded shrilly. "I've got to find him. My *hand*!"

"He should be here soon," Jay offered.

I could still hear the strange howls through the open window. "Do you hear that?" I asked, walking over to the window and listening hard.

"Probably a prairie cat," Colin said.

"Prairie cats don't howl," Mike told him. "Prairie cats screech, but they don't howl."

"How do you know?" Colin asked, walking over to Larry's bunk and sitting down on the bottom bed.

"We studied them in school," Mike replied.

Another howl made us all stop and listen.

"It sounds like a man," Jay offered, his eyes

lighting up excitedly. "A man who's been locked up in the Forbidden Bunk for years and years."

Mike swallowed hard. "Do you really think so?"

Jay and Colin laughed.

"What should I do about my hand?" Mike asked, holding it up. It was definitely swollen.

"Go wash it again," I told him. "And put a fresh bandage on it." I peered out the window into the darkness. "Maybe Larry will show up soon. He probably knows where to get something to put on it."

"I can't believe there's no nurse," Mike whined. "Why would my parents send me to a camp where there's no nurse or infirmary or anything?"

"Uncle Al doesn't like to coddle us," Colin said, repeating Larry's words.

Jay stood up and broke into an imitation of Uncle Al. "Stay away from the Forbidden Bunk!" he cried in a booming deep voice. He sounded a lot like him. "We don't talk about it and we don't ever go near it!"

We all laughed at Jay's impression. Even Mike.

"We should go there tonight!" Colin said enthusiastically. "We should check it out immediately!"

We heard another long, sorrowful howl roll down the hill from the direction of the Forbidden Bunk.

"I — I don't think we should," Mike said softly, examining his hand. He started to the door. "I'm going to go wash this." The door slammed behind him.

"He's scared," Jay scoffed.

"I'm a little scared, too," I admitted. "I mean, those awful howls . . ."

Jay and Colin both laughed. "Every camp has something like the Forbidden Bunk. The camp director makes it up," Colin said.

"Yeah," Jay agreed. "Camp directors love scaring kids. It's the only fun they have."

He puffed out his chest and imitated Uncle Al again. "Don't go out after lights out or you'll never be seen again!" he thundered, then burst out laughing.

"There's nothing in that Forbidden Bunk," Colin said, shaking his head. "It's probably completely empty. It's all just a joke. You know. Like camp ghost stories. Every camp has its own ghost story."

"How do you know?" I asked, dropping down onto Mike's bed. "Have you been to camp before?"

"No," Colin replied. "But I have friends who told me about *their* camp." He reached up and pulled off his silver sunglasses for the first time. He had bright sky-blue eyes, like big blue marbles.

We suddenly heard the sound of a bugle, repeating a slow, sad-sounding tune.

"That must be the signal for lights out," I said, yawning. I started to pull off my shoes. I was too tired to change or wash up. I planned to sleep in my clothes.

"Let's sneak out and explore the Forbidden Bunk," Jay urged. "Come on. We can be the first ones to do it!"

I yawned again. "I'm really too tired," I told them.

"Me, too," Colin said. He turned to Jay. "How about tomorrow night?"

Jay's face fell in disappointment.

"Tomorrow," Colin insisted, kicking his shoes into the corner and starting to pull off his socks.

"I wouldn't do it if I were you!"

The voice startled all three of us. We turned to the window where Larry's head suddenly appeared from out of the darkness. He grinned in at us. "I'd listen to Uncle Al if I were you," he said.

How long had he been out there listening to us? I wondered. Was he deliberately *spying* on us?

The door opened. Larry lowered his head as he loped in. His grin had faded. "Uncle Al wasn't kidding around," he said seriously.

"Yeah. Sure," Colin replied sarcastically. He climbed up to his bed and slid beneath the wool blanket.

"I guess the camp ghost will get us if we go out after lights out," Jay joked, tossing a towel across the room.

"No. No ghost," Larry said softly. "But Sabre

will." He pulled out his drawer and began searching for something inside it.

"Huh? Who's Sabre?" I asked, suddenly wide awake.

"Sabre is an *it*," Larry answered mysteriously.

"Sabre is a red-eyed monster who eats a camper every night," Colin sneered. He stared down at me. "There *is* no Sabre. Larry's just giving us another phony camp story."

Larry stopped searching his drawer and gazed up at Colin. "No, I'm not," he insisted in a low voice. "I'm trying to save you guys some trouble. I'm not trying to scare you."

"Then what is Sabre?" I asked impatiently.

Larry pulled a sweater from the drawer, then pushed the drawer shut. "You don't want to find out," he replied.

"Come on. Tell us what it is," I begged.

"He isn't going to," Colin said.

"I'll tell you guys only one thing. Sabre will rip your heart out," Larry said flatly.

Jay snickered. "Yeah. Sure."

"I'm serious!" Larry snapped. "I'm not kidding, you guys!" He pulled the sweater over his head. "You don't believe me? Go out one night. Go out and meet Sabre." He struggled to get his arm into the sweater sleeve. "But before you do," he warned, "leave me a note with your address so I'll know where to send your stuff."

8

We had fun the next morning.

We all woke up really early. The sun was just rising over the horizon to the south, and the air was still cool and damp. I could hear birds chirping.

The sound reminded me of home. As I lowered myself to the floor and stretched, I thought of my mom and dad and wished I could call them and tell them about the camp. But it was only the second day. I'd be too embarrassed to call them on the second day.

I was definitely homesick. But luckily there wasn't any time to feel sad. After we pulled on fresh clothes, we hurried up to the lodge on the hill, which served as a meeting hall, theater, and mess hall.

Long tables and benches were set up in straight rows in the center of the enormous room. The floorboards and walls were all dark redwood. Redwood ceiling beams crisscrossed high above our heads. There were no windows, so it felt as if we were in an enormous, dark cave.

The clatter of dishes and cups and silverware was deafening. Our shouts and laughter rang off the high ceiling, echoed off the hardwood walls. Mike shouted something to me from across the table, but I couldn't hear him because of the racket.

Some guys complained about the food, but I thought it was okay. We had scrambled egg squares, bacon strips, fried potatoes, and toast, with tall cups of juice. I never eat a breakfast that big at home. But I found that I was really starved, and I gobbled it up.

After breakfast we lined up outside the lodge to form different activity groups. The sun had climbed high in the sky. It was going to be really hot. Our excited voices echoed off the sloping hill. We were all laughing and talking, feeling good.

Larry and two other counselors, clipboards in hand, stood in front of us, shielding their eyes from the bright sun as they divided us into groups. The first group of about ten boys headed off to the river for a morning swim.

Some people have all the luck, I thought. I was eager to get to the waterfront and see what the river was like.

As I waited for my name to be called, I spotted a pay phone on the wall of the lodge. My parents flashed into my mind again. Maybe I *will* call them later, I decided. I was so eager to describe the camp to them and tell them about my new friends.

"Okay, guys. Follow me to the ball field," Larry instructed us. "We're going to play our first game of scratchball."

About twelve of us, including everyone from my bunk, followed Larry down the hill toward the flat grassy area that formed the playing field.

I jogged to catch up to Larry, who always seemed to walk at top speed, stretching out his long legs as if he were in a terrible hurry. "Are we going to swim after this?" I asked.

Without slowing his pace, he glanced at his clipboard. "Yeah. I guess," he replied. "You guys'll need a swim. We're going to work up a sweat."

"You ever play scratchball before?" Jay asked me as we hurried to keep up with Larry.

"Yeah. Sure," I replied. "We play it a lot in school."

Larry stopped at the far corner of the wide, green field, where the bases and batter's square had already been set up. He made us line up and divided us into two teams.

Scratchball is an easy game to learn. The batter throws the ball in the air as high and as far as he can. Then he has to run the bases before someone on the other team catches the ball, tags him with it, or throws him out.

Larry started calling out names, dividing us into teams. But when he called out Mike's name,

Mike stepped up to Larry, holding his bandaged hand tenderly. "I — I don't think I can play, Larry," Mike stammered.

"Come on, Mike. Don't whine," Larry snapped.

"But it really hurts," Mike insisted. "It's throbbing like crazy, Larry. The pain is shooting all the way up and down my side. And, look" — he raised the hand to Larry's face — "It's all swelled up!"

Larry pushed the arm away gently with his clipboard. "Go sit in the shade," he told Mike.

"Shouldn't I get some medicine or something to put on it?" Mike asked shrilly. I could see the poor guy was really in bad shape.

"Just sit over there by that tree," Larry ordered, pointing to a clump of short, leafy trees at the edge of the field. "We'll talk about it later."

Larry turned away from Mike and blew a whistle to start the game. "I'll take Mike's place on the Blue team," he announced, jogging onto the field.

I forgot about Mike as soon as the game got underway. We were having a lot of fun. Most of the guys were pretty good scratchball players, and we played much faster than my friends do back home at the playground.

My first time up at the batter's square, I heaved the ball really high. But it dropped right into a fielder's hands, and I was out. My second time up, I made it to three bases before I was tagged out.

Larry was a great player. When he came up to the batter's square, he tossed the ball harder than I ever saw anyone toss it. It sailed over the fielders' heads and, as they chased after it, Larry rounded all the bases, his long legs stretching out gracefully as he ran.

By the fourth inning, our team, the Blue team, was ahead twelve to six. We had all played hard and were really hot and sweaty. I was looking forward to that swim at the waterfront.

Colin was on the Red team. I noticed that he was the only player who wasn't enjoying the game. He had been tagged out twice, and he'd missed an easy catch in the field.

I realized that Colin wasn't very athletic. He had long, skinny arms without any muscles, and he also ran awkwardly.

In the third inning Colin got into an argument with a player on my team about whether a toss had been foul or not. A few minutes later, Colin argued angrily with Larry about a ball that he claimed should have been out.

He and Larry shouted at each other for a few minutes. It was no big deal, a typical sports argument. Larry finally ordered Colin to shut up and get back to the outfield. Colin grudgingly obeyed, and the game continued.

I didn't think about it again. I mean, that kind of arguing happens all the time in ball games. And there are guys who enjoy the arguments as much as the game.

But then, in the next inning, something strange happened that gave me a really bad feeling and made me stop and wonder just what was going on.

Colin's team came to bat. Colin stepped up to the batter's square and prepared to toss the ball.

Larry was playing the outfield. I was standing nearby, also in the field.

Colin tossed the ball high, but not very far.

Larry and I both came running in to get it.

Larry got there first. He picked up the small, hard ball on the first bounce, drew back his arm — and then I saw his expression change.

I saw his features tighten in anger. I saw his eyes narrow, his copper-colored eyebrows lower in concentration.

With a loud grunt of effort, Larry heaved the ball as hard as he could.

It struck Colin in the back of the head, making a loud *crack* sound as it hit.

Colin's silver sunglasses went flying in the air.

Colin stopped short and uttered a short, high-pitched cry. His arms flew up as if he'd been shot. Then his knees buckled.

He collapsed in a heap, facedown on the grass. He didn't move.

The ball rolled away over the grass.

I cried out in shock.

Then I saw Larry's expression change again. His eyes opened wide in disbelief. His mouth dropped open in horror.

"No!" he cried. "It slipped! I didn't mean to throw it at him!"

I knew Larry was lying. I had seen the anger on his face before he threw the ball.

I sank down to my knees on the ground as Larry went running toward Colin. I felt dizzy and upset and confused. I had this sick feeling in my stomach.

"The ball slipped!" Larry was yelling. "It just slipped."

Liar, I thought. Liar. Liar. Liar.

I forced myself up on my feet and hurried to join the circle of guys around Colin. When I got there, Larry was kneeling over Colin, raising Colin's head off the ground gently with both hands.

Colin's eyes were open wide. He stared up at Larry groggily, and uttered low moans.

"Give him room," Larry was shouting. "Give him room." He gazed down at Colin. "The ball slipped. I'm real sorry. The ball slipped."

Colin moaned. His eyes rolled around in his head. Larry pulled off Colin's red bandanna and mopped Colin's forehead with it.

Colin moaned again. His eyes closed.

"Help me carry him to the lodge," Larry instructed two guys from the Red team. "The rest of you guys get changed for your swim. The waterfront counselor will be waiting for you."

I watched as Larry and the two guys hoisted Colin up and started to carry him toward the lodge. Larry gripped him under the shoulders. The two boys awkwardly took hold of his legs.

The sick feeling in my stomach hadn't gone away. I kept picturing the intense expression of anger on Larry's face as he heaved the ball at the back of Colin's head.

I knew it had been deliberate.

I started to follow them. I don't know why. I guess I was so upset, I wasn't thinking clearly.

They were nearly to the bottom of the hill when I saw Mike catch up to them. He ran alongside Larry, holding his swollen hand.

"Can I come, too?" Mike pleaded. "Someone has to look at my hand. It's really bad, Larry. Please — can I come, too?"

"Yeah. You'd better," I heard Larry reply curtly.

Good, I thought. Finally someone was going to pay some attention to Mike's snakebite wound.

Ignoring the sweat pouring down my forehead, I watched them make their way up the hill to the lodge.

This shouldn't have happened, I thought, suddenly feeling a chill despite the hot sun.

Something is wrong. Something is terribly wrong here.

How was I to know that the horrors were just beginning?

9

Later that afternoon, Jay and I were writing our letters to our parents. I was feeling pretty upset about things. I kept seeing the angry expression on Larry's face as he heaved the ball at the back of Colin's head.

I wrote about it in my letter, and I also told my mom and dad about how there was no nurse here, and about the Forbidden Bunk.

Jay stopped writing and looked up at me from his bunk. He was really sunburned. His cheeks and forehead were bright red.

He scratched his red hair. "We're dropping like flies," he said, gesturing around the nearly empty cabin.

"Yeah," I agreed wistfully. "I hope Colin and Mike are okay." And then I blurted out, "Larry deliberately hit Colin."

"Huh?" Jay stopped scratching his hair and lowered his hand to the bunk. "He *what*?"

"He deliberately threw at Colin's head. I *saw*

him," I said, my voice shaky. I wasn't going to tell anyone, but now I was glad I did. It made me feel a little bit better to get it out.

But then I saw that Jay didn't believe me. "That's impossible," he said quietly. "Larry's our counselor. His hand slipped. That's all."

I started to argue when the cabin door opened and Colin entered, with Larry at his side.

"Colin! How *are* you?" I cried. Jay and I both jumped up.

"Not bad," Colin replied. He forced a thin smile. I couldn't see his eyes. They were hidden once again behind his silver sunglasses.

"He's still a little wobbly, but he's okay," Larry said cheerfully, holding Colin's arm.

"I'm sort of seeing double," Colin admitted. "I mean, this cabin looks really crowded to me. There are two of each of you."

Jay and I uttered short, uncomfortable laughs.

Larry helped Colin over to the lower bunk where Jay had been sitting. "He'll be just fine in a day or two," Larry told us.

"Yeah. The headache is a little better already," Colin said, gently rubbing the back of his head, then lying down on top of the bedcovers.

"Did you see a doctor?" I asked.

"Huh-uh. Just Uncle Al," Colin replied. "He looked it over and said I'd be fine."

I cast a suspicious glance at Larry, but he turned his back on us and crouched down to search for something in the duffel bag he kept under his bed.

"Where's Mike? Is he okay?" Jay asked Larry.

"Uh-huh," Larry answered without turning around. "He's fine."

"But where is he?" I demanded.

Larry shrugged. "Still at the lodge, I guess. I don't really know."

"But is he coming back?" I insisted.

Larry shoved the bag under his bed and stood up. "Have you guys finished your letters?" he asked. "Hurry and get changed for dinner. You can mail your letters at the lodge."

He started to the door. "Hey, don't forget tonight is Tent Night. You guys are sleeping in a tent tonight."

We all groaned. "But, Larry, it's too cold out!" Jay protested.

Larry ignored him and turned away.

"Hey, Larry, do you have anything I can put on this sunburn?" Jay called after him.

"No," Larry replied and disappeared out the door.

Jay and I helped Colin up to the lodge. He was still seeing double, and his headache was pretty bad.

The three of us sat at the end of the long table nearest the window. A strong breeze blew cool air over the table, which felt good on our sun-burned skin.

We had some kind of meat with potatoes and gravy for dinner. It wasn't great, but I was so hungry, it didn't matter. Colin didn't have much appetite. He picked at the edges of his gray meat.

The mess hall was as noisy as ever. Kids were laughing and shouting to friends across the long tables. At one table, the guys were throwing breadsticks back and forth like javelins.

As usual, the counselors, dressed in their green and white, ate together at a table in the far corner and ignored us campers completely.

The rumor spread that we were going to learn all of the camp songs after dinner. Guys were groaning and complaining about that.

About halfway through dinner, Jay and the boy across the table, a kid named Roger, started horsing around, trying to wrestle a breadstick from each other. Jay pulled hard and won the bread-stick — and spilled his entire cup of grape juice on my tan shorts.

"Hey!" I jumped up angrily, staring down as the purple stain spread across the front of my shorts.

"Billy had an accident!" Roger cried out. And everyone laughed.

"Yeah. He purpled in his pants!" Jay added.

Everyone thought that was hilarious. Someone

threw a breadstick at me. It bounced off my chest and landed on my dinner plate. More laughter.

The food fight lasted only a few minutes. Then two of the counselors broke it up. I decided I'd better run back to the bunk and change my shorts. As I hurried out, I could hear Jay and Roger calling out jokes about me.

I ran full-speed down the hill toward the bunks. I wanted to get back up to the mess hall in time for dessert.

Pushing open the bunk door with my shoulder, I darted across the small room to the dresser and pulled open my drawer.

"Huh?"

To my surprise, I stared into an empty drawer. It had been completely cleaned out.

"What's going on here?" I asked aloud. "Where's my stuff?"

Confused, I took a step back — and realized I had opened the wrong drawer. This wasn't my drawer.

It was Mike's.

I stared for a long while into the empty drawer.

Mike's clothes had all been removed. I turned and looked for his trunk, which had been stacked on its side behind our bunk.

Mike's trunk was gone, too.

Mike wasn't coming back.

* * *

I was so upset, I ran back to the mess hall without changing my shorts.

Panting loudly, I made my way to the counselors' table and came up behind Larry. He was talking to the counselor next to him, a fat guy with long, scraggly blond hair. "Larry — Mike's gone!" I cried breathlessly.

Larry didn't turn around. He kept talking to the other counselor as if I weren't there.

I grabbed Larry's shoulder. "Larry — listen!" I cried. "Mike — he's gone!"

Larry turned around slowly, his expression annoyed. "Go back to your table, Billy," he snapped. "This table is for counselors only."

"But what about Mike?" I insisted shrilly. "His stuff is gone. What happened to him? Is he okay?"

"How should I know?" Larry replied impatiently.

"Did they send him home?" I asked, refusing to back away until I had some kind of an answer.

"Yeah. Maybe." Larry shrugged and lowered his gaze. "You spilled something on your shorts."

My heart was pounding so hard, I could feel the blood pulsing at my temples. "You really don't know what happened to Mike?" I asked, feeling defeated.

Larry shook his head. "I'm sure he's fine," he replied, turning back to his pals.

"He probably went for a swim," the scragglyhaired guy next to him snickered.

Larry and some of the other counselors laughed, too.

I didn't think it was funny. I felt pretty sick. And a little frightened.

Don't the counselors at this camp care what happens to us? I asked myself glumly.

I made my way back to the table. They were passing out chocolate pudding for dessert, but I wasn't hungry.

I told Colin, and Jay, and Roger about Mike's dresser drawer being cleaned out, and about how Larry pretended he didn't know anything about it. They didn't get as upset about it as I was.

"Uncle Al probably had to send Mike home because of his hand," Colin said quietly, spooning up his pudding. "It was pretty swollen."

"But why wouldn't Larry tell me the truth?" I asked, my stomach still feeling as if I had eaten a giant rock for dinner. "Why did he say he didn't know what happened to Mike?"

"Counselors don't like to talk about bad stuff," Jay said, slapping the top of his pudding with his spoon. "It might give us poor little kids nightmares." He filled his spoon with pudding, tilted it back, and flung a dark gob of pudding onto Roger's forehead.

"Jay — you're dead meat now!" Roger cried, plunging his spoon into the chocolate goo. He shot a gob of it onto the front of Jay's sleeveless T-shirt.

That started a pudding war that spread down the long table.

There was no more talk about Mike.

After dinner, Uncle Al talked about Tent Night and what a great time we were going to have sleeping in tents tonight. "Just be very quiet so the bears can't find you!" he joked. Some joke.

Then he and the counselors taught us the camp songs. Uncle Al made us sing them over and over until we learned them.

I didn't feel much like singing. But Jay and Roger began making up really gross words to the songs. And pretty soon, a whole bunch of us joined in, singing our own versions of the songs as loudly as we could.

Later, we were all making our way down the hill toward our tents. It was a cool, clear night. A wash of pale stars covered the purple-black sky.

I helped Colin down the hill. He was still seeing double and feeling a little weak.

Jay and Roger walked a few steps ahead of us, shoving each other with their shoulders, first to the left, then to the right.

Suddenly, Jay turned back to Colin and me. "Tonight's the night," he whispered, a devilish grin spreading across his face.

"Huh? Tonight's *what* night?" I demanded.

"Ssshhh." He raised a finger to his lips. "When everyone's asleep, Roger and I are going to go check out the Forbidden Bunk." He turned to Colin. "You with us?"

Colin shook his head sadly. "I don't think I can, Jay."

Walking backwards in front of us, Jay locked his eyes on mine. "How about you, Billy? You coming?"

10

"I — I think I'll stay with Colin," I told him.

I heard Roger mutter something about me being a chicken. Jay looked disappointed. "You're going to miss out," he said.

"That's okay. I'm kind of tired," I said. It was true. I felt so weary after this long day, every muscle ached. Even my hair hurt!

Jay and Roger made whispered plans all the way back to the tent.

At the bottom of the hill, I stopped and gazed up at the Forbidden Bunk. It appeared to lean toward me in the pale starlight. I listened for the familiar howls that seemed to come from inside it. But tonight there was only a heavy silence.

The large plastic tents were lined up in the bunk area. I crawled into ours and lay down on top of my sleeping bag. The ground was really hard. I could see this was going to be a long night.

Jay and Colin were messing around with their

sleeping bags at the back of the tent. "It seems weird without Mike here," I said, feeling a sudden chill.

"Now you'll have more room to put your stuff," Jay replied casually. He sat hunched against the tent wall, his expression tense, his eyes on the darkness outside the tent door, which was left open a few inches.

Larry was nowhere in sight. Colin sat quietly. He still wasn't feeling right.

I shifted my weight and stretched out, trying to find a comfortable position. I really wanted to go to sleep. But I knew I wouldn't be able to sleep until after Jay and Roger returned from their adventure.

Time moved slowly. It was cold outside, and the air was heavy and wet inside the tent.

I stared up at the dark plastic tent walls. A bug crawled across my forehead. I squashed it with my hand.

I could hear Jay and Colin whispering behind me, but I couldn't make out their words. Jay snickered nervously.

I must have dozed off. An insistent whispering sound woke me up. It took me a while to realize it was someone whispering outside the tent.

I lifted my head and saw Roger's face peering in. I sat up, alert.

"Wish us luck," Jay whispered.

"Good luck," I whispered back, my voice clogged from sleep.

In the darkness I saw Jay's large, shadowy form crawl quickly to the tent door. He pushed it open, revealing a square of purple sky, then vanished into the darkness.

I shivered. "Let's sneak back to the bunk," I whispered to Colin. "It's too cold out here. And the ground feels like solid rock."

Colin agreed. We both scrambled out of the tent and made our way silently to our nice, warm bunk. Inside, we headed to the window to try to see Jay and Roger.

"They're going to get caught," I whispered. "I just know it."

"They won't get caught," Colin disagreed. "But they won't see anything, either. There's nothing to see up there. It's just a stupid cabin."

Poking my head out the window, I could hear Jay and Roger giggling quietly out somewhere in the dark. The camp was so silent, so eerily silent. I could hear their whispers, their legs brushing through the tall grass.

"They'd better be quiet," Colin muttered, leaning against the window frame. "They're making too much noise."

"They must be up to the hill by now," I whispered. I stuck my head out as far as I could, but I couldn't see them.

Colin started to reply, but the first scream made him stop.

It was a scream of horror that cut through the silent air.

"Oh!" I cried out and pulled my head in.

"Was that Jay or Roger?" Colin asked, his voice trembling.

The second scream was more terrifying than the first.

Before it died down, I heard animal snarls. Loud and angry. Like an eruption of thunder.

Then I heard Jay's desperate plea: "Help us! Please — somebody help us!"

My heart thudding in my chest, I lurched to the cabin door and pulled it open. The hideous screams still ringing in my ears, I plunged out into the darkness, the dew-covered ground soaking my bare feet.

"Jay — where are you?" I heard myself calling, but I didn't recognize my shrill, frightened voice.

And then I saw a dark form running toward me, running bent over, arms outstretched.

"Jay!" I cried. "What — *is* it? What *happened*?"

He ran up to me, still bent forward, his face twisted in horror, his eyes wide and unblinking. His bushy hair appeared to stand straight up.

"It — it got Roger," he moaned, his chest heaving as he struggled to straighten up.

"What did?" I demanded.

"What was it?" Colin asked, right behind me.

"I — I don't know!" Jay stammered, shutting his eyes tight. "It — it tore Roger to pieces."

Jay uttered a loud sob. Then he opened his eyes and spun around in terror. "Here it comes!" he shrieked. "Now it's coming after *us*!"

11

In the pale starlight, I saw Jay's eyes roll up in his head. His knees collapsed, and he began to slump to the ground.

I grabbed him before he fell and dragged him into the cabin. Colin slammed the door behind us.

Once inside, Jay recovered slowly. The three of us froze in place and listened hard. I was still holding onto Jay's heaving shoulders. He was as pale as a bedsheet, and his breath came out in short, frightened moans.

We listened.

Silence.

The air hung hot and still.

Nothing moved.

No footsteps. No animal approaching.

Just Jay's frightened moans and the pounding of my heart.

And then, somewhere far in the distance, I heard the howl. Soft and low at first, then rising on the wind. A howl that chilled my blood and made me cry out.

"It's Sabre!"

"Don't let it get me!" Jay shrieked, covering his face with his hands. He dropped to his knees on the cabin floor. "Don't let it get me!"

I raised my eyes to Colin, who was huddled against the wall, away from the window. "We have to get Larry," I managed to choke out. "We have to get help."

"But how?" Colin demanded in a trembling voice.

"Don't let it get me!" Jay repeated, crumpled on the floor.

"It isn't coming here," I told him, trying to sound certain, trying to sound soothing. "We're okay inside the bunk, Jay. It isn't coming here."

"But it got Roger and — " Jay started. His entire body convulsed in a shudder of terror.

Thinking about Roger, I felt a stab of fear in my chest.

Was it really true? Was it true that Roger had been attacked by some kind of creature? That he'd been slashed to pieces?

I'd heard the screams from the hillside. Two bloodcurdling screams.

They'd been so loud, so horrifying. Hadn't anyone else in camp heard them, too? Hadn't any other kids heard Roger's cries? Hadn't any counselors heard?

I froze in place and listened.

Silence. The whisper of the breeze rustling the tree leaves.

No voices. No cries of alarm. No hurried footsteps.

I turned back toward the others. Colin had helped Jay to his bunk. "Where can Larry be?" Colin asked. His eyes, for once not hidden behind the silver sunglasses, showed real fear.

"Where can *everyone* be?" I asked, crossing my arms over my chest and starting to pace back and forth in the small space between the beds. "There isn't a sound out there."

I saw Jay's eyes go wide with horror. He was staring at the open window. "The creature — " he cried. "Here it comes! It's coming through the window!"

12

All three of us gaped in horror at the open window.

But no creature jumped in.

As I stared, frozen in the center of the cabin, I could see only darkness and a fringe of pale stars.

Outside in the trees, crickets started up a shrill clatter. There was no other sound.

Poor Jay was so frightened and upset, he was seeing things.

Somehow Colin and I got him a little calmed down. We made him take off his sneakers and lie down on the lower bed. And we covered him up with three blankets to help him to stop trembling.

Colin and I wanted to run for help. But we were too frightened to go outside.

The three of us were up all night. Larry never showed up.

Except for the crickets and the brush of the wind through the trees, the camp was silent.

I think I must have finally dozed off just before

dawn. I had strange nightmares about fires and people trying to run away.

I was awakened by Colin shaking me hard. "Breakfast," he said hoarsely. "Hurry. We're late."

I sat up groggily. "Where's Larry?"

"He never showed," Colin replied, motioning to Larry's unused bunk.

"We've got to find him! We've got to tell him what happened!" Jay cried, hurrying to the cabin door with his sneakers untied.

Colin and I stumbled after him, both of us only half-awake. It was a cool, gray morning. The sun was trying hard to poke through high white clouds.

The three of us stopped halfway up the hill to the mess hall. Reluctantly, our eyes searched the ground around the Forbidden Bunk.

I don't know what I expected to see. But there was no sign of Roger.

No sign of any struggle. No dried blood on the ground. The tall grass wasn't bent or matted down.

"Weird," I heard Jay mutter, shaking his head. "That's weird."

I tugged his arm to get him moving, and we hurried the rest of the way up to the lodge.

The mess hall was as noisy as ever. Kids were laughing and shouting to each other. It all seemed perfectly normal. I guessed that no one had made an announcement about Roger yet.

Some kids called to Colin and me. But we ignored them and searched for Roger, moving quickly through the aisles between the tables.

No sign of him.

I had a heavy, queasy feeling in my stomach as we hurried to the counselors' table in the corner.

Larry glanced up from a big plate of scrambled eggs and bacon as the three of us advanced on him.

"What happened to Roger?"

"Is he okay?"

"Where were you last night?"

"Roger and I were attacked."

"We were afraid to go find you."

All three of us bombarded Larry at once.

His face was filled with confusion, and he raised both hands to silence us. "Whoa," he said. "Take a breath, guys. What are you talking about?"

"About Roger!" Jay screamed, his face turning bright red. "The creature — it jumped on him. And — and — "

Larry glanced at the other counselors at the table, who looked as confused as he did. "Creature? What creature?" Larry demanded.

"It attacked Roger!" Jay screamed. "It was coming after me and — "

Larry stared up at Jay. "Someone was attacked? I don't think so, Jay." He turned to the counselor next to him, a pudgy boy named Derek.

"Did you hear anything in your area?"

Derek shook his head.

"Isn't Roger in your group?" Larry asked Derek.

Derek shook his head. "Not in *my* group."

"But Roger — !" Jay insisted.

"We didn't get any report about any attack," Larry said, interrupting. "If a camper was attacked by a bear or something, we'd hear about it."

"And we'd hear the noise," Derek offered. "You know. Screams or something."

"I heard screams," I told them.

"We both heard screams," Colin added quickly. "And Jay came running back, crying for help."

"Well, why didn't anyone else hear it?" Larry demanded, turning his gaze on Jay. His expression changed. "Where did this happen? When?" he asked suspiciously.

Jay's face darkened to a deeper red. "After lights out," he admitted. "Roger and I went up to the Forbidden Bunk, and — "

"Are you sure it wasn't a bear?" Derek interrupted. "Some bears were spotted downriver yesterday afternoon."

"It was a *creature*!" Jay screamed angrily.

"You shouldn't have been out," Larry said, shaking his head.

"Why won't you listen to me?" Jay screamed.

"Roger was attacked. This big thing jumped on him and — "

"We would've heard something," Derek said calmly, glancing at Larry.

"Yeah," Larry agreed. "The counselors were all up here at the lodge. We would've heard any screams."

"But, Larry — you've got to check it out!" I cried. "Jay isn't making it up. It really happened!"

"Okay, okay," Larry replied, raising his hands as if surrendering. "I'll go ask Uncle Al about it, okay?"

"Hurry," Jay insisted. "Please!"

"I'll ask Uncle Al after breakfast," Larry said, turning back to his eggs and bacon. "I'll see you guys at morning swim later. I'll report what Uncle Al says."

"But, Larry — " Jay pleaded.

"I'll ask Uncle Al," Larry said firmly. "If anything happened last night, he'll know about it." He raised a strip of bacon to his mouth and chewed on it. "I think you just had a bad nightmare or something," he continued, eyeing Jay suspiciously. "But I'll let you know what Uncle Al says."

"It wasn't a nightmare!" Jay cried shrilly. Larry turned his back on us and continued eating his breakfast. "Don't you *care*?" Jay screamed at him. "Don't you *care* what happens to us?"

I saw that a lot of kids had stopped eating their breakfast to gawk at us. I pulled Jay away, and tried to get him to go to our table. But he insisted on searching the entire mess hall again. "I know Roger *isn't* here," he insisted. "He — he *can't* be!"

For the second time, the three of us made our way up and down the aisles between the tables, studying every face.

One thing was for sure: Roger was nowhere to be seen.

The sun burned through the high clouds just as we reached the waterfront for morning swim. The air was still cool. The thick, leafy shrubs along the riverbank glistened wetly in the white glare of sunlight.

I dropped my towel under a bush and turned to the gently flowing green water. "I'll bet it's cold this morning," I said to Colin, who was re-tying the string on his swim trunks.

"I just want to go back to the bunk and go to sleep," Colin said, plucking at a knot. He wasn't seeing double any longer, but he was tired from being up all night.

Several guys were already wading into the river. They were complaining about the cold water, splashing each other, shoving each other forward.

"Where's Larry?" Jay demanded breathlessly,

pushing his way through the clump of shrubs to get to us. His auburn hair was a mess, half of it standing straight up on the side of his head. His eyes were red-rimmed and bloodshot.

"Where's Larry? He promised he'd be here," Jay said, frantically searching the waterfront.

"Here I am." The three of us spun around as Larry appeared from the bushes behind us. He was wearing baggy green Camp Nightmoon swim trunks.

"Well?" Jay demanded. "What did Uncle Al say? About Roger?"

Larry's expression was serious. His eyes locked on Jay's. "Uncle Al and I went all around the Forbidden Bunk," he told Jay. "There wasn't any attack there. There couldn't have been."

"But it — it got Roger," Jay cried shrilly. "It slashed him. I saw it!"

Larry shook his head, his eyes still burning into Jay's. "That's the other thing," he said softly. "Uncle Al and I went up to the office and checked the records, Jay. And there *is* no camper here this year named Roger. Not a first name or a middle name. No Roger. No Roger at all."

13

Jay's mouth dropped open and he uttered a low gasp.

The three of us stared in disbelief at Larry, letting this startling news sink in.

"Someone's made a mistake," Jay said finally, his voice trembling with emotion. "We searched the mess hall for him, Larry. And he's gone. Roger isn't here."

"He never *was* here," Larry said without any emotion at all.

"I — I just don't believe this!" Jay cried.

"How about a swim, guys," Larry said, motioning to the water.

"Well, what do *you* think?" I demanded of Larry. I couldn't believe he was being so calm about this. "What do *you* think happened last night?"

Larry shrugged. "I don't know what to think," he replied, his eyes on a cluster of swimmers farthest from the shore. "Maybe you guys are trying to pull a weird joke on me."

"Huh? Is *that* what you think?" Jay cried. "That it's a *joke*?!"

Larry shrugged again. "Swim time, guys. Get some exercise, okay?"

Jay started to say more, but Larry quickly turned and went running into the green water. He took four or five running steps off the shore, then dove, pulling himself quickly through the water, taking long, steady strokes.

"I'm not going in," Jay insisted angrily. "I'm going back to the bunk." His face was bright red. His chin was trembling. I could see that he was about to cry. He turned and began running through the bushes, dragging his towel along the ground.

"Hey, wait up!" Colin went running after him.

I stood there trying to decide what to do. I didn't want to follow Jay to the bunk. There wasn't anything I could do to help him.

Maybe a cold swim will make me feel better, I thought.

Maybe *nothing* will make me feel better, I told myself glumly.

I stared out at the other guys in the water. Larry and another counselor were setting up a race. I could hear them discussing what kind of stroke should be used.

They all seem to be having a great time, I thought, watching them line up.

So why aren't I?

Why have I been so frightened and unhappy since I arrived here? Why don't the other campers see how weird and frightening this place is?

I shook my head, unable to answer my questions.

I need a swim, I decided.

I took a step toward the water.

But someone reached out from the bushes and grabbed me roughly from behind.

I started to scream out in protest.

But my attacker quickly clamped a hand over my mouth to silence me.

14

I tried to pull away, but I'd been caught off guard.

As the hands tugged me, I lost my balance and I was pulled back into the bushes.

Is this a joke? What's going on? I wondered.

Suddenly, as I tried to tug myself free, the hands let go.

I went sailing headfirst into a clump of fat green leaves.

It took me a long moment to pull myself up. Then I spun around to face my attacker.

"Dawn!" I cried.

"Ssshhhh!" She leapt forward and clamped a hand over my mouth again. "Duck down," she whispered urgently. "They'll see you."

I obediently ducked behind the low bush. She let go of me again and moved back. She was wearing a blue, one-piece bathing suit. It was wet. Her blonde hair was also wet, dripping down onto her bare shoulders.

"Dawn — what are you *doing* here?" I whispered, settling onto my knees.

Before Dawn could reply, another figure in a bathing suit moved quickly from the bushes, crouching low. It was Dawn's friend Dori.

"We swam over. Early this morning," Dori whispered, nervously pushing at her curly red hair. "We waited here. In the bushes."

"But it's not allowed," I said, unable to hide my confusion. "If you're caught — "

"We had to talk to you," Dawn interrupted, raising her head to peek over the top of the bushes, then quickly ducking back down.

"We decided to risk it," Dori added.

"What — what's wrong?" I stammered. A red-and-black bug crawled up my shoulder. I brushed it away.

"The girls' camp. It's a nightmare," Dori whispered.

"Everyone calls it Camp *Nightmare* instead of Camp Nightmoon," Dawn added. "Strange things have been happening."

"Huh?" I gaped at her. Not far from us in the water, I could hear the shouts and splashes of the swim race beginning. "What kinds of strange things?"

"Scary things," Dori replied, her expression solemn.

"Girls have disappeared," Dawn told me. "Just vanished from sight."

"And no one seems to care," Dori added in a trembling whisper.

"I don't believe it!" I uttered. "The same thing has happened here. At the boys' camp." I swallowed hard. "Remember Mike?"

Both girls nodded.

"Mike disappeared," I told them. "They removed his stuff, and he just disappeared."

"It's unbelievable," Dori said. "Three girls are gone from our camp."

"They announced that one was attacked by a bear," Dawn whispered.

"What about the other two?" I asked.

"Just gone," Dawn replied, the words catching in her throat.

I could hear whistles blowing in the water. The race had ended. Another one was being organized.

The sun disappeared once again behind high white clouds. Shadows lengthened and grew darker.

I told them quickly about Roger and Jay and the attack at the Forbidden Bunk. They listened in open-mouthed silence. "Just like at our camp," Dawn said.

"We have to do something," Dori said heatedly.

"We have to get together. The boys and the girls," Dawn whispered, peering once again over the tops of the leaves. "We have to make a plan."

"You mean to escape?" I asked, not really understanding.

The two girls nodded. "We can't stay here," Dawn said grimly. "Every day another girl disappears. And the counselors act as if nothing is happening."

"I think they *want* us to get killed or something," Dori added with emotion.

"Have you written to your parents?" I asked.

"We write every day," Dori replied. "But we haven't heard from them."

I suddenly realized that I hadn't received any mail from my parents, either. They had both promised to write every day. But I had been at camp for nearly a week, and I hadn't received a single piece of mail.

"Visitors Day is next week," I said. "Our parents will be here. We can tell them everything."

"It may be too late," Dawn said grimly.

"Everyone is so scared!" Dori declared. "I haven't slept in two nights. I hear these horrible screams outside every night."

Another whistle blew, closer to shore. I could hear the swimmers returning. Morning swim was ending.

"I — I don't know what to say," I told them. "You've got to be careful. Don't get caught."

"We'll swim back to the girls' camp when everyone has left," Dawn said. "But we have to meet again, Billy. We have to get more guys together. You know. Maybe if we all get organized . . ." Her voice trailed off.

"There's something bad going on at this camp," Dori said with a shiver, narrowing her eyes. "Something evil."

"I — I know," I agreed. I could hear boys' voices now. Close by. Just on the other side of the leafy bushes. "I've got to go."

"We'll try to meet here again the day after tomorrow," Dawn whispered. "Be careful, Billy."

"*You* be careful," I whispered. "Don't get caught."

They slipped back, deeper in the bushes.

Crouching low, I made my way away from the shore. When I was past the clump of bushes, I stood up and began to run. I couldn't wait to tell Colin and Jay about what the girls had said.

I felt frightened and excited at the same time. I thought maybe it would make Jay feel a little better to know that the same kinds of horrible things were happening across the river at the girls' camp.

Halfway to the bunks, I had an idea. I stopped and turned toward the lodge.

I suddenly remembered seeing a pay phone on the wall on the side of the building. Someone had told me that phone was the only one campers were allowed to use.

I'll call Mom and Dad, I decided.

Why hadn't I thought of it before?

I can call my parents, I realized, and tell them everything. I could ask them to come and get me.

And they could get Jay, Colin, Dawn, and Dori, too.

Behind me, I saw my group heading toward the scratchball field, their swimming towels slung over their shoulders. I wondered if anyone had noticed that I was missing.

Jay and Colin were missing, too, I told myself. Larry and the others probably think I'm with them.

I watched them trooping across the tall grass in twos and threes. Then I turned and started jogging up the hill toward the lodge.

The idea of calling home had cheered me up already.

I was so eager to hear my parents' voices, so eager to tell them the strange things that were happening here.

Would they believe me?

Of *course* they would. My parents always believed me. Because they trusted me.

As I ran up the hill, the dark pay phone came into view on the white lodge wall. I started to run at full speed. I wanted to *fly* to the phone.

I hope Mom and Dad are home, I thought.

They've *got* to be home.

I was panting loudly as I reached the wall. I lowered my hands to my knees and crouched there for a moment, waiting to catch my breath.

Then I reached up to take the receiver down.

And gasped.

The pay phone was plastic. Just a stage prop. A phony.

It was a thin sheet of molded plastic held to the wall by a nail, made to look just like a telephone.

It wasn't real. It was a fake.

They don't want us to call out, I thought with a sudden chill.

My heart thudding, my head spinning in bitter disappointment, I turned away from the wall — and bumped right into Uncle Al.

15

"Billy — what are you doing up here?" Uncle Al asked. He was wearing baggy green camp shorts and a sleeveless white T-shirt that revealed his meaty pink arms. He carried a brown clipboard filled with papers. "Where are you supposed to be?"

"I . . . uh . . . wanted to make a phone call," I stammered, taking a step back. "I wanted to call my parents."

He eyed me suspiciously and fingered his yellow mustache. "Really?"

"Yeah. Just to say hi," I told him. "But the phone — "

Uncle Al followed my gaze to the plastic phone. He chuckled. "Someone put that up as a joke," he said, grinning at me. "Did it fool you?"

"Yeah," I admitted, feeling my face grow hot. I raised my eyes to his. "Where is the real phone?"

His grin faded. His expression turned serious.

"No phone," he replied sharply. "Campers aren't allowed to call out. It's a rule, Billy."

"Oh." I didn't know what to say.

"Are you really homesick?" Uncle Al asked softly.

I nodded.

"Well, go write your mom and dad a long letter," he said. "It'll make you feel a lot better."

"Okay," I said. I didn't think it *would* make me feel better. But I wanted to get away from Uncle Al.

He raised his clipboard and gazed at it. "Where are you supposed to be now?" he asked.

"Scratchball, I think," I replied. "I didn't feel too well, see. So I — "

"And when is your canoe trip?" he asked, not listening to me. He flipped through the sheets of paper on the clipboard, glancing over them quickly.

"Canoe trip?" I hadn't heard about any canoe trip.

"Tomorrow," he said, answering his own question. "Your group goes tomorrow. Are you excited?" He lowered his eyes to mine.

"I — I didn't really know about it," I confessed.

"Lots of fun!" he exclaimed enthusiastically. "The river doesn't look like much up here. But it gets pretty exciting a few miles down. You'll find yourself in some good rapids."

He squeezed my shoulder briefly. "You'll enjoy it," he said, grinning. "Everyone always enjoys the canoe ride."

"Great," I said. I tried to sound a little excited, but my voice came out flat and uncertain.

Uncle Al gave me a wave with his clipboard and headed around toward the front of the lodge, taking long strides. I stood watching him till he disappeared around the corner of the building. Then I made my way down the hill to the bunk.

I found Colin and Jay on the grass at the side of the cabin. Colin had his shirt off and was sprawled on his back, his hands behind his head. Jay sat cross-legged beside him, nervously pulling up long, slender strands of grass, then tossing them down.

"Come inside," I told them, glancing around to make sure no one else could hear.

They followed me into the cabin. I closed the door.

"What's up?" Colin asked, dropping onto a lower bunk. He picked up his red bandanna and twisted it in his hands.

I told them about Dawn and Dori and what they had reported about the girls' camp.

Colin and Jay both reacted with shock.

"They really swam over here and waited for you?" Jay asked.

I nodded. "They think we have to get organized or escape or something," I said.

"They could get in big trouble if they get caught," Jay said thoughtfully.

"We're all in big trouble," I told him. "We have to get *out*!"

"Visitors Day is next week," Colin muttered.

"I'm going to write to my parents right now," I said, pulling out the case from under my bunk where I kept my paper and pens. "I'm going to tell them I *have* to come home on Visitors Day."

"I guess I will, too," Jay said, tapping his fingers nervously against the bunk frame.

"Me, too," Colin agreed. "It's just too . . . weird here!"

I pulled out a couple of sheets of paper and sat down on the bed to write. "Dawn and Dori were really scared," I told them.

"So am I," Jay admitted.

I started to write my letter. I wrote *Dear Mom and Dad, HELP!*, then stopped. I raised my eyes across the cabin to Jay and Colin. "Do you guys know about the canoe trip tomorrow?" I asked.

They stared back at me, their expressions surprised.

"Whoa!" Colin declared. "A three-mile hike this afternoon, and a canoe trip tomorrow?"

It was my turn to be surprised. "Hike? What hike?"

"Aren't you coming on it?" Jay asked.

"You know that really tall counselor? Frank? The one who wears the yellow cap?" Colin asked.

"He told Jay and me we're going on a three-mile hike after lunch."

"No one told me," I replied, chewing on the end of my pen.

"Maybe you're not in the hike group," Jay said.

"You'd better ask Frank at lunch," Colin suggested. "Maybe he couldn't find you. Maybe you're supposed to come, too."

I groaned. "Who wants to go on a three-mile hike in this heat?"

Colin and Jay both shrugged.

"Frank said we'd really like it," Colin told me, knotting and unknotting the red bandanna.

"I just want to get out of here," I said, returning to my letter.

I wrote quickly, intensely. I wanted to tell my parents all the frightening, strange things that had happened. I wanted to make them see why I couldn't stay at Camp Nightmoon.

I had written nearly a page and a half, and I was up to the part where Jay and Roger went out to explore the Forbidden Bunk, when Larry burst in. "You guys taking the day off?" he asked, his eyes going from one of us to the other. "You on vacation or something?"

"Just hanging out," Jay replied.

I folded up my letter and started to tuck it under my pillow. I didn't want Larry to see it. I realized I didn't trust Larry at all. I had no reason to.

"What are *you* doing, Billy?" he asked suspiciously, his eyes stopping on the letter I was shoving under the pillow.

"Just writing home," I replied softly.

"You homesick or something?" he asked, a grin spreading across his face.

"Maybe," I muttered.

"Well, it's lunchtime, guys," he announced. "Let's hustle, okay?"

We all climbed out of our bunks.

"Jay and Colin are going on a hike with Frank this afternoon, I heard," Larry said. "Lucky guys." He turned and started out the door.

"Larry!" I called to him. "Hey, Larry — what about me? Am I supposed to go on the hike, too?"

"Not today," he called back.

"But why not?" I said.

But Larry disappeared out the door.

I turned back to my two bunk mates. "Lucky guys!" I teased them.

They both growled back at me in reply. Then we headed up the hill to lunch.

They served pizza for lunch, which is usually my favorite. But today, the pizza was cold and tasted like cardboard, and the cheese stuck to the roof of my mouth.

I wasn't really hungry.

I kept thinking about Dawn and Dori, how frightened they were, how desperate. I wondered when I'd see them again. I wondered if they would swim over and hide at the boys' camp again before Visitors Day.

After lunch, Frank came by our table to pick up Jay and Colin. I asked him if I was supposed to come, too.

"You weren't on the list, Billy," he said, scratching at a mosquito bite on his neck. "I can only take two at a time, you know? The trail gets a little dangerous."

"Dangerous?" Jay asked, climbing up from the table.

Frank grinned at him. "You're a big strong guy," he told Jay. "You'll do okay."

I watched Frank lead Colin and Jay out of the mess hall. Our table was empty now, except for a couple of blond-haired guys I didn't know who were arm-wrestling down at the end near the wall.

I pushed my tray away and stood up. I wanted to go back to the bunk and finish the letter to my parents. But as I took a few steps toward the door, I felt a hand on my shoulder.

I turned to see Larry grinning down at me. "Tennis tournament," he said.

"Huh?" I reacted with surprise.

"Billy, you're representing Bunk 4 in the tennis tournament," Larry said. "Didn't you see the lineup? It was posted on the announcements board."

"But I'm a terrible tennis player!" I protested.

"We're counting on you," Larry replied. "Get a

racquet and get your bod to the courts!"

I spent the afternoon playing tennis. I beat a little kid in straight sets. I had the feeling he had never held a tennis racquet before. Then I lost a long, hard-fought match to one of the blond-haired boys who'd been arm-wrestling at lunch.

I was drowning in sweat, and every muscle in my body ached when the match was over. I headed to the waterfront for a refreshing swim.

Then I returned to the bunk, changed into jeans and a green-and-white Camp Nightmoon T-shirt, and finished my letter to my parents.

It was nearly dinnertime. Jay and Colin weren't back from their hike yet. I decided to go up to the lodge and mail my letter. As I headed up the hill, I saw clusters of kids hurrying to their bunks to change for dinner. But no sign of my two bunk mates.

Holding the letter tightly, I headed around to the back of the lodge building where the camp office was located. The door was wide open, so I walked in. A young woman was usually behind the counter to answer questions and to take the letters to be mailed.

"Anyone here?" I called, leaning over the counter and peering into the tiny back room, which was dark.

No reply.

"Hi. Anyone here?" I repeated, clutching the envelope.

No. The office was empty.

Disappointed, I started to leave. Then I glimpsed the large burlap bag on the floor just inside the tiny back room.

The mailbag!

I decided to put my letter in the bag with the others to be mailed. I slipped around the counter and into the back room and crouched down to put my envelope into the bag.

To my surprise, the mailbag was stuffed full with letters. As I pulled the bag open and started to shove my letter inside, a bunch of letters fell out onto the floor.

I started to scoop them up when a letter caught my eye.

It was one of mine. Addressed to my parents.

One I had written yesterday.

"Weird," I muttered aloud.

Bending over the bag, I reached in and pulled out a big handful of letters. I sifted through them quickly. I found a letter Colin had written.

I pulled out another pile.

And my eyes fell upon two other letters I had written nearly a week ago when I first arrived in camp.

I stared at them, feeling a cold chill run down my back.

All of our letters, all of the letters we had written since the first day of camp, were here. In this mailbag.

None of them had been mailed.

We couldn't call home.

And we couldn't *write* home.

Frantically, my hands trembling, I began shoving the envelopes back into the mailbag.

What is going on here? I wondered. *What is going on?*

16

By the time I got into the mess hall, Uncle Al was finishing the evening announcements. I slid into my seat, hoping I hadn't missed anything important.

I expected to see Jay and Colin across the table from me. But their places on the bench were empty.

That's strange, I thought, still shaken from my discovery about the mailbag. They should be back by now.

I wanted to tell them about the mail. I wanted to share the news that our parents weren't getting any of the letters we wrote.

And we weren't getting any of theirs.

The camp had to be keeping our mail from us, I suddenly realized.

Colin and Jay — where are you?

The fried chicken was greasy, and the potatoes were lumpy and tasted like paste. As I forced the food down, I kept turning to glance at the mess hall door, expecting to see my two bunk mates.

But they didn't show up.

A heavy feeling of dread formed in my stomach. Through the mess hall window, I could see that it was already dark outside.

Where could they be?

A three-mile hike and back shouldn't take this many hours.

I pulled myself up and made my way to the counselors' table in the corner. Larry was having a loud argument about sports with two of the other counselors. They were shouting and gesturing with their hands.

Frank's chair was empty.

"Larry, did Frank get back?" I interrupted their discussion.

Larry turned, a startled expression on his face. "Frank?" He motioned to the empty chair at the table. "Guess not."

"He took Jay and Colin on the hike," I said. "Shouldn't they be back by now?"

Larry shrugged. "Beats me." He returned to his argument, leaving me standing there staring at Frank's empty chair.

After the trays had been cleared, we pushed the tables and benches against the wall and had indoor relay races. Everyone seemed to be having a great time. The shouts and cheers echoed off the high-raftered ceiling.

I was too worried about Jay and Colin to enjoy the games.

Maybe they decided to camp out overnight, I told myself.

But I had seen them leave, and I knew they hadn't taken any tents or sleeping bags or other overnight supplies.

So where *were* they?

The games ended a little before lights out. As I followed the crowd to the door, Larry appeared beside me. "We're leaving early tomorrow," he said. "First thing."

"Huh?" I didn't understand what he meant.

"The canoe trip. I'm the canoe counselor. I'll be taking you guys," he explained, seeing my confusion.

"Oh. Okay," I replied without enthusiasm. I was so worried about Jay and Colin, I'd nearly forgotten about the canoe trip.

"Right after breakfast," Larry said. "Wear a bathing suit. Bring a change of clothes. Meet me at the waterfront." He hurried back to help the other counselors pull the tables into place.

"After breakfast," I muttered. I wondered if Jay and Colin were also coming on the canoe trip. I had forgotten to ask Larry.

I headed quickly down the dark hill. The dew had already fallen, and the tall grass was slippery and wet. Halfway down, I could see the dark outline of the Forbidden Bunk, hunched forward as if preparing to strike.

Forcing myself to look away, I jogged the rest of the way to Bunk 4.

To my surprise, I could see through the window that someone was moving around inside.

Colin and Jay are back! I thought.

Eagerly, I pushed open the door and burst inside. "Hey — where've you guys been?" I cried.

I stopped short. And gasped.

Two strangers stared back at me.

One was sitting on the edge of Colin's top bunk, pulling off his sneakers. The other was leaning over the dresser, pulling a T-shirt from one of the drawers.

"Hi. You in here?" the boy at the dresser stood up straight, his eyes studying me. He had very short black hair, and a gold stud in one ear.

I swallowed hard. "Am I in the wrong bunk? Is this Bunk 4?"

They both stared at me, confused.

I saw that the other boy, the one in Colin's bunk, also had black hair, but his was long and scraggly and fell over his forehead. "Yeah. This is Bunk 4," he said.

"We're new," the short-haired boy added. "I'm Tommy, and he's Chris. We just started today."

"Hi," I said uncertainly. "My name's Billy." My heart was pounding like a tom-tom in my chest. "Where's Colin and Jay?"

"Who?" Chris asked. "They told us this bunk was mostly empty."

"Well, Colin and Jay — " I started.

"We just arrived. We don't know anyone," Tommy interrupted. He pushed the drawer shut.

"But that's Jay's drawer," I said, bewildered, pointing. "What did you do with Jay's stuff?"

Tommy gazed back at me in surprise. "The drawer was empty," he replied.

"Almost all the drawers were empty," Chris added, tossing his sneakers down to the floor. "Except for the bottom two drawers."

"That's my stuff," I said, my head spinning. "But Colin and Jay — their stuff was here," I insisted.

"The whole cabin was empty," Tommy said. "Maybe your friends got moved."

"Maybe," I said weakly. I sat down on the lower bunk beneath my bed. My legs felt shaky. A million thoughts were whirring through my mind, all of them frightening.

"This is weird," I said aloud.

"It's not a bad bunk," Chris said, pulling down his blanket and settling in. "Kind of cozy."

"How long you staying at camp?" Tommy asked, pulling on an oversized white T-shirt. "All summer?"

"No!" I exclaimed with a shudder. "I'm not staying!" I sputtered. "I mean — I mean . . . I'm leaving. On . . . uh . . . I'm leaving on Visitors Day next week."

Chris flashed Tommy a surprised glance. "Huh? When are you leaving?" he asked again.

"On Visitors Day," I repeated. "When my parents come up for Visitors Day."

"But didn't you hear Uncle Al's announcement before dinner?" Tommy asked, staring hard at me. "Visitors Day has been canceled!"

17

I drifted in and out of a troubled sleep that night.
Even with the blanket pulled up to my chin, I felt
chilled and afraid.

It felt so weird to have two strange guys in the
bunk, sleeping where Jay and Colin slept. I was
worried about my missing friends.

What had happened to them? Why hadn't they
come back?

As I tossed restlessly in my top bunk, I heard
howls off in the distance. Animal cries, probably
coming from the Forbidden Bunk. Long, frightening howls carried by the wind into our open
bunk window.

At one point, I thought I heard kids screaming.
I sat up straight, suddenly alert, and listened.

Had I dreamed the frightful shrieks? I was so
scared and confused, it was impossible to tell what
was real and what was a nightmare.

It took hours to fall back to sleep.

I awoke to a gray, overcast morning, the air

heavy and cold. Pulling on swim trunks and a T-shirt, I raced to the lodge to find Larry. I had to find out what had happened to Jay and Colin.

I searched everywhere for him without success. Larry wasn't at breakfast. None of the other counselors admitted to knowing anything. Frank, the counselor who had taken my two friends on the hike, was also not there.

I finally found Larry at the waterfront, preparing a long metal canoe for our river trip. "Larry — where are they?" I cried out breathlessly.

He gazed up at me, holding an armload of canoe paddles. His expression turned to bewilderment. "Huh? Chris and Tommy? They'll be here soon."

"No!" I cried, grabbing his arm. "Jay and Colin! Where are they? What happened to them, Larry? You've *got* to tell me!"

I gripped his arm tightly. I was gasping for breath. I could feel the blood pulsing at my temples. "You've got to tell me!" I repeated shrilly.

He pulled away from me and let the paddles fall beside the canoe. "I don't know anything about them," he replied quietly.

"But Larry!"

"Really, I don't," he insisted in the same quiet voice. His expression softened. He placed a hand on my trembling shoulder. "Tell you what, Billy," he said, staring hard into my eyes. "I'll ask Uncle Al about it after our trip, okay? I'll find out for you. When we get back."

I stared back at him, trying to decide if he was being honest.

I couldn't tell. His eyes were as calm and cold as marbles.

He leaned forward and pushed the canoe into the shallow river water. "Here. Take one of those life preservers," he said, pointing to a pile of blue rubber vests behind me. "Strap it on. Then get in."

I did as he instructed. I saw that I had no choice.

Chris and Tommy came running up to us a few seconds later. They obediently followed Larry's instructions and strapped on the life-preserver vests.

A few minutes later, the four of us were seated cross-legged inside the long, slender canoe, drifting slowly away from the shore.

The sky was still charcoal-gray, the sun hidden behind hovering, dark clouds. The canoe bumped over the choppy river waters. The current was stronger than I had realized. We began to pick up speed. The low trees and shrubs along the riverbank slid past rapidly.

Larry sat facing us in the front of the canoe. He demonstrated how to paddle as the river carried us away.

He watched us carefully, a tight frown on his face, as the three of us struggled to pick up the rhythm he was showing us. Then, when we finally seemed to catch on, Larry grinned and carefully turned around, gripping the sides of the canoe as he shifted his position.

"The sun is trying to come out," he said, his voice muffled in the strong breeze over the rippling water.

I glanced up. The sky looked darker than before.

He stayed with his back to us, facing forward, allowing the three of us to do the paddling. I had never paddled a canoe before. It was harder than I'd imagined. But as I fell into the rhythm of it with Tommy and Chris, I began to enjoy it.

Dark water smacked against the prow of the canoe, sending up splashes of white froth. The current grew stronger, and we picked up speed. The air was still cold, but the steady work of rowing warmed me. After a while, I realized I was sweating.

We rowed past tangles of yellow- and gray-trunked trees. The river suddenly divided in two, and we shifted our paddles to take the left branch. Larry began paddling again, working to keep us off the tall rocks that jutted between the river branches.

The canoe bobbed up and slapped down. Bobbed

up and slapped down. Cold water poured over the sides.

The sky darkened even more. I wondered if it was about to storm.

As the river widened, the current grew rapid and strong. I realized we didn't really need to paddle. The river current was doing most of the work.

The river sloped down. Wide swirls of frothing white water made the canoe leap and bounce.

"Here come the rapids!" Larry shouted, cupping his hands around his mouth so we could hear him. "Hang on! It gets pretty wild!"

I felt a tremor of fear as a wave of icy water splashed over me. The canoe rose up on a shelf of white water, then hit hard as it landed.

I could hear Tommy and Chris laughing excitedly behind me.

Another icy wave rolled over the canoe, startling me. I cried out and nearly let go of my paddle.

Tommy and Chris laughed again.

I took a deep breath and held on tightly to the paddle, struggling to keep up the rhythm.

"Hey, look!" Larry cried suddenly.

To my astonishment, he climbed to his feet. He leaned forward, pointing into the swirling, white water.

"Look at those fish!" he shouted.

As he leaned down, the canoe was jarred by a powerful rush of current. The canoe spun to the right.

I saw the startled look on Larry's face as he lost his balance. His arms shot forward, and he plunged headfirst into the tossing waters.

"Noooooo!" I screamed.

I glanced back at Tommy and Chris, who had stopped paddling and were staring into the swirling, dark waters, their expressions frozen in open-mouthed horror.

"Larry! Larry!" I was screaming the name over and over without realizing it.

The canoe continued to slide rapidly down the churning waters.

Larry didn't come up.

"Larry!"

Behind me, Tommy and Chris also called out his name, their voices shrill and frightened.

Where was he? Why didn't he swim to the surface?

The canoe was drifting farther and farther downriver.

"Larrrrrry!"

"We have to stop!" I screamed. "We have to slow down!"

"We can't!" Chris shouted back. "We don't know how!"

Still no sign of Larry. I realized he must be in trouble.

Without thinking, I tossed my paddle into the river, climbed to my feet, and plunged into the dark, swirling waters to save him.

18

I jumped without thinking and swallowed a mouthful of the brown water as I went down.

My heart thudded in my chest as I struggled frantically to the surface, sputtering and choking.

Gasping in a deep breath, I lowered my head and tried to swim against the current. My sneakers felt as if they weighed a thousand pounds.

I realized I should have pulled them off before I jumped.

The water heaved and tossed. I moved my arms in long, desperate strokes, pulling myself toward the spot where Larry had fallen. Glancing back, I saw the canoe, a dark blur growing smaller and smaller.

"Wait!" I wanted to shout to Tommy and Chris. "Wait for me to get Larry!"

But I knew that they didn't know how to slow the canoe. They were helpless as the current carried them away.

Where was Larry?

I sucked in another mouthful of air — and froze as I felt a sharp cramp in my right leg.

The pain shot up through my entire right side.

I slid under the water and waited for the pain to lessen.

The cramp seemed to tighten until I could barely move the leg. Water rushed over me. I struggled to pull myself up to the surface.

As I choked in more air, I stroked rapidly and hard, pulling myself up, ignoring the sharp pain in my leg.

Hey!

What was that object floating just ahead of me? A piece of driftwood being carried by the current?

Brown water washed over me, blinding me, tossing me back. Sputtering, I pulled myself back up.

Water rolled down my face. I struggled to see.

Larry!

He came floating right to me.

"Larry! Larry!" I managed to scream.

But he didn't answer me. I could see clearly

The leg cramp miraculously vanished as I reached out with both arms and grabbed Larry's shoulders. I pulled his head up from the water, rolled him onto his back, and wrapped my arm around his neck. I was using the lifesaving technique my parents had taught me.

Turning downriver, I searched for the canoe. But the current had carried it out of sight.

I swallowed another mouthful of icy water. Choking, I held onto Larry. I kicked hard. My right leg still felt tight and weak, but at least the pain had gone. Kicking and pulling with my free hand, I dragged Larry toward the shore.

To my relief, the current helped. It seemed to pull in the same direction.

A few seconds later, I was close enough to shore to stand. Wearily, panting like a wild animal, I tottered to my feet and dragged Larry onto the wet mud of the shore.

Was he dead? Had he drowned before I reached him?

I stretched him out on his back and, still panting loudly, struggling to catch my breath, to stop my entire body from trembling, I leaned over him.

And he opened his eyes.

He stared up at me blankly, as if he didn't recognize me.

Finally, he whispered my name. "Billy," he choked out, "are we okay?"

Larry and I rested for a bit. Then we walked back to camp, following the river upstream.

We were soaked clear through and drenched with mud, but I didn't care. We were alive. We were okay. I had saved Larry's life.

We didn't talk much all the way back. It was taking every ounce of strength we had just to walk.

I asked Larry if he thought Tommy and Chris would be okay.

"Hope so," he muttered, breathing hard. "They'll probably ride to shore and walk back like us."

I took this opportunity to ask him again about Jay and Colin. I thought maybe Larry would tell me the truth since we were completely alone and since I had just saved his life.

But he insisted he didn't know anything about my two bunk mates. As we walked, he raised one hand and swore he didn't know anything at all.

"So many frightening things have happened," I muttered.

He nodded, keeping his eyes straight ahead. "It's been strange," he agreed.

I waited for him to say more. But he walked on in silence.

It took three hours to walk back. We hadn't traveled downriver as far as I had thought, but the muddy shore kept twisting and turning, making our journey longer.

As the camp came into view, my knees buckled and my legs nearly collapsed under me.

Breathing hard, drenched in perspiration, our

clothes still damp and covered in mud, we trudged wearily onto the waterfront.

"Hey — !" a voice called from the swim area. Uncle Al, dressed in baggy, green sweats, came hurrying across the dirt to us. "What happened?" he asked Larry.

"We had an accident!" I cried before Larry had a chance to reply.

"I fell in," Larry admitted, his face reddening beneath the splattered mud. "Billy jumped in and saved me. We walked back."

"But Tommy and Chris couldn't stop the canoe. They drifted away!" I cried.

"We both nearly drowned," Larry told the frowning camp director. "But, Billy — he saved my life."

"Can you send someone to find Tommy and Chris?" I asked, suddenly starting to shake all over, from exhaustion, I guess.

"The two boys floated on downriver?" Uncle Al asked, staring hard at Larry, scratching the back of his fringe of yellow hair.

Larry nodded.

"We have to find them!" I insisted, trembling harder.

Uncle Al continued to glare at Larry. "What about my canoe?" he demanded angrily. "That's our best canoe! How am I supposed to replace it?"

Larry shrugged unhappily.

"We'll have to go look for that canoe tomorrow," Uncle Al snapped.

He doesn't care about the two boys, I realized. *He doesn't care about them at all.*

"Go get into dry clothes," Uncle Al instructed Larry and me. He stormed off toward the lodge, shaking his head.

I turned and started to the cabin, feeling chilled, my entire body still trembling. I could feel a strong wave of anger sweep over me.

I had just saved Larry's life, but Uncle Al didn't care about that.

And he didn't care that two campers were lost on the river.

He didn't care that two campers and a counselor never returned from their hike.

He didn't care that boys were attacked by *creatures!*

He didn't care that kids disappeared and were never mentioned again.

He didn't care about any of us.

He only cared about his canoe.

My anger quickly turned to fear.

Of course, I had no way of knowing that the *scariest* part of my summer was still to come.

19

I was all alone in the bunk that night.

I pulled an extra blanket onto my bed and slid into a tight ball beneath the covers. I wondered if I'd be able to fall asleep. Or if my frightened, angry thoughts would keep me tossing and turning for another night.

But I was so weary and exhausted, even the eerie, mournful howls from the Forbidden Bunk couldn't keep me awake.

I fell into deep blackness and didn't wake up until I felt someone shaking my shoulders.

Startled alert, I sat straight up. "Larry!" I cried, my voice still clogged with sleep. "What's happening?"

I squinted across the room. Larry's bed was rumpled, the blanket balled up at the end. He had obviously come in late and slept in the bunk.

But Tommy's and Chris's beds were still untouched from the day before.

"Special hike," Larry said, walking over to his bunk. "Hurry. Get dressed."

"Huh?" I stretched and yawned. Outside the window, it was still gray. The sun hadn't risen. "What kind of hike?"

"Uncle Al called a special hike," Larry replied, his back to me. He grabbed the sheet and started to make his bed.

With a groan, I lowered myself to the cabin floor. It felt cold beneath my bare feet. "Don't we get to rest? I mean, after what happened yesterday?" I glanced once again at Tommy's and Chris's unused beds.

"It's not just us," Larry replied, smoothing the sheet. "It's the whole camp. Everyone's going. Uncle Al is leading it."

I pulled on a pair of jeans, stumbling across the cabin with one leg in. A sudden feeling of dread fell over me. "It wasn't scheduled," I said darkly. "Where is Uncle Al taking us?"

Larry didn't reply.

"Where?" I repeated shrilly.

He pretended he didn't hear me.

"Tommy and Chris — they didn't come back?" I asked glumly, pulling on my sneakers. Luckily, I had brought two pairs. My shoes from yesterday sat in the corner, still soaked through and mud-covered.

"They'll turn up," Larry replied finally. But he didn't sound as if he meant it.

I finished getting dressed, then ran up the hill to get breakfast. It was a warm, gray morning. It must have rained during the night. The tall grass glistened wetly.

Yawning and blinking against the harsh gray light, campers headed quietly up the hill. I saw that most of them had the same confused expression I had.

Why were we going on this unscheduled hike so early in the morning? How long was it going to be? Where were we going?

I hoped that Uncle Al or one of the counselors would explain everything to us at breakfast, but none of them appeared in the mess hall.

We ate quietly, without the usual joking around.

I found myself thinking about the terrifying canoe trip yesterday. I could almost taste the brackish brown water again. I saw Larry floating toward me, facedown, floating on the churning water like a clump of seaweed.

I pictured myself trying to get to him, struggling to swim, struggling to go against the current, to keep afloat in the swirls of white water.

And I saw the blur of the canoe as the strong river current carried it out of sight.

Suddenly Dawn and Dori burst into my thoughts. I wondered if they were okay. I wondered if they were going to try and meet me again by the waterfront.

Breakfast was French toast with syrup. It was usually my favorite. But this morning, I just poked at it with my fork.

"Line up outside!" a counselor cried from the doorway.

Chairs scraped loudly. We all obediently climbed to our feet and began making our way outside.

Where are they taking us?

Why doesn't anyone tell us what this is about?

The sky had brightened to pink, but the sun still hadn't risen over the horizon.

We formed a single line along the side wall of the lodge. I was near the end of the line toward the bottom of the hill.

Some kids were cracking jokes and playfully shoving each other. But most were standing quietly or leaning against the wall, waiting to see what was going to happen.

Once the line was formed, one of the counselors walked the length of it, pointing his finger and moving his lips in concentration as he counted us. He counted us twice to make sure he had the right number.

Then Uncle Al appeared at the front of the line. He wore a brown-and-green camouflage outfit, the kind soldiers wear in movies. He had on very black sunglasses, even though the sun wasn't up yet.

He didn't say a word. He signaled to Larry and

another counselor, who were both carrying very large, heavy-looking brown bags over their shoulders. Then Uncle Al strode quickly down the hill, his eyes hidden behind the dark glasses, his features set in a tight frown.

He stopped in front of the last camper. "This way!" he announced loudly, pointing toward the waterfront.

Those were his only words. "This way!"

And we began to follow, walking at a pretty fast clip. Our sneakers slid against the wet grass. A few kids were giggling about something behind me.

To my surprise, I realized I was now nearly at the front of the line. I was close enough to call out to Uncle Al. So I did. "Where are we going?" I shouted.

He quickened his pace and didn't reply.

"Uncle Al — is this a long hike?" I called.

He pretended he hadn't heard.

I decided to give up.

He led us toward the waterfront, then turned right. Thick clumps of trees stood a short way up ahead where the river narrowed.

Glancing back to the end of the line, I saw Larry and the other counselor, bags on their shoulders, hurrying to catch up to Uncle Al.

What is this about? I wondered.

And as I stared at the clumps of low, tangled

trees up ahead, a thought pushed its way into my head.

I can escape.

The thought was so frightening — but suddenly so real — it took a long time to form.

I can escape into these trees.

I can run away from Uncle Al and this frightening camp.

The idea was so exciting, I nearly stumbled over my own feet. I bumped into the kid ahead of me, a big bruiser of a guy named Tyler, and he turned and glared at me.

Whoa, I told myself, feeling my heart start to pound in my chest. Think about this. Think carefully. . . .

I kept my eyes locked on the woods. As we drew closer, I could see that the thick trees, so close together that their branches were all intertwined, seemed to stretch on forever.

They'd never find me in there, I told myself. It would be really easy to hide in those woods.

But then what?

I couldn't stay in the woods forever.

Then what?

Staring at the trees, I forced myself to concentrate, forced myself to think clearly.

I could follow the river. Yes. Stay on the shore. Follow the river. It was bound to come to a town eventually. It *had* to come to a town.

I'd walk to the first town. Then I'd call my parents.

I can do it, I thought, so excited I could barely stay in line.

I just have to run. Make a dash for it. When no one is looking. Into the woods. Deep into the woods.

We were at the edge of the trees now. The sun had pulled itself up, brightening the rose-colored morning sky. We stood in the shadows of the trees.

I can do it, I told myself.

Soon.

My heart thudded loudly. I was sweating even though the air was still cool.

Calm down, Billy, I warned myself. *Just calm down.*

Wait your chance.

Wait till the time is right.

Then leave Camp Nightmare behind. Forever.

Standing in the shade, I studied the trees. I spotted a narrow path into the woods a few yards up ahead.

I tried to calculate how long it would take me to reach the path. Probably ten seconds at most. And, then, in another five seconds, I could be into the protection of the trees.

I can do it, I thought.

I can be gone in less than ten seconds.

I took a deep breath. I braced myself. I tensed my leg muscles, preparing to run.

Then I glanced to the front of the line.

To my horror, Uncle Al was staring directly at me. And he held a rifle in his hands.

20

I cried out when I saw the rifle in his hands.

Had he read my thoughts? Did he know I was about to make a run for it?

A cold chill slid down my back as I gaped at the rifle. As I raised my eyes to Uncle Al's face, I realized he wasn't looking at me.

He had turned his attention to the two counselors. They had lowered the bags to the ground and were bending over them, trying to get them open.

"Why did we stop?" Tyler, the kid ahead of me, asked.

"Is the hike over?" another kid joked. A few kids laughed.

"Guess we can go back now," another kid said.

I stood watching in disbelief as Larry and the other counselor began unloading rifles from the two bags.

"Line up and get one," Uncle Al instructed us, tapping the handle of his own rifle against the ground. "One rifle per boy. Come on — hurry!"

No one moved. I think everyone thought Uncle Al was kidding or something.

"What's *wrong* with you boys? I said *hurry!*" he snapped angrily. He grabbed up an armload of rifles and began moving down the line, pushing one into each boy's hands.

He pushed a rifle against my chest so hard, I staggered back a few steps. I grabbed it by the barrel before it fell to the ground.

"What's going on?" Tyler asked me.

I shrugged, studying the rifle with horror. I'd never held any kind of real gun before. My parents were both opposed to firearms of all kinds.

A few minutes later, we were all lined up in the shadow of the trees, each holding a rifle. Uncle Al stood near the middle of the line and motioned us into a tight circle so we could hear him.

"What's going on? Is this target practice?" one boy asked.

Larry and the other counselor snickered at that. Uncle Al's features remained hard and serious.

"Listen up," he barked. "No more jokes. This is serious business."

The circle of campers tightened around him. We grew silent. A bird squawked noisily in a nearby tree. Somehow it reminded me of my plan to escape.

Was I about to be really sorry that I hadn't made a run for it?

"Two girls escaped from the girls' camp last night," Uncle Al announced in a flat, businesslike tone. "A blonde and a redhead."

Dawn and Dori! I exclaimed to myself. I'll bet it was them!

"I believe," Uncle Al continued, "that these are the same two girls who sneaked over to the boys' camp and hid near the waterfront a few days ago."

Yes! I thought happily. It *is* Dawn and Dori! They escaped!

I suddenly realized a broad smile had broken out on my face. I quickly forced it away before Uncle Al could see my happy reaction to the news.

"The two girls are in these woods, boys. They're nearby," Uncle Al continued. He raised his rifle. "Your guns are loaded. Aim carefully when you see them. They won't get away from us!"

21

"Huh?" I gasped in disbelief. "You mean we're supposed to *shoot* them?"

I glanced around the circle of campers. They all looked as dazed and confused as I did.

"Yeah. You're supposed to shoot them," Uncle Al replied coldly. "I *told* you — they're trying to escape."

"But we can't!" I cried.

"It's easy," Uncle Al said. He raised his rifle to his shoulder and pretended to fire it. "See? Nothing to it."

"But we can't kill people!" I insisted.

"Kill?" His expression changed behind the dark glasses. "I didn't say anything about killing, did I? These guns are loaded with tranquilizer darts. We just want to stop these girls — not hurt them."

Uncle Al took two steps toward me, the rifle still in his hands. He stood over me menacingly, lowering his face close to mine.

"You got a problem with that, Billy?" he demanded.

He was challenging me.

I saw the other boys back away.

The woods grew silent. Even the bird stopped squawking.

"You got a problem with that?" Uncle Al repeated, his face so close to mine, I could smell his sour breath.

Terrified, I took a step back, then another.

Why was he doing this to me? Why was he challenging me like this?

I took a deep breath and held it. Then I screamed as loudly as I could: "I — I won't do it!"

Without completely realizing what I was doing, I raised the rifle to my shoulder and aimed the barrel at Uncle Al's chest.

"You're gonna be sorry," Uncle Al growled in a low voice. He tore off the sunglasses and heaved them into the woods. Then he narrowed his eyes furiously at me. "Drop the rifle, Billy. I'm gonna make you sorry."

"No," I told him, standing my ground. "You're not. Camp is over. You're not going to do anything."

My legs were trembling so hard, I could barely stand.

But I wasn't going to go hunting Dawn and Dori. I wasn't going to do anything else Uncle Al said. Ever.

"Give me the rifle, Billy," he said in his low, menacing voice. He reached out a hand toward my gun. "Hand it over, boy."

"No!" I cried.

"Hand it over now," he ordered, his eyes narrowed, burning into mine. "Now!"

"No!" I cried.

He blinked once. Twice.

Then he leapt at me.

I took a step back with the rifle aimed at Uncle Al — and pulled the trigger.

22

The rifle emitted a soft *pop.*

Uncle Al tossed his head back and laughed. He let his rifle drop to the ground at his feet.

"Hey — !" I cried out, confused. I kept the rifle aimed at his chest.

"Congratulations, Billy," Uncle Al said, grinning warmly at me. "You passed." He stepped forward and reached out his hand to shake mine.

The other campers dropped their rifles. Glancing at them, I saw that they were all grinning, too. Larry, also grinning, flashed me a thumbs-up sign.

"What's going on?" I demanded suspiciously. I slowly lowered the rifle.

Uncle Al grabbed my hand and squeezed it hard. "Congratulations, Billy. I *knew* you'd pass."

"Huh? I don't understand!" I screamed, totally frustrated.

But instead of explaining anything to me, Uncle Al turned to the trees and shouted, "Okay, everyone! It's over! He passed! Come out and congratulate him!"

And as I stared in disbelief, my wide-open mouth hanging down around my knees, people began stepping out from behind the trees.

First came Dawn and Dori.

"You *were* hiding in the woods!" I cried.

They laughed in response. "Congratulations!" Dawn cried.

And then others came out, grinning and congratulating me. I screamed when I recognized Mike. He was okay!

Beside him were Jay and Roger!

Colin stepped out of the woods, followed by Tommy and Chris. All smiling and happy and okay.

"What — what's going *on* here?" I stammered. I was totally stunned. I felt dizzy.

I didn't get it. I really didn't get it.

And then my mom and dad stepped out from the trees. Mom rushed up and gave me a hug. Dad patted the top of my head. "I knew you'd pass, Billy," he said. I could see happy tears in his eyes.

Finally, I couldn't take it anymore. I pushed Mom gently away. "Passed *what*?" I demanded. "What *is* this? What's going on?"

Uncle Al put his arm around my shoulder and guided me away from the group of campers. Mom and Dad followed close behind.

"This isn't really a summer camp," Uncle Al explained, still grinning at me, his face bright pink. "It's a government-testing lab."

"Huh?" I swallowed hard.

"You know your parents are scientists, Billy," Uncle Al continued. "Well, they're about to leave on a very important expedition. And this time they wanted to take you along with them."

"How come you didn't tell me?" I asked my parents.

"We couldn't!" Mom exclaimed.

"According to government rules, Billy," Uncle Al continued, "children aren't allowed to go on official expeditions unless they pass certain tests. That's what you've been doing here. You've been taking tests."

"Tests to see what?" I demanded, still dazed.

"Well, we wanted to see if you could obey orders," Uncle Al explained. "You passed when you refused to go to the Forbidden Bunk." He held up two fingers. "Second, we had to test your bravery. You demonstrated that by rescuing Larry." He held up a third finger. "Third, we had to see if you knew when *not* to follow orders. You passed that test by refusing to hunt for Dawn and Dori."

"And everyone was in on it?" I asked. "All the campers? The counselors? Everyone? They were all actors?"

Uncle Al nodded. "They all work here at the testing lab." His expression turned serious. "You see, Billy, your parents want to take you to a very dangerous place, perhaps the most dangerous place in the known universe. So we had to make sure you can handle it."

The most dangerous place in the universe?

"Where?" I asked my parents. "Where are you taking me?"

"It's a very strange planet called Earth," Dad replied, glancing at Mom. "It's very far from here. But it could be exciting. The inhabitants there are weird and unpredictable, and no one has ever studied them."

Laughing, I stepped between my mom and dad and put my arms around them. "Earth?! It sounds pretty weird. But it could *never* be as dangerous or exciting as Camp Nightmoon!" I exclaimed.

"We'll see," Mom replied quietly. "We'll see."

The Horror
at Camp
Jellyjam

GOOSEBUMPS #33

Mom pointed excitedly out the car window. "Look! A cow!"

My brother, Elliot, and I both groaned. We had been driving through farmland for four hours, and Mom had pointed out every single cow and horse.

"Look out your side, Wendy!" Mom cried from the front seat. "Sheep!"

I stared out the window and saw about a dozen gray sheep — fat, woolly ones — grazing on a grassy green hill. "Nice sheep, Mom," I said, rolling my eyes.

"There's a cow!" Elliot exclaimed.

Now *he* was doing it!

I reached across the backseat and gave him a hard shove. "Mom, is it possible to explode from boredom?" I moaned.

"BOOOOOOM!" Elliot shouted. The kid is a riot, isn't he?

"I told you," Dad muttered to Mom. "A twelve-year-old is too old to go on a long car trip."

"So is an eleven-year-old!" Elliot protested.

I'm twelve. Elliot is eleven.

"How can you two be bored?" Mom asked. "Look — horses!"

Dad sped up to pass a huge yellow truck. The road curved through high, sloping hills. In the far distance, I could see gray mountains, rising up in a heavy mist.

"There's so much beautiful scenery to admire," Mom gushed.

"After a while, it all looks like some boring old calendar," I complained.

Elliot pointed out of his window. "Look! No horses!"

He doubled over, laughing. He thought that was the funniest thing anyone had ever said. Elliot really cracks himself up.

Mom turned in the front seat. She narrowed her eyes at my brother. "Are you making fun of me?" she demanded.

"Yes!" Elliot replied.

"Of course not," I chimed in. "Who would ever make fun of *you*, Mom?"

"When do you ever stop?" Mom complained.

"We're leaving Idaho," Dad announced. "That's Wyoming up ahead. We'll be up in those mountains soon."

"Maybe we'll see Mountain Cows!" I exclaimed sarcastically.

Elliot laughed.

Mom sighed. "Go ahead. Ruin our first family vacation in three years."

We hit a bump. I heard the trailer bounce behind us. Dad had hooked one of those big, old-fashioned trailers to the back of our car. We had dragged it all over the West.

The trailer was actually kind of fun. It had four narrow beds built into the sides. And it had a table we could sit around to eat or play cards. It even had a small kitchen.

At night, we'd pull into a trailer camp. Dad would hook the trailer up to water and electricity. And we spent the night inside, in our own private little house.

We hit another bump. I heard the trailer bounce behind us again. The car lurched forward as we started to climb into the mountains.

"Mom, how do I know if I'm getting carsick or not?" Elliot asked.

Mom turned back to us, frowning. "Elliot, you never get carsick," she said in a low voice. "Did you forget?"

"Oh. Right," Elliot replied. "I just thought it might be something to do."

"Elliot!" Mom screamed. "If you're so bored, take a nap!"

"That's boring," my brother muttered.

I could see Mom's face turning an angry red. Mom doesn't look like Dad, Elliot, and me. She is blond and has blue eyes and very fair skin, which turns red very easily. And she's kind of plump.

My dad, brother, and I are skinny and sort of dark. The three of us have brown hair and brown eyes.

"You kids don't know how lucky you are," Dad said. "You're getting to see some amazing sights."

"Bobby Harrison got to go to baseball camp," Elliot grumbled. "And Jay Thurman went to sleepaway camp for eight weeks!"

"I wanted to go to sleepaway camp, too!" I protested.

"You'll go to camp *next* summer," Mom replied sharply. "This is the chance of a lifetime!"

"But the chance of a lifetime is so boring!" Elliot complained.

"Wendy, entertain your brother," Dad ordered.

"Excuse me?" I cried. "How am I supposed to entertain him?"

"Play Car Geography," Mom suggested.

"Oh, no! Not again!" Elliot wailed.

"Go ahead. I'll start," Mom said. "Atlanta."

Atlanta ends with an A. So I had to think of a city that starts with an A. "Albany," I said. "Your turn, Elliot."

"Hmmmmm. A city that starts with a Y . . ." My brother thought for a moment. Then he twisted up his face. "I quit!"

My brother is such a bad sport. He takes games too seriously, and he really hates to lose. Sometimes he gets so intense when he's playing soccer or softball, I really worry about him.

Sometimes when he thinks he can't win, he just quits. Like now.

"What about Youngstown?" Mom asked.

"What about it?" Elliot grumbled.

"I have an idea!" I said. "How about letting Elliot and me ride in the trailer for a while?"

"Yeah! Cool!" Elliot cried.

"I don't think so," Mom replied. She turned to Dad. "It's against the law to ride in a trailer, isn't it?"

"I don't know," Dad said, slowing the car. We were climbing through thick pine woods now. The air smelled so fresh and sweet.

"Let us!" Elliot pleaded. "Come on — let us!"

"I don't see any harm in letting them ride back there for a while," Dad told Mom. "As long as they're careful."

"We'll be careful!" Elliot promised.

"Are you sure it's safe?" Mom asked Dad.

Dad nodded. "What could happen?"

He pulled the car to the side of the highway. Elliot and I slid out. We ran to the trailer, pulled open the door, and hurried inside.

A few seconds later, the car pulled back onto the highway. We bounced along behind it in the big trailer.

"This is so cool!" Elliot declared, making his way to the back window.

"Do I have good ideas or what?" I asked, following him. He slapped me a high five.

We stared out the back window. The highway seemed to tilt down as we headed up to the mountains.

The trailer bounced and swayed as the car tugged it.

The road tilted up steeper. And steeper.

And that's when all our troubles began.

2

"I win!" Elliot cried. He jumped up and raised both fists in triumph.

"Three out of five!" I demanded, rubbing my wrist. "Come on — three out of five. Unless you're chicken."

I knew that would get him. Elliot can't stand to be called a chicken. He settled back in the seat.

We leaned over the narrow table and clasped hands. We had been arm wrestling for about ten minutes. It was kind of fun because the table bounced every time the trailer rolled over a bump in the road.

I am as strong as Elliot. But he's more determined. A *lot* more determined. You never saw anyone groan and sweat and strain so much in arm wrestling!

To me, a game is just a game. But to Elliot, every game is life or death.

He had won two out of three about five times.

My wrist was sore, and my hand ached. But I really wanted to beat him in this final match.

I leaned over the table and squeezed his hand harder. I gritted my teeth and stared menacingly into his dark brown eyes.

"Go!" he cried.

We both strained against each other. I pushed hard. Elliot's hand started to bend back.

I pushed harder. I nearly had him. Just a little harder.

He let out a groan and pushed back. He shut his eyes. His face turned beet-red. I could see the veins push out at the sides of his neck.

My brother just can't stand to lose.

SLAM!

The back of my hand hit the table hard.

Elliot had won again.

Actually, I let him win. I didn't want to see his whole head explode because of a stupid arm-wrestling match.

He jumped up and pumped his fists, cheering for himself.

"Hey — !" he cried out as the trailer swayed hard, and he went crashing into the wall.

The trailer lurched again. I grabbed the table to keep from falling off my seat. "What's going on?"

"We changed direction. We're heading down now," Elliot replied. He edged his way back toward the table.

But we bumped hard, and he toppled to the floor. "Hey — we're going backwards!"

"I'll bet Mom's driving," I said, holding on to the table edge with both hands.

Mom always drives like a crazy person. When you warn her that she's going eighty, she always says, "That can't be right. It feels as if I'm going thirty-five!"

The trailer was bouncing and bumping, rolling downhill. Elliot and I were bouncing and bumping with the trailer.

"What is their problem?" Elliot cried, grabbing on to one of the beds, struggling to keep his balance. "Are they backing up? Why are we going backwards?"

The trailer roared downhill. I pushed myself up from the table and stumbled to the front to see the car. Shoving aside the red plaid curtain, I peered out through the small window.

"Uh . . . Elliot . . ." I choked out. "We've got a problem."

"Huh? A problem?" he replied, bouncing harder as the trailer picked up speed.

"Mom and Dad aren't pulling us anymore," I told him. "The car is gone."

3

Elliot's face filled with confusion. He didn't understand me. Or maybe he didn't believe me!

"The trailer has come loose!" I screamed, staring out the bouncing window. "We're rolling downhill — on our own!"

"N-n-n-no!" Elliot chattered. He wasn't stuttering. He was bouncing so hard, he could barely speak. His sneakers hopped so hard on the trailer floor, he seemed to be tap dancing.

"OW!" I let out a pained shriek as my head bounced against the ceiling. Elliot and I stumbled to the back. Gripping the windowsill tightly, I struggled to see where we were heading.

The road curved steeply downhill, through thick pine woods on both sides. The trees were a bouncing blur of greens and browns as we hurtled past.

Picking up speed. Bouncing and tumbling.

Faster.

Faster.

The tires roared beneath us. The trailer tilted and dipped.

I fell to the floor. Landed hard on my knees. Reached to pull myself up. But the trailer swayed, and I went sprawling on my back.

Pulling myself to my knees, I saw Elliot bouncing around on the floor like a soccer ball. I threw myself at the back of the trailer and peered out the window.

The trailer bumped hard. The road curved sharply — but we didn't curve with it!

We shot off the side of the road. Swerved into the trees.

"Elliot!" I shrieked. "We're going to crash!"

4

The trailer jolted hard. I heard a cracking sound.

It's going to break in half! I thought.

I pressed both hands against the front and stared out the window. Dark trees flew past.

A hard bump sent me sprawling to the floor.

I heard Elliot calling my name. "Wendy! Wendy! Wendy!"

I shut my eyes and tensed every muscle. And waited for the crash.

Waited . . .

Waited . . .

Silence.

I opened my eyes. It took me a few seconds to realize that we were no longer moving. I took a deep breath and climbed to my feet.

"Wendy?" I heard Elliot's weak cry from the back of the trailer.

My legs were trembling as I turned around. My whole body felt weird. As if we were still bouncing. "Elliot — are you okay?"

He had been thrown into one of the bottom bunks. "Yeah. I guess," he replied. He lowered his feet to the floor and shook his head. "I'm kind of dizzy."

"Me, too," I confessed. "What a ride!"

"Better than Space Mountain!" Elliot exclaimed. He climbed to his feet. "Let's get *out* of this thing!"

We both started to the door at the front. It was an uphill climb. The trailer tilted up.

I reached the door first. I grabbed the handle.

A loud knock on the door made me jump back. "Hey . . . !" I cried.

Three more knocks.

"It's Mom and Dad!" Elliot cried. "They found us! Open it up! Hurry!"

He didn't have to tell me to hurry. My heart skipped. I was so glad to see them!

I turned the handle, pushed open the trailer door —

— and gasped.

5

I stared into the face of a blond-haired man. His blue eyes sparkled in the bright sunlight.

He was dressed all in white. He wore a crisp white T-shirt tucked into baggy white shorts. A small round button pinned to his T-shirt read **ONLY THE BEST** in bold black letters.

"Uh . . . hi," I finally managed to choke out.

He flashed me a gleaming smile. He seemed to have about two thousand teeth. "Hey, guys — everyone okay in there?" he asked. His blue eyes sparkled even brighter.

"Yeah. We're okay," I told him. "A little shaken up, but — "

"Who are *you?*" Elliot cried, poking his head out the door.

The guy's smile didn't fade. "My name is Buddy."

"I'm Wendy. He's Elliot. We thought you were our parents," I explained. I hopped down to the ground.

Elliot followed me. "Where are Mom and Dad?" he asked, frowning.

"I haven't seen anyone, guy," Buddy told him. He studied the trailer. "What happened here? You came unhitched?"

I nodded, brushing my dark hair off my face. "Yeah. On the steep hills, I guess."

"Dangerous," Buddy muttered. "You must have been really scared."

"Not me!" Elliot declared.

What a kid. First, he's shaking in terror and calling out my name over and over. Now he's Mister Macho.

"I've never been so scared in all my life!" I admitted.

I took a few steps away from the trailer and searched the woods. The trees creaked and swayed in a light breeze. The sun beamed down brightly. I shielded my eyes with one hand as I peered around.

No sign of Mom and Dad. I couldn't see the highway through the thick trees.

I could see the tire tracks our trailer had made through the soft dirt. Somehow we had shot through a clear path between the trees. The trailer had come to rest at the foot of a sharp, sloping hill.

"Wow. We were lucky," I muttered.

"You're very lucky," Buddy declared cheerfully. He stepped up beside me, placed his hands on my shoulders, and turned me around. "Check it out. Look where you guys landed!"

Gazing up the hill, I saw a wide clearing between the trees. And then I saw a huge, red-and-white banner, stretched high on two poles. I had to squint to read the words on the banner.

Elliot read them aloud: "King Jellyjam's Sports Camp."

"The camp is on the other side of the hill," Buddy told us, flashing us both a friendly smile. "Come on! Follow me!"

"But — but — " my brother sputtered. "We have to find our parents!"

"Hey — no problem, guy. You can wait for them at the camp," Buddy assured him.

"But how will they know where to find us?" I protested. "Should we leave a note?"

Buddy flashed me another dazzling smile. "No. I'll take care of it," he told me. "No problem."

He stepped past the trailer and started up the hill. His white T-shirt and white shorts gleamed in the sunlight. I saw that his socks and high-tops were sparkling white, too.

That's his uniform. He must work at the camp, I decided.

Buddy turned back. "You guys coming?" He motioned with both hands. "Come on. You're going to like it!"

Elliot and I hurried to catch up to him. My legs

trembled as I ran. I could still feel the trailer floor bouncing and jolting beneath me. I wondered if I would ever feel normal again.

As we made our way up the grassy hill, the red-and-white banner came into clearer view. "King Jellyjam's Sports Camp," I read the words aloud.

A funny, purple cartoon character had been drawn beside the words on the banner. He looked like a blob of grape bubble gum. He had a big smile on his face. He wore a gold crown on his head.

"Who's *that*?" I asked Buddy.

Buddy glanced up at the banner. "That's King Jellyjam," he replied. "He's our little mascot."

"Weird-looking mascot for a *sports* camp," I declared, staring up at the purple, blobby king.

Buddy didn't reply.

"Do you work at the camp?" Elliot asked.

Buddy nodded. "It's a great place to work. I'm the head counselor, guys. So — welcome!"

"But we can't go to your camp," I protested. "We have to find our parents. We have to . . ."

Buddy put a hand on my shoulder and a hand on Elliot's shoulder. He guided us up the hill. "You guys have had a close call. You might as well stay and have some fun. Enjoy the camp. Until I can hook up with your parents."

As we neared the top of the hill, I heard voices. Kids' voices. Shouting and laughing.

The clearing narrowed. Tall pine trees, birch trees, and maples clustered over the hill.

"What kind of sports camp is it?" Elliot asked Buddy.

"We play all kinds of sports," Buddy replied. "From Ping-Pong to football. From croquet to soccer. We have swimming. We have tennis. We have archery. We even have a marbles tournament!"

"Sounds like a cool place!" my brother declared, grinning at me.

"Only the best!" Buddy said, slapping Elliot on the shoulder.

I reached the top of the hill first and peered down through the trees to the camp. It seemed to stretch for miles!

I could see two long, white, two-story buildings on either side. Between them, I saw several playing fields, a baseball diamond, a long row of tennis courts, and two enormous swimming pools.

"Those long, white buildings are the dorms," Buddy explained, pointing. "That's the girls' dorm, and that's the boys'. You guys can stay in them while you're here."

"Wow! It looks awesome!" Elliot exclaimed. "Two swimming pools!"

"Olympic size," Buddy told him. "We have diving competitions, too. Are you into diving?"

"Only inside the trailer!" I joked.

"Wendy is into swimming," Elliot told Buddy.

"I think there's a four-lap swim race this afternoon," Buddy told me. "I'll check the schedule for you."

The sun beamed on us as we followed the path down the hill. The back of my neck started to prickle. A cool swim sounded pretty good to me.

"Can anyone sign up for baseball?" Elliot asked Buddy. "I mean, do you have to be on a team or something?"

"You can play any sport you want," Buddy told him. "The only rule at King Jellyjam's Sports Camp is to try hard." Buddy tapped the button on his T-shirt. "Only The Best," he said.

The breeze blew my hair back over my face. I *knew* I should have had it cut before vacation! I decided I'd have to find something to tie it back with as soon as I got into the dorm.

A soccer match was under way on the nearest field. Whistles blew. Kids shouted. I saw a long row of archery targets at the far end of the soccer field.

Buddy started jogging toward the field. Elliot stepped up beside me. "Hey — we wanted to go to camp, right?" he said, grinning. "Well? We made it!"

Before I could reply, he trotted after Buddy.

I brushed back my hair one more time, then followed. But I stopped when I saw a little girl poke her head out from behind a wide tree trunk.

She appeared to be about six or seven. She had bright red hair and a face full of freckles. She wore a pale blue T-shirt pulled down over black tights.

"Hey — " she called in a loud whisper. "Hey — !"

I turned toward her, startled.

"Don't come in!" she called. "Run away! Don't come in!"

6

Buddy turned back quickly. "What's the problem, Wendy?" he called.

When I returned my eyes to the tree, the red-haired girl had vanished. I blinked a couple of times. No trace of her.

What was that girl doing out here? I wondered. Did she hide behind that tree just to scare people?

"Uh . . . no problem," I called to Buddy. I followed Elliot and the counselor into the camp.

I quickly forgot all about the girl as we made our way around the soccer field and past a long row of fenced-in tennis courts. The *thwack* of tennis balls followed us as we turned on to the main path that led through the camp.

So many sports! So much activity!

We pushed our way through kids of all ages, eagerly hurrying to the swimming pools, to the baseball diamond, to the bowling lanes!

"Awesome!" Elliot kept repeating. "Totally awesome!"

And for once, he was right.

We passed several other camp counselors. They were all young men and women, dressed completely in white, all of them good-looking and smiling cheerfully.

And we passed dozens of little triangular signs showing the purple, blobby face of King Jellyjam, smiling out from under his shiny gold crown. Under each face was the camp slogan: Only The Best.

He's kind of cute, I decided. I realized I was starting to like *everything* about this amazing sports camp.

And I have to confess I found myself secretly hoping that Mom and Dad wouldn't be able to find Elliot and me for at least a day or two.

Isn't that terrible?

I felt really guilty about it. But I couldn't help thinking it. This camp was just too exciting. Especially after days of riding in the backseat of the car, staring out at cows!

We dropped my brother off at the boys' dorm first. Another counselor, a tall, dark-haired guy named Scooter, greeted Elliot and took my brother off to find a dorm room.

Then Buddy led me to the girls' dorm on the other side of the camp. We passed a gymnastics competition being held in an outdoor arena. Beyond that, one of the swimming pools was jammed with kids watching a diving contest off the high board.

Buddy and I chatted as we walked. I told him about my school and about how my favorite sports are swimming and biking.

We stopped at the white double-door entrance to the dorm. "Where are you from?" I asked him.

Buddy stared back at me. He had such a confused expression on his face. For a moment, I thought he didn't understand the question.

"Do you come from around here?" I asked.

He swallowed hard. He squinted his blue eyes. "Weird . . ." he muttered finally.

"What's weird?" I demanded.

"I . . . I don't remember," he stammered. "I don't remember where I'm from. Is that weird or what?" He raised his right hand to his mouth and nibbled his pointer finger.

"Hey, I forget stuff all the time," I told him, seeing how upset he was.

I didn't get a chance to say anything else. A young woman counselor with very short, straight black hair and bright purple-lipsticked lips came trotting up to us. "Hello. I'm Holly. Are you ready for some sports?"

"I guess," I replied uncertainly.

"This is Wendy," Buddy told her, his expression still troubled. "She needs a room."

"No problem!" Holly declared cheerfully. "Only The Best!"

"Only The Best," Buddy repeated quietly. He flashed me a smile. But I could see he was still struggling to remember where his home was. Weird, huh?

Holly led the way into the dorm. I followed her down a long, white-tiled hall. Several girls came running past, on their way to different sports. They were all shouting and laughing excitedly.

I peeked into some of the open rooms as we passed by them. Wow! I thought. This place is so modern and luxurious! It's not exactly your basic, rustic summer camp.

"We don't stay in the rooms much at all," Holly told me. "Everyone is always outdoors, competing."

She pushed open a white door and motioned for me to step in. Bright sunlight flooded the room from a wide window on the opposite wall.

I saw two bright blue bunk beds against each wall. A sleek white dresser between them. Two white leather armchairs.

The walls were white. They were bare except for a small, framed drawing of King Jellyjam above the dresser.

"Nice room!" I exclaimed, squinting against the bright sunlight.

Holly smiled. Her bright purple lips made the rest of her features seem to disappear. "Glad you like it, Wendy. You can take that bottom bunk over there." She pointed. She had purple finger-nails that matched her lipstick.

"Do I have roommates?" I asked.

Holly nodded. "You'll meet them soon. They'll get you started with some activities. I think they're playing soccer on the lower field. I'm not sure."

She started out of the room, but turned at the doorway. "You'll like Dierdre. I think she's about your age."

"Thanks," I said, gazing around the room.

"Catch you later," Holly replied. She vanished into the hall.

I stood in the center of the sunlit room, thinking hard. What am I supposed to do for clothes? I wondered. What about swimsuits? Sweats?

All I had were the denim short-shorts and pink-and-blue-striped T-shirt I was wearing.

And why didn't Holly tell me where to go next? I asked myself. Why did she just leave me by myself in this empty room?

I didn't have long to ask myself questions.

I started to cross to the window when I heard voices. Whispered voices outside the door.

I turned to the door. Were my roommates returning?

I listened to the excited buzz of whispers.

Then I heard a girl loudly instruct the others. "Come on. We've got her trapped in there. Let's *get* her!"

7

I gasped and searched frantically for a place to hide.

No time.

Three girls burst into the room, their eyes narrowed, their mouths twisted into menacing sneers. They formed a line and moved toward me quickly.

"Whoa! Wait!" I cried. I raised both hands as if to shield myself from their attack.

The tall girl with streaky blond hair was the first to laugh. Then the other two joined in.

"Gotcha," the blond girl declared, tossing back her long hair triumphantly.

I glared back at her, my mouth hanging open.

"Did you really think we were going to attack?" one of the others asked. She was thin and wiry, with very short black hair cut into bangs. She wore gray sweats and a torn gray T-shirt.

"Well . . ." I started. I could feel my face growing hot. Their little joke had really fooled me. I felt like a total jerk.

"Don't look at me," the third girl said, shaking her head. She had frizzy blond hair tumbling out from beneath a blue and red Chicago Cubs cap. "It was all Dierdre's idea." She pointed to the girl with streaky blond hair.

"Don't feel bad," Dierdre told me, grinning. Her green eyes flashed. "You're the third girl this week."

The other two snickered.

"And did the others think you were attacking?" I asked.

Dierdre nodded, very pleased with herself. "It's kind of a mean joke," she admitted. "But it's funny."

This time I joined in the laughter.

"I have a younger brother. I'm used to dumb jokes," I told Dierdre.

She swept back her hair again. Rummaged around on the dresser top. Found a hair scrunchy to hold it back. "This is Jan and this is Ivy," she said, motioning to the other girls.

Jan was the one with the short black bangs. She slumped on to a lower bunk. "I'm whipped," she sighed. "What a workout. Look at me. I'm sweating like a pig."

"Ever hear of deodorant?" Ivy cracked.

Jan stuck out her tongue at Ivy in reply.

"Get changed," Dierdre instructed them both. "We've only got ten minutes."

"Ten minutes till what?" Jan demanded, bending down and rubbing her calf muscles.

"Did you forget the four-lap race?" Dierdre replied.

"Oh, wow!" Jan cried, jumping up. "I *did* forget." She hurried to the dresser. "Where's my swimsuit?"

Ivy followed her. They began frantically sifting through the drawers.

Dierdre turned to me. "Do you want to enter the race?" she asked.

"I — I don't have a swimsuit," I replied.

She shrugged. "No problem. I have about a dozen." She studied me. "We're about the same size. I'm just a little taller."

"Well, I'd *love* a swim," I told her. "Maybe I'll just go to the pool and splash around for a while."

"Huh? Not compete?" Dierdre cried.

All three girls turned to me, stunned expressions on their faces.

"I'll do some sports later," I said. "Right now, I just want to dive in and swim a little. You know. Cool off."

"But — you can't!" Jan cried. She gaped at me as if I had suddenly grown a second head.

"No way," Ivy said, shaking her head.

"You *have* to compete," Dierdre added. "You can't just swim."

"Only The Best," Ivy recited.

"Right. Only The Best," Jan agreed.

I felt totally confused. "What do you *mean*?" I demanded. "Why do you keep saying that?"

Dierdre tossed me a blue swimsuit. "Put it on. We're going to be late."

"But . . . but — " I sputtered.

The three girls hurried to get into their swimsuits.

I saw that I had no choice. I went into the bathroom and started to change.

But my questions repeated in my mind. I really wanted them answered.

Why did I have to compete in the race? Why couldn't I just have a swim?

And why did everyone keep repeating "Only The Best"?

What did they mean?

8

The enormous blue pool sparkled under the bright sunlight. The sun hovered high overhead. The concrete burned the soles of my bare feet. I couldn't wait to get into the water.

Shielding my eyes with one hand, I searched for Elliot. But I couldn't find him in the crowd of kids who were waiting to watch the race.

Elliot has probably already played three sports, I told myself. This had to be the perfect camp for my brother!

I gazed down the line of girls waiting to compete in the four-lap race. We all stood on the edge of the deep end of the pool, waiting to jump in.

I silently counted. There were at least two dozen girls in this race. And the pool was wide enough for all of us to have a lane to swim in.

"Hey, you look terrific in my suit," Dierdre said. Her green eyes studied me. "You should have tied your hair back, Wendy. It's going to slow you down."

Wow, I thought. Dierdre really cares about winning.

"Are you a good swimmer?" I asked her.

She swatted a fly on the back of her calf. "The best," she replied, grinning. "How about you?"

"I've never really raced," I told her.

The pool counselors were all young women. They wore white two-piece swimsuits. Across the pool, I saw Holly sitting on the edge of the diving board, talking to another counselor.

A tall, red-haired counselor moved to the edge of the pool and blew her whistle. "Everyone ready?" she called.

We all shouted back that we were ready. Then the long line of girls grew silent. We turned to the pool, leaned forward, and prepared to dive in.

The water shimmered beneath me. The sun burned down on my back and shoulders. I felt about to melt. I couldn't wait to jump in.

The whistle blew. I sprang forward and hit the water hard.

I gasped from the shock of the cold against my hot skin. My arms churned hard as I pulled myself forward.

The splash of thrashing arms and kicking feet sounded like the roar of a waterfall. I dipped my face into the water, feeling tne refreshing coldness.

Turning my head, I glimpsed Dierdre a few lengths behind me. She swam in a steady rhythm, her arms and legs moving smoothly, gracefully.

I'm ahead of everyone, I realized, glancing across the pool. I'm winning the race!

With a hard kick, I reached the other end of the pool. I made a sharp turn and pushed off. As I started back to the deep end, the other girls were still approaching the shallow end wall.

I pulled myself harder. My heart started to pound.

I knew I'd win the first lap easily. Then there were three laps to go.

Three laps . . .

I suddenly realized how dumb I was. The other girls were pacing themselves. They weren't swimming full speed because they knew it was a four-lap race.

If I kept swimming this hard, I wouldn't survive two laps!

I sucked in a deep breath, then let it out slowly. Slowly . . . slowly . . .

That was the word of the day.

I slowed my kicking. Shot my arms out and pulled them back slowly. Took long breaths. Long, slow breaths.

As I made my turn and started the second lap, several other swimmers had moved beside me. I caught Dierdre's eye as she swam past.

She never broke her steady rhythm. Stroke. Stroke. Breath. Stroke.

On the other side of Dierdre, I saw Jan swimming comfortably, easily. Jan was so small and light. She seemed to float over the water.

Into the third lap. I kept a few lengths behind Dierdre. I had to concentrate on keeping a slow, even pace. I pretended I was a robot, programmed to swim slowly.

Dierdre turned into the fourth lap a few seconds ahead of me. I saw her expression change as she made her turn. She narrowed her eyes. Her entire face grew tight and tense.

Dierdre really wants to win, I saw.

I wondered if I could catch her. I wondered if I could *beat* her.

I made my turn and put on the speed.

I ignored the aching in my arms.

I ignored the cramp in my left foot.

I thrust myself forward, kicking hard from the waist. My hands cut through the water.

Faster.

I glimpsed Jan fall behind. I saw the disappointment on her face as I passed by.

Pounding, thrusting arms and legs churned the water to froth. The splashing became a roar. The roar nearly drowned out the cheers of the kids watching from around the pool.

My heart thudded so hard, I thought my chest might explode.

My arms ached. They felt as if they each weighed a thousand pounds.

Faster . . .

I pulled up beside Dierdre. Close. So close, I could hear her gasping breaths.

I glimpsed her face, tight with concentration.

She's just like Elliot, I decided. She wants to win so badly.

Lots of times I *let* Elliot win a game. Because he cared about it so much more than I did. And so did Dierdre.

As we neared the wall at the deep end, I let Dierdre pull ahead.

I saw how much it meant to her. I saw how desperate she was to finish first.

What the heck, I thought. There's nothing wrong with coming in second.

I heard the cheers ring out as Dierdre won the race.

I touched the wall, then dipped below the surface. I pulled myself up and grabbed the wall.

My entire body ached and throbbed. I gasped in breath after breath. I shut my eyes and pulled my hair back with both hands, squeezing the water out of it.

My arms were so tired, I could barely pull myself out of the pool. I was one of the last swimmers out.

The others had all formed a circle around Dierdre. I pushed my way into the crowd of girls to see what was happening.

My eyes burned. I brushed water out of them.

I saw the red-haired counselor hand something to Dierdre. Something gold and shiny.

Everyone cheered. Then the circle broke, and the girls all headed in different directions.

I made my way up to Dierdre. "Way to go!" I exclaimed. "I came close. But you're really fast."

"I'm on the swim team at school," she replied. She held up the gold object the counselor had given her.

I could see it clearly now. A shiny gold coin. It had a smiling King Jellyjam engraved on it. I couldn't read the words around the edge of the coin. But I could guess what they were.

"It's my fifth King Coin!" Dierdre declared proudly.

Why is she so excited about it? I wondered. It wasn't a real coin. It probably wasn't even real gold!

"What's a King Coin?" I asked. The coin gleamed in the sunlight.

"If I win one more King Coin, I can walk in the Winners Walk," Dierdre explained.

I started to ask what the Winners Walk was. But Jan and Ivy came running up to congratulate Dierdre. And the three of them all started talking at once.

I suddenly remembered my brother. Where *is* Elliot? I wondered. What has he been doing?

I turned away from Dierdre and the other girls

and started toward the pool exit. But I had only taken a few steps when I heard someone calling my name.

I spun around to see Holly jogging toward me. Her purple-lipsticked lips were knotted in a fretful expression. "Wendy, you'd better come with me," the counselor told me.

My heart skipped. "Huh? What's wrong?" I asked.

"I'm afraid there's a problem," Holly said softly.

9

Something happened to Mom and Dad!

That's the first thought that burst into my head.

"What's wrong?" I cried. "My parents! Are they okay? Are they — "

"We haven't found your parents yet," Holly said. She wrapped a towel around my trembling shoulders. Then she led me to a bench at the side of the pool.

"Is it Elliot?" I cried, dropping down beside her. "What is wrong?"

Holly kept one arm around my shoulders. She leaned close. Her brown eyes stared into mine.

"Wendy, the problem is that you didn't really try very hard to win the race," she said.

I swallowed hard. "Excuse me?"

"I watched you," Holly continued. "I saw you slow your strokes in the last lap. I don't think you tried your best to win."

"But — but — I — " I sputtered.

Holly continued to stare at me without blinking. "Am I right?" she demanded softly.

"I — I'm not used to swimming that far," I stammered. "It was my first race. I didn't think — "

"I know you're new at camp," Holly said, brushing a fly off my leg. "But you know the camp slogan, right?"

"For sure," I replied. "It's everywhere I look! But what does it mean? 'Only The Best!' "

"I guess it's kind of a warning," Holly replied thoughtfully. "That's why I decided to talk to you now, Wendy."

"A warning?" I cried. I felt more confused than ever. "A warning about what?"

Holly didn't reply. She forced a smile to her face and stood up. "Catch you later, okay?"

She turned and hurried away.

I wrapped the towel tighter around my shoulders and started back to the dorm to change. As I walked past the tennis courts, I thought hard about Holly's warning.

Why was it so important for me to win the race?

So that I could be awarded one of those gold coins with the blobby purple king on it?

Why should I care about winning coins? Why couldn't I just play some games, make new friends, and have fun?

Why did Holly say she was giving me a warning? A warning about what?

I shook my head, trying to shake away all these puzzling questions. I'd heard about sports camps from some of my friends back home. Some camps, they said, were really tough. The kids were all serious jock types who wanted to win, win, win.

I guessed this was one of those camps.

Oh, well, I thought, sighing. I don't have to love this camp. Mom and Dad will be here soon to take Elliot and me away.

I glanced up — and saw Elliot.

Sprawled face down on the ground. His arms and legs spread out awkwardly. His eyes closed.

Unconscious.

10

"Ooooh!" I let out a frightened wail.

"Elliot! Elliot!" I dropped down beside him.

He sat up and grinned at me. "How many times are you going to fall for that?" he asked. He started to laugh.

I slugged him in the shoulder as hard as I could. "You creep!"

That made him laugh even harder. It really cracks him up when he makes me look like a jerk.

Why do I always fall for the stupid joke? Elliot pulls it on me all the time. And I always believe he's been knocked out cold.

"I'm never falling for that again. Never!" I cried.

Elliot pulled himself to his feet. "Come watch me play Ping-Pong," he said, tugging my hand. "I'm in the tournament. I'm beating this kid Jeff. He thinks he's good because he puts a spin on his serve. But he's pitiful."

"I can't," I replied. I pulled out of his grasp. "I'm dripping wet. I have to change."

"Come watch," he insisted. "It won't take long. I'll beat him really fast, okay?"

"Elliot — " He certainly was excited.

"If I beat Jeff, I win a King Coin," he announced. "Then I'm going to win five more. I want to win six so I can walk in the Winners Walk before Mom and Dad come for us."

"Good luck," I mumbled, rubbing my wet hair with the towel.

"Were you in a swim race? Did you win?" Elliot asked, tugging my hand again.

"No. I came in second," I told him.

He snickered. "You're a loser. Come watch me beat this kid."

I rolled my eyes. "Okay, okay."

Elliot pulled me to a row of outdoor Ping-Pong tables. They were shielded from the sun by a broad, white canvas awning.

He hurried up to the table on the end. Jeff was waiting for him there, softly bouncing a Ping-Pong ball in the air with his paddle.

I had pictured a little shrimpy guy that Elliot could beat easily. But Jeff was a *big*, red-faced, blond kid with bulging muscles. He had to be twice the size of my brother!

I took a seat on a white wooden bench across from the tables. Elliot can't beat this big guy, I thought. My poor brother is in for a major defeat.

As they started to play, Buddy came walking over and sat down beside me. He flashed me a smile. "No word from your parents yet," he said. "But we'll find them."

We watched the Ping-Pong match. Jeff did his serve with the special spin. Elliot slammed it back at him.

To my surprise, the match was really even. I think Jeff was surprised, too. His returns became more and more wild. And a lot of his special serves missed the table entirely!

They had already played two games, Buddy told me. Jeff had won the first, Elliot the second. This was the third and deciding match.

The game was a tie at sixteen, then a tie at seventeen and eighteen.

I watched Elliot become more and more intense. He wanted desperately to win. He leaned stiffly over the table, gripping the paddle so tightly, his hand was white.

Sweat poured off his forehead. He began ducking and dodging, groaning with each hit, trying to slam every ball.

The more frantic and wild Elliot became, the calmer Jeff appeared.

The game was a tie at nineteen.

Elliot missed a shot and angrily slammed his paddle against the table.

I could see that he was losing it. I'd seen this

happen to my brother many times before. He could never win if he stayed this intense.

As he held the ball and prepared to serve, I raised two fingers to the sides of my mouth and blew hard. He lowered the paddle when he heard my loud whistle.

That was my signal. I'd used it many times before. It meant, "Cool it, Elliot. Calm down."

Elliot turned and gave me a quick thumbs-up.

I saw him take a deep breath. Then another.

My whistle signal always helped him.

He raised the ball and served it to Jeff. Jeff sent back a weak return. Elliot smacked it back into the right corner. Jeff swung off balance and missed.

Jeff served the next one. Elliot backhanded it. Very soft. The ball tipped over the net and dribbled several times on Jeff's side.

Elliot had won!

He let out a gleeful cheer and raised his fists in victory.

Jeff angrily heaved his paddle to the ground and stomped away.

"Your brother is good," Buddy said, climbing to his feet. "I like his style. He's intense."

"For sure," I muttered.

Buddy hurried over to award Elliot his King Coin. "Hey, guy — you only need five more," Buddy said, slapping Elliot a high five, then a low five.

"No problem," Elliot bragged. He held the coin up so I could see it. King Jellyjam smiled out at me, engraved on the coin.

Why did the camp pick this silly little blob for a mascot? I wondered again. He looked like a fat hunk of pudding wearing a crown.

"I've got to get changed," I told Elliot.

He slid the gold coin into the pocket of his shorts. "I'm going to find another sport!" he declared. "I want to win another King Coin before tonight!"

I waved good-bye, then started toward the dorm.

I had walked only a few steps when I heard a low rumbling.

Then the ground started to shake.

I froze. Every muscle in my body locked as the rumbling grew louder.

"Earthquake!" I cried.

11

The ground shook hard. The awning over the Ping-Pong tables shook. The tables bounced on the ground.

My knees buckled. I struggled to stay on my feet.

"Earthquake!" I choked out again.

"It's okay!" Buddy called, running toward me.

He was right. The rumbling sound faded quickly. The ground stopped shaking.

"That happens sometimes," Buddy explained. "It's no problem."

My heart still thudded in my chest. My legs wobbled as if they were rubber bands. "No problem?"

"See?" Buddy motioned around the crowded camp. "No one pays any attention. It lasts only a few seconds.

I gazed around quickly. Buddy was right again. The kids in the chess tournament in front of the lodge didn't glance up from their chessboards. The kickball game on the field across from the pool continued without a pause.

"It usually happens once or twice a day," Buddy told me.

"But what causes it?" I demanded.

He shrugged. "Beats me."

"But — everything shook so hard! Isn't it dangerous?" I asked.

Buddy didn't hear me. He was already jogging over to watch the kickball game.

I turned and started walking to the dorm. I felt kind of shaky. I could still hear that strange rumbling sound in my ears.

As I pulled open the door to the dorm, I bumped into Jan and Ivy. They both had changed into white tennis outfits, and they both carried tennis rackets over their shoulders.

"What sports have you been playing?"

"Did you win a King Coin?"

"Wasn't that a great swim race?"

"Are you having fun, Wendy?"

"Do you play tennis?"

They both talked at once and shot out half a dozen questions. They seemed really excited. They didn't give me a chance to answer.

"We need more girls for the tennis tournament," Ivy said. "We're having a two-day tournament. Come to the courts after lunch, okay?"

"Okay," I agreed. "I'm not that good, but — "

"See you later!" Jan cried. They both hurried away.

Actually, I am a pretty good tennis player. I have a decent serve. And I do all right with my two-handed backhand.

But I'm not great.

Back home, my friend Allison and I always play for fun. We don't try to kill each other. Sometimes we just keep volleying back and forth. We don't even keep score.

I'll enter the tennis tournament, I decided. And if I lose in the first round, it's no big deal.

Besides, I told myself, Mom and Dad will be here any minute. And Elliot and I will have to leave.

Mom and Dad . . . their faces flashed into my mind.

They must be frantic, I realized. They must be worried sick. I hoped they were okay.

I suddenly had an idea.

I'll call home, I decided. I should have thought of this before. I'll call home and leave a message on our answering machine. I'll tell Mom and Dad on the machine where Elliot and I are.

No matter where he goes, Dad checks for phone messages every hour. Mom always makes fun of him for being so nervous about missing a call.

But they'll both be glad to get this message! I told myself.

What a good idea! I congratulated myself.

Now all I needed was a phone.

There *have* to be phones in the dorm, I decided. I searched the small front lobby. But I didn't see any pay phones.

No one at the front desk. No one I could ask.

I peered down a long hallway. Rooms on both sides. No phones.

I tried the other hallway. No pay phones there, either.

Eager to make my call, I turned and hurried back outside. I let out a long sigh of relief when I spotted two pay phones beside the long white dorm building.

My heart pounding, I jogged over to them.

I picked up the phone closest to me. And I started to raise the receiver to my ear —

— when two strong hands grabbed me from behind.

"Get off the phone!" a voice demanded.

12

"Huh?" I shrieked in surprise and dropped the phone. It spun crazily on its cord.

I turned around. "Dierdre! You scared me to death!" I cried.

Her green eyes flashed excitedly. "Sorry, Wendy. I just had to tell you my news! Look!"

She held out her hand. I saw a stack of gold King Coins.

"I just won my sixth coin!" Dierdre declared breathlessly. "Isn't that awesome?"

"I — I guess," I replied uncertainly. I still couldn't figure out why it was such a big deal.

"I'll be in the Winners Walk tonight!" Dierdre exclaimed. "I can't believe I made it!"

"That's great," I told her. "Congratulations."

"Have you won any King Coins yet?" Dierdre asked, still holding out her hand.

"Uh . . . not yet," I replied.

"Well, get going!" Dierdre urged. "Show them what you've got, Wendy. Only The Best!" She flashed me a thumbs-up with her free hand.

"Right. Only The Best," I repeated.

"We'll have a party," Dierdre continued. "In our room. Right after the Winners Walk. Okay? We'll celebrate."

"Great!" I replied. "Maybe we can get a pizza from the mess hall or something."

"Tell Jan and Ivy," Dierdre instructed. "Or I'll tell them. Whoever sees them first! See you later!"

She ran off, holding the six gold coins tightly in her fist.

I realized I was smiling. Dierdre had been so excited, she'd gotten *me* excited. So excited, I forgot about my phone call.

I have to give this camp a chance, I decided. I have to get into the spirit of things and start having some fun. Only The Best! I'm going to *win* that tennis tournament!

We all ate dinner at long wooden tables in the huge mess hall inside the main camp lodge. The long, high-ceilinged room seemed to stretch on forever.

Loud voices and laughter echoed off the walls over the clatter of plates and silverware. Everyone had a story to tell. Everyone wanted to talk about the games of the day.

After dinner, the counselors led us all to the running track. I searched for Elliot. But I couldn't find him in the crowd.

It was a warm, clear night. A pale sliver of a moon floated low over the darkening trees. As the sun set, the sky faded from pink to purple to gray.

When darkness fell, I saw two flickering yellow lights at the far end of the track, moving toward me. As they came near, I could see that they were torches, carried by two counselors.

A blaring trumpet fanfare made us all grow quiet.

I stepped closer to Jan, who stood at my side. "They sure make a big deal of this," I whispered.

"It *is* a big deal," Jan replied, her eyes straight ahead as the torches approached.

"Do we have any food for the party later?" I whispered.

Jan raised a finger to her lips. "Ssshhhh."

Several more torches had been lighted. The yellow balls of light glowed like tiny suns.

I heard a drumroll. Then a loud march blared from the loudspeaker, all trumpets and pounding drums.

We stood in silence as the parade of torches passed by. And, then, in the flickering yellow light, I saw faces. The smiling faces of the kids who had won their sixth King Coin that day.

I counted eight kids. Five boys and three girls.

Their gold coins had been strung as necklaces around their necks. The coins caught the light of the torches and made the faces of the winners appear to glow as they marched by.

Dierdre marched second in line. She seemed so happy and excited! Her coins jangled at her throat. Her smile never faded.

Jan and I waved and called to her, but she marched right past.

A counselor's voice suddenly boomed over the loudspeaker: "Let's hear it for our winners who are taking the Winners Walk tonight!"

A deafening cheer rose up from the kids watching the parade. We all clapped and shouted and whistled until the winners had marched past and the final torches had floated out of sight.

"Only The Best!" the voice shouted over the loudspeaker.

"Only The Best!" we all chanted back. "Only The Best!"

That ended the Winners Walk parade. The lights came on. We all scrambled toward the dorms. The boys ran in one direction, the girls in the other.

"The torches were really cool," I said to Jan as we followed the crowd of girls down the path to the dorm.

"I only need two more King Coins," Jan replied.

"Maybe I can win them tomorrow. Are you playing in the softball tournament?"

"No. Tennis," I told her.

"There are too many good tennis players," Jan replied. "It'll be too hard to win a coin. You should play softball, too."

"Well . . . maybe," I replied.

Ivy was already waiting for us in the room. "Where's Dierdre?" she demanded as Jan and I entered.

"We didn't see her," Jan replied.

"Probably hanging out with the other winners," I added.

"I found two bags of tortilla chips, but I couldn't find any salsa," Ivy reported, holding up the bags.

"Do we have anything to drink?" I asked.

Ivy held up two cans of diet Coke.

"Wow! Great party!" Jan exclaimed, laughing.

"Maybe we should invite some girls in from other rooms," I suggested.

"No way! Then we'd have to share the Cōkes!" Jan protested.

We all laughed.

The three of us joked and kidded around for about half an hour, waiting for Dierdre. We sat down on the floor and opened one of the bags of tortilla chips.

Without realizing it, we finished off the whole bag. Then we passed around one of the cans of soda.

"Where *is* she?" Jan demanded, glancing at her watch.

"It's nearly time for lights-out," Ivy sighed. "We won't have much time for a party."

"Maybe Dierdre forgot we were having a party," I suggested, crinkling up the tortilla chip bag and tossing it toward the trash basket.

I missed. Basketball is definitely not my sport.

"But the party was her idea!" Ivy replied. She climbed to her feet and started pacing back and forth. "Where can she be? Everyone is inside by now."

"Let's go find her," I said. The words just popped out of my mouth. That happens to me sometimes. I get a bright idea before I know what I'm saying.

"Yes! Let's go!" Ivy eagerly agreed.

"Whoa. Hold it," Jan said, stepping in front of us, blocking our way to the door. "We're not allowed. You know the rules, Ivy. We're not allowed outside after ten."

"We'll sneak out, find Dierdre, and sneak back in," Ivy replied. "Come on, Jan. What could happen?"

"Right. What could happen?" I chimed in.

Jan was outnumbered. "Okay, okay. But I hope we don't get caught," she muttered. She followed Ivy and me to the door.

"What could happen?" I asked myself, leading the way into the empty hall.

"What could happen?" I repeated as we sneaked out the door, into the night.

"What could happen?"

I didn't know it. But the answer to the question was: *A LOT!*

13

The night had grown warmer. And steamier. As I crept out the door, I felt as if I were stepping into a hot shower.

A mosquito buzzed around my head. I tried to clap it between my hands. Missed.

Jan, Ivy, and I edged our way around the side of the building. My shoes slid on the dew-wet grass. Bright spotlights shone down from the trees, lighting the path.

We crept in the shadows.

"Where should we look first?" Ivy whispered.

"Let's start at the lodge," I suggested. "Maybe all of tonight's winners are partying there."

"I don't hear any partying," Jan whispered. "It's so quiet out here!"

She was right. The only sounds I could hear were the steady chirp of crickets and the whisper of the warm wind through the trees.

Keeping in the shadows, we followed the path

toward the lodge. We passed the swimming pool, empty and silent. The water shimmered like silver under the bright spotlights.

It was such a hot, wet night, I imagined myself jumping into the pool with all of my clothes on.

But we were on a mission: To find Dierdre. No time to think about late-night swims.

Staying close together, we passed the row of Ping-Pong tables. They made me think of Elliot. I wondered what he was doing. Probably tucked into bed.

Like any sensible person.

We were approaching the first row of tennis courts when Ivy suddenly cried out, "Whoa! Get back!" She grabbed me and shoved me hard against the fence.

I heard soft footsteps on the path. Someone humming.

The three of us held our breath as a counselor walked past. He had curly black hair and wore dark blue sunglasses even though it was night. He wore the white T-shirt and white shorts that made up the counselor's uniform.

We pressed our backs against the tennis court fence. "That's Billy," Jan whispered. "He's kind of cute. He's always so happy."

"He won't be too happy if he catches us," Ivy whispered. "We'll be in major trouble."

Humming to himself, snapping his fingers, Billy

walked past us. The path curved around the other side of the tennis courts. I watched him until he disappeared.

I took a deep breath. I hadn't been breathing the whole time!

"Where's he going?" Ivy wondered.

"Maybe he's going to the party at the lodge," I suggested.

"Why don't we ask him?" Jan joked.

"For sure," I muttered.

We checked out the path in both directions. Then we started walking again.

We made our way past the tennis courts. The spotlights in the trees cast long shadows across the path. The shadows shifted and moved as the tree limbs bobbed in the wind. They looked like dark creatures crawling and slithering over the ground.

Despite the heat of the night, I shivered.

It was kind of creepy walking over these moving shadows. I had the feeling one of them might reach up, grab me, and pull me down.

Weird thought, huh?

I turned back in time to see the lights in the dorm windows start to go out. Lights-out.

I tapped Jan on the shoulder. She turned and watched the dorm, too. As the lights all went out, the building seemed to disappear in front of our eyes. It faded into the black of the night sky.

"M-maybe this wasn't such a good idea," I whispered.

Ivy didn't reply. She bit her lower lip. Her eyes were darting around the darkness.

Jan laughed. "Don't wimp out now," she scolded. "We're almost to the lodge."

We cut through the soccer field. The main lodge stood on a low, sloping hill, hidden by wide, old maple and sassafras trees.

We didn't have to climb very far up the hill to see that the lodge was as dark as the dorm.

"No party up there," I whispered.

Ivy sighed, disappointed. "Well, where could Dierdre be?"

"We could try the boys' dorm!" I joked.

They both laughed.

Our laughter was cut short by a loud fluttering sound, very close by.

"What's that?" Ivy cried.

"Ohhh!" I let out a low moan as I raised my eyes and saw them.

The sky was thick with bats. Dozens of black bats.

Fluttering over the spotlights in the old trees. And, then — swooping down to get us!

14

I couldn't help myself. I let out a scream. Then I shielded my face with both hands.

I heard Jan and Ivy gasp.

The fluttering grew louder. Closer.

I could feel the bats' hot breath on the back of my neck. Then I could feel them clawing at my hair, tearing at my face.

I've got a real good imagination when it comes to bats.

"Wendy, it's okay," Jan whispered. She tugged my hands from my face. She pointed. "Look."

I followed her gaze up to the fluttering black wings. The bats were swooping low. But they weren't swooping at us. They were swooping down and landing on the swimming pool at the bottom of the hill.

In the bright spotlights, I could see them dart into the water — for less than a second. Then sweep back up to the sky.

"I — I don't like bats," I whispered.

"Neither do I," Ivy confessed. "I know they're supposed to be good. I know they eat insects and stuff. But I still think they're creepy."

"Well, they won't bother us," Jan said. "They're just taking a drink." She gave Ivy and me a push to get us started down the hill.

We were lucky. Nobody had heard me scream. But we had walked only a few steps when we spotted another counselor coming down the path. I recognized her. She had straight white-blond hair that tumbled down to her waist from under a blue baseball cap.

Without making a sound, all three of us dove behind a tall evergreen shrub and crouched down.

Did she see us?

I held my breath again.

She kept walking.

"Where are these counselors going?" Ivy whispered.

"Let's follow her," I suggested.

"Stay far back," Jan instructed.

We slowly climbed back to our feet. And stepped out from behind the shrub.

And stopped when we heard the low, rumbling sound.

As the rumbling grew louder, the ground began to shake.

I caught the frightened expressions on my two friends' faces. Ivy and Jan were just as scared as I was.

The ground shook harder, so hard that we dropped to our knees. I leaned on all fours, holding on to the grass. The ground trembled and shook. The rumbling became a roar.

I shut my eyes.

The sound slowly faded.

The ground gave a final tremble, then remained still.

I opened my eyes and turned to Ivy and Jan. They started to stand. Slowly.

"I hate when that happens!" Jan muttered.

"What *is* it?" I whispered. I stood up on shaky legs.

"Nobody knows," Jan replied, brushing grass stains off her knees. "It just happens. A few times a day."

"I think we should give up on Dierdre," Ivy said quietly. "I want to go back. To the dorm."

"Yeah. I'm with you," I replied wearily. "We can have our celebration with Dierdre tomorrow."

"She can tell us all about where she was tonight and what she did," Jan said.

"This was a crazy idea," I muttered.

"It was *your* idea!" Jan exclaimed.

"Most of my ideas are crazy!" I replied.

Hiding in the shadows, we made our way down to the path. I gazed toward the pool. The bats had disappeared. Maybe the rumbling sound had scared them back into the woods.

The crickets had stopped chirping. The air remained hot, but silent and still.

The only sound was the scrape of our sneakers on the soft dirt path.

And, then — before we could move or hide — we heard someone else's footsteps.

Rapid footsteps. Running hard. Running toward us.

I stopped short when I heard a girl's desperate cry. "Help me! Please — somebody! Help me!"

15

A hot gust of wind shook the trees, making their eerie dark shadows dance.

I leaped back, startled by the girl's terrified cries.

"Help me! Please — !"

She came running around from the side of the tennis courts. She wore tight blue short-shorts and a magenta midriff top.

Her arms were stretched out in front of her. Her long hair flew wildly behind her head.

I recognized her as soon as she burst into view.

The little red-haired girl with all the freckles. The one who had hidden in the woods and warned Elliot and me not to come into the camp.

"Help me!"

She ran right into me, sobbing hard. I threw my arms around her tiny shoulders and held her. "You're okay," I whispered. "You're okay."

"No!" she shrieked. She tugged away from me.

"What's wrong?" Jan demanded. "Why are you out here?"

"Why aren't you in bed?" Ivy added, stepping up beside me.

The little girl didn't answer. Her entire body trembled.

She grabbed my hand and pulled me behind the bushes beside the path. Jan and Ivy followed.

"I'm not okay," she started, wiping the tears off her freckled cheeks with both hands. "I'm not. I — I — "

"What's your name?" Jan asked in a whisper.

"Why are you out here?" Ivy repeated.

I heard the flutter of bat wings again, low overhead. But I stared at the little girl and forced myself to ignore them.

"My name — it's Alicia," the girl replied, sobbing. "We've got to go. Fast!"

"Huh?" I cried. "Take a deep breath, Alicia. You're okay. Really."

"No!" she cried again, shaking her head.

"You're safe now. You're with us," I insisted.

"We're not safe," she cried. "No one. No one here. I tried to warn people. I tried to tell you . . ." Her words were cut off once again by her loud sobs.

"What *is* it?" Ivy demanded.

"What did you try to warn us about?" Jan asked, leaning down to the crying girl.

"I — I saw something *terrible!*" Alicia stammered. "I — "

"What did you see?" I asked impatiently.

"I followed them," Alicia replied. "And I saw it. Something horrible. I — I can't talk about it. We just have to run. We have to tell the others. Everyone. We have to run. We have to get away from here!"

She let out a long breath. Her entire body trembled again.

"But *why* do we have to run?" I asked, placing my hands gently on her shoulders.

I felt so bad. I wanted to calm her. I wanted to tell her that everything would be okay. But I didn't know how to convince her.

What had she seen? What had frightened her so much?

Had she had a bad dream?

"We have to go now!" she repeated shrilly. Her red hair was matted to her face by her tears. She grabbed my arm and pulled hard. "Hurry! We've got to run! I saw it!"

"Saw *what?*" I cried.

Alicia had no time to reply.

A dark-haired counselor stepped up in front of the bushes. "Caught you!" he cried.

16

I froze. My entire body went cold.

The counselor's dark eyes flashed in the light of a spotlight. "What are *you* doing out here?" he demanded.

I sucked in a deep breath and started to answer.

But another voice replied before I could. "Kind of nosy, aren't you?" It was another counselor. A woman with short, black hair.

Breathing hard, trying not to make a sound, I ducked lower behind the bushes. My two friends dropped to their knees.

"You aren't following me — are you?" the first counselor teased.

"Why would I follow you? Maybe you're following me!" the woman teased back.

They didn't see us, I realized happily. We were two feet away from them. But they didn't see us behind the bushes.

A few seconds later, the two counselors strolled off together. My friends and I waited a long while, listening hard until we could no longer hear their voices. Then we climbed slowly to our feet.

"Alicia?" I asked. "Are you okay?"

"Alicia?" Ivy and Jan cried.

The little girl had vanished.

We sneaked back into the dorm through a side door. Luckily, there were no counselors patrolling the halls. No one in sight.

"Dierdre — are you back?" Jan called as we stepped into our room.

No reply.

I clicked on the light. Dierdre's bunk remained empty.

"Better turn off the light," Ivy warned. "It's after lights-out."

I clicked the light back off. Then I stumbled toward my bunk, waiting for my eyes to adjust to the darkness.

"Where is Dierdre?" Ivy asked. "I'm a little worried about her. Maybe we should tell a counselor that she's missing."

"What counselor?" Jan asked, slumping onto her bed. "There's no one around. The counselors are all out somewhere."

"I'm sure she's partying somewhere and forgot all about us," I said, yawning. I bent to pull down the covers on my bed.

"What do you think that little girl saw?" Ivy asked, peering out the window.

"Alicia? I think she had a bad dream," I replied.

"But she was so frightened!" Jan said, shaking her head. "And what was she doing outside?"

"And why did she run away from us like that?" Ivy added.

"Weird," I mumbled.

"Weird is right," Jan agreed. Weird is the word of the night. She made her way to the dresser. "I'm getting changed for bed. Big day tomorrow. I've got to win two more King Coins."

"Me, too," Ivy said, yawning.

Jan pulled out a dresser drawer. "Oh, no!" she shrieked. "No! I don't *believe* it!"

17

"Jan — what is it?" I cried.

Ivy and I tore across the room to the dresser.

Jan continued to stare down into the open drawer. "It's so dark," she said. "I opened Dierdre's drawer by mistake. And — and — it's *empty*!"

"Huh?" Ivy and I both uttered our surprise.

Squinting through the dim gray light, I studied the dresser drawer. Totally empty. "Check the closet," I suggested.

Ivy crossed the room in three or four quick strides. She pulled open the closet door.

"Dierdre's stuff — it's all gone!" Ivy declared.

"Weird," I muttered. It was still the word of the night.

"Why would she move out and not tell us?" Jan demanded.

"Where did she go?" Ivy added.

Good question, I thought, staring at the empty closet.

Where did Dierdre go?

*　　*　　*

Breakfast was the noisiest meal of the day. Spoons clattered against cereal bowls. Orange juice pitchers banged on the long wooden tables.

Voices rang out as if someone had turned up the volume all the way. Everyone talked excitedly about the sports they planned to play today, the games they planned to win.

I had taken the last shower. So Jan and Ivy were already eating breakfast when I made my way into the mess hall.

As I pushed through the narrow aisle between the tables, I searched for Dierdre. No sign of her.

I hadn't slept very well, even though I was really tired. I kept thinking about Dierdre — and about Alicia. And I kept wondering what was taking Mom and Dad so long to get in touch with us.

I spotted Elliot at the end of a table filled with boys about his age. He had a stack of waffles in front of him, and he was pouring dark syrup over them.

"Elliot — what's up?" I called, squeezing through the aisle to get over to him.

My brother didn't bother saying good morning. "I've got a one-on-one tournament this morning," he reported excitedly. "I could win my third King Coin!"

"Thrills and chills," I replied, rolling my eyes. "You haven't heard anything about Mom and Dad, have you?"

215

He stared at me as if he didn't remember who they were. Then he shook his head. "Not yet. Isn't this a great camp? Did we luck out, or what?"

I didn't reply. My eyes were on the next table. I thought I had spotted Dierdre. But it was just another girl with streaky blond hair.

"Have you won any coins yet?" Elliot asked. He had a mouth full of waffle. Syrup dripped down his chin.

"Not yet," I replied.

He snickered. "They should change the camp slogan for you, Wendy. Only The Worst!"

Elliot laughed. The other boys at the table laughed, too.

As I said, Elliot really cracks himself up.

I wasn't in the mood for his lame jokes. My mind was still on Dierdre. "Catch you later," I said.

I squeezed past the table and headed toward the girls' side of the room. Cheers and laughter rang out at a table near the wall. A scrambled-egg tossing battle had broken out. Three counselors rushed to stop it.

Jan and Ivy's table was full. I found an empty space at the next table. I poured myself a glass of juice and a bowl of cornflakes. But I didn't feel too hungry.

"Hey — !" I called out when I saw Buddy walk by. He didn't hear me over the noise, so I jumped up and ran after him.

"Hi. What's up?" He greeted me with a smile.

His blond hair was still wet from the shower. He smelled kind of flowery. Aftershave, I guessed.

"Do you know where Dierdre went?" I demanded.

He narrowed his eyes in surprise. "Dierdre?"

"A girl in my dorm room," I explained. "She didn't come back to the room last night. Her closet is empty."

"Dierdre," he repeated, thinking hard. He raised his clipboard to his face and ran his finger down it slowly. "Oh, yeah. She's gone." His cheeks turned bright pink.

"Excuse me?" I stared up at him. "Dierdre is gone? Where did she go? Home?"

He studied the sheet on his clipboard. "I guess. It just says she's gone." His cheeks darkened from pink to red.

"That's so weird," I told him. "She didn't say good-bye or anything."

Buddy shrugged. A smile spread over his face. "Have a nice day!"

He started toward the counselors' table at the front of the huge room. But I ran after him. I grabbed his arm.

"Buddy, one more question," I said. "Do you know where I can find a little girl named Alicia?"

Buddy waved to some boys across the room. "Go get 'em, guys! Only The Best!" he shouted to them. Then he turned back to me. "Alicia?"

"I don't know her last name. She's probably six

or seven," I told him. "She has beautiful, long red hair and a face full of freckles."

"Alicia . . ." He chewed his bottom lip. Then he raised the clipboard again.

I watched as he ran his finger down the list of names. When his finger stopped, his cheeks turned pink again.

"Oh, yeah. Alicia," he said, lowering the clipboard. He grinned at me. A strange grin. A chilling grin. "She's gone, too."

18

"Jan! Ivy!" I saw them hurrying from the mess hall, and I chased after them. "We've got to talk!" I cried breathlessly.

"We can't. We're late." Jan straightened her bangs with one hand. "If we don't get to the volleyball nets in time, we can't be in the tournament."

"But it's *important*!" I called as they jogged to the doors.

They didn't seem to hear me. I watched them disappear into the morning sunlight.

My heart pounded in my chest. I suddenly felt cold all over.

I caught up with my brother, who was playfully boxing a tall, skinny boy with short blond hair. "Elliot — come here," I instructed. "Just for a minute."

"I can't," he called. "Remember? My one-on-one contest?"

The tall, skinny boy hurried out the door. I stepped in front of Elliot, blocking his path.

"Give me a break!" he cried. "I don't want to be late. I'm going against Jeff. Remember him? I can beat him. He's big, but he's real slow."

"Elliot, something strange is going on here," I said, backing him against the wall. Kids were staring at us as they made their way outside. But I didn't care.

"*You're* the only one who's strange!" Elliot shot back. "Are you going to let me go to the basketball court or not?"

He started to push past me. I pinned his shoulders to the wall with both hands.

"Just give me one second!" I insisted. "There's something wrong with this camp, Elliot." I let go of him.

"You mean the rumbling noises?" he asked, brushing back his dark hair with one hand. "That's just gas under the ground or something. A counselor explained it to me."

"That's not what I'm talking about," I replied. "Kids are disappearing."

He laughed. "Invisible kids? You mean like a magic trick?"

"Stop making fun of me!" I snapped. "It isn't funny, Elliot. Kids are disappearing. Dierdre from my dorm room? She was in the Winners Walk last night. Then she didn't come back to the room."

Elliot's grin faded.

"This morning, Buddy told me she was gone," I continued. I snapped my fingers. "Just like that. And a little girl named Alicia — she disappeared, too."

Elliot's brown eyes studied me. "Kids have to go home *sometime*," he insisted. "What's the big deal?"

"And what about Mom and Dad?" I demanded. "They couldn't have driven very far before they realized the trailer had come loose. Why haven't they found us? Why hasn't the camp found them?"

Elliot shrugged. "Beats me," he replied casually. He dodged past me and started to the door. "Wendy, you're just unhappy because you stink at sports. But I'm having a great time here. Don't mess it up for me — okay?"

"But — but — Elliot — !" I sputtered.

Shaking his head, he pushed the door open with both hands and escaped into the sunlight.

I balled both hands into tight fists. I really wanted to pound him. Why wouldn't he listen to me? Couldn't he see how upset and frightened I was?

Elliot is the kind of kid who never worries about anything. Everything always seems to go his way. So why should he sweat it?

But you'd think he'd be just a *little* worried about Mom and Dad.

Mom and Dad . . .

I had a heavy feeling in my stomach as I made

my way slowly out the door. Had they been in a car accident or something? Is that why they hadn't found Elliot and me yet?

No. Stop making things worse, I scolded myself. Don't let your imagination run away with you, Wendy.

I suddenly remembered my plan to call home. Yes, I decided, I will do that right now. I will call home and leave a message for Mom and Dad on the answering machine.

I stopped in the middle of the path and searched for a pay phone. A group of girls carrying hockey sticks passed by. I heard a long whistle coming from the pool across from the tennis courts. Then I heard the splash of kids diving into the water.

Everyone is having fun, I thought — except me.

I decided to make the call, then find a sport to play. Something to take my mind off all my crazy worries.

I returned to the row of blue and white pay phones at the side of the lodge. I ran full speed and picked up the nearest phone.

I raised the receiver to my ear and started to punch in our number.

Then I cried out in surprise.

19

"Hi there, Camper!" boomed a cheerful, deep voice. *"Have a wonderful day at camp. This is King Jellyjam greeting you. Work hard. Play hard. And win. And always remember — Only The Best!"*

"Oh, no!" I cried. "A stupid message — !"

"Hi there, Camper! Have a wonderful day — " The tape started to repeat in my ear.

I slammed the receiver down and picked up the next phone.

"Hi there, Camper! Have a wonderful day at camp." The same jolly, booming voice. The same recorded message.

I tried every phone in the row. They all played the same message. None of the phones were real.

Where are the real phones? I wondered. There *have* to be phones that actually work.

I turned away from the lodge and wandered down the dirt path. As I passed the bushes where

Jan, Ivy, and I had hid last night, I felt a chill. And thought about Alicia.

Bright sunlight washed over the sloping, grassy hill. I shielded my eyes and watched a black-and-gold monarch butterfly. It fluttered toward a patch of red and pink geraniums.

I walked aimlessly, searching for a telephone. All around, kids were shouting, laughing, playing hard. I didn't really hear them. I was deep into my own troubled thoughts.

"Hey! Hey! Hey!"

My brother's voice startled me into stopping. I blinked several times, struggling to focus.

I saw that I had wandered down to the basketball court. Elliot and Jeff were having their one-on-one basketball competition.

Jeff dribbled the ball. It thudded loudly on the asphalt court. My brother waved both arms in Jeff's face. Made a grab for the ball.

Missed.

Jeff lowered his shoulder. Bumped Elliot out of the way. Dribbled to the basket — and shot.

"Two points!" he cried, grinning.

Elliot scowled and shook his head. "You fouled me."

Jeff pretended not to hear. He was twice as big as Elliot. A big hulk. He could push Elliot all over the court, if he wanted to.

Whatever made Elliot think he could win?

"What's the score?" Jeff demanded, wiping

sweat off his forehead with the back of one hand.

"Eighteen to ten," Elliot reported unhappily. I didn't need twenty guesses to figure out that my brother was losing.

The basketball court was closed off by a mesh-wire fence. I grabbed the fence with both hands, pressed my face up against it, and watched.

Elliot dribbled, moving back, back, giving himself some space. Jeff moved with him, leaning forward, adjusting his basketball shorts with one hand as he moved.

Suddenly, Elliot burst forward, his eyes on the basket. He started his jump, raised his right hand to shoot — and Jeff grabbed the ball away.

Elliot jumped and shot nothing but air.

Jeff dribbled twice. Put up a two-handed layup. *Swish*. The score was twenty to ten.

Jeff won the game a few seconds later. He let out a cheer and slapped Elliot a high five.

Elliot frowned and shook his head. "Lucky shots," he muttered.

"Yeah. For sure," Jeff replied, using the front of his sleeveless blue T-shirt to mop his sweating face. "Hey, congratulate me, man. You're my sixth victim!"

"Huh?" Elliot stared at him, hands pressed against his knees, struggling to catch his breath. "You mean — ?"

"Yeah." Jeff grinned. "My sixth King Coin. I get to march in the Winners Walk tonight!"

"Wow. That's cool," Elliot replied without enthusiasm. "I still have three coins to go."

I had the sudden feeling that I was being watched. I let go of the wire fence and took a step back.

Buddy had been staring at me from the path. His eyes were narrowed, and his mouth was set in a stern, unhappy expression.

How long had he been standing there?

Why did he look so unhappy? His grim expression gave me a chill.

As I turned to him, he stepped forward. His blue eyes stared hard into mine.

"I'm sorry, Wendy," the counselor said softly. "But you have to go."

20

"Excuse me?" I gaped at him. My mouth dropped open.

What was he saying? *Where* did I have to go?

Did he mean I had to go — *like Dierdre and Alicia?*

"You have to go find a sport," Buddy repeated, still speaking softly. His solemn expression didn't change. "You can't stand around watching other kids play. King Jellyjam would never approve of that."

I'd like to *step* on that ugly little blob! I thought angrily. What a stupid name. King Jellyjam. Yuck!

Buddy had just scared me to death. Was he *trying* to frighten me? I wondered.

No, I quickly decided. Buddy doesn't know that I'm upset about things. How could he know?

Buddy hurried on to the basketball court. He slapped Jeff on the back and handed him a gold King Coin. "Way to go, guy!" he cried, flashing

Jeff a thumbs-up. "I'll see you in the Winners Walk tonight. Only The Best!"

Buddy said a few words to my brother. Elliot shrugged a few times. Then he said something that made Buddy laugh. I couldn't hear their words.

When Elliot trotted off to find his next sport, Buddy strode quickly back to me. He put an arm around my shoulders and guided me away from the basketball court.

"I guess you're just not a self-starter, Wendy," he said.

"I guess," I replied. What was I supposed to say?

"Well, I'm going to give you a schedule for today. See if you like it," Buddy said. "First, I have a tennis match lined up for you. You play tennis, right?"

"A little," I told him. "I'm not that great, but — "

"After tennis, come down to the softball diamond, okay?" Buddy continued. "We'll get you on one of the softball teams."

He flashed me a warm smile. "I think you'll have a lot more fun if you join in — don't you?"

"Yeah. Probably," I replied. I wanted to sound more enthusiastic. But I just couldn't.

Buddy led me onto one of the back tennis courts. An African-American girl about my age was warming up by hitting a tennis ball against a backboard.

She turned and greeted me as I approached. "How's it going?"

"Fine," I replied. We introduced ourselves.

Her name was Rose. She was tall and pretty. She wore a purple tank top over black shorts. I saw a silver ring dangling from one ear.

Buddy handed me a racket. "Have fun," he said. "And watch out, Wendy. Rose already has five King Coins!"

"Are you a good tennis player?" I asked, twirling the racket in my hand.

Rose nodded. "Yeah. Pretty good. How about you?"

"I don't know," I told her honestly. "My friend and I always play just for fun."

Rose laughed. She had a deep, throaty laugh that I liked. It made me want to laugh, too. "I *never* play for fun!" she declared.

She told the truth.

We volleyed back and forth for a while, to get warmed up. Rose leaned forward, tensed her body, narrowed her dark eyes — then started slamming the ball back at me as if we were playing the final set of a championship!

She played even harder once we started our match.

I found out very quickly that I was no match

for her. I was lucky to return a few of her serves!

Rose was a good sport about it. I caught her snickering a few times at my two-handed backhand. But she didn't make fun of my pitiful game. And she gave me some really helpful tips as the match continued.

She won in straight sets.

I congratulated her. She seemed really excited about winning her sixth King Coin.

A woman counselor I hadn't seen before appeared on the court and presented the coin to Rose. "See you at the Winners Walk tonight," she said, grinning.

Then the counselor turned to me. "The softball diamond is right over that hill, Wendy." She pointed.

I thanked her and began walking in that direction. "Don't walk — run!" she called. "Let's see some spirit! Only The Best!"

I let out an unhappy groan. I don't think she heard me. Then I obediently started to run.

Why was everyone always rushing me around here? I complained silently. Why can't I go lie down by the pool and work on my tan?

As the softball diamond came into view, I started to cheer up a little. I actually like softball. I'm not much of a fielder. But I'm a pretty good slugger.

The teams, I saw, had boys and girls on them.

I recognized two of the girls from my breakfast table this morning.

One of them tossed me a bat. "Hi. I'm Ronni. You can be on our team," she said. "Can you pitch?"

"I guess," I replied, wrapping my hands around the bat. "Sometimes I pitch after school on the playground."

She nodded. "Okay. You can pitch the first couple of innings."

Ronni called the other kids together and we huddled. We went around the circle, giving our names. Then the kids who didn't have fielding positions chose their spots.

"If we win, do we *all* get King Coins?" a boy with a fake tattoo of an eagle on his shoulder asked.

"Yes. All of us," Ronni told him.

Everyone cheered.

"Don't start cheering yet. We've got to win first!" Ronni exclaimed.

She went around the circle, giving the batting order. Since I was the pitcher, I batted ninth.

But since I had a bat, I decided to take a few practice swings. I stepped away from the others, behind the third base line.

Easing my hands up on the bat, I took a soft swing. I like to choke up pretty high. I'm not very strong, and it gives me a harder swing.

The bat felt pretty good. I took a few more soft swings.

Then I pulled it behind my shoulder — and swung as hard as I could.

I didn't see Buddy standing there.

The bat smacked him hard in the chest.

It made a sickening *thocccck* as it crashed into his ribs.

I let the bat fall from my hands. Then I staggered back. Stunned. Horrified.

21

Buddy's smile faded. He narrowed his blue eyes at me.

He raised a hand and pointed a finger at me.

"I like the way you choke up," he said. "But maybe we could find you a lighter bat."

"Huh?" My mouth hung open. I couldn't move. I stood there, gaping at him. "Buddy — ?"

He picked up the bat from the ground. "Does it feel comfortable? Let me see you swing again, Wendy." He handed the bat to me.

My hands trembled as I took it from him. I kept my eyes on him. Waited for him to cry out. To grab his chest and collapse in a heap on the ground.

"Some of the aluminum bats are lighter," he said. He brushed back his blond hair with one hand. "Go ahead. Swing again."

I took a few shaky steps away from him. I wanted to make sure I didn't hit him again. Then I choked up on the bat and swung.

"How is it?" he asked.

"F-fine," I stammered.

He flashed me a thumbs-up and went to talk to Ronni.

Whoa! I thought. What is the story here?

I swung that bat into his chest, hard enough to break a few ribs. Or at least knock his breath out.

But Buddy didn't even seem to notice!

What is the story here?

I told Jan and Ivy about it at dinner.

Jan snickered. "I guess your swing isn't as hard as you think."

"But it made a horrible sound! Like eggs breaking or something!" I exclaimed. "And he just went on smiling and talking."

"He probably waited until he was out of sight. Then he screamed his head off!" Ivy suggested.

I forced myself to laugh along with my two friends. But I didn't feel like laughing.

It was all too strange.

I mean, *no one* could take a blow like that right in the chest and not even say "Ouch!"

Our team lost by ten points. But after that *thocccck*, who could think about the game?

I glanced across the room to the counselors' table. Buddy sat at one end, talking and laughing with Holly. He seemed perfectly okay.

I kept glancing at him all through dinner. Again and again, I heard the sickening *thocccck* the bat made as it smashed into his chest. I just couldn't get it out of my mind.

I kept thinking about it as we trooped out to the track after dinner for the Winners Walk. It was a windy night. The torches flickered and nearly went out.

The trees around the track shivered and bent. Their branches seemed to reach down for the ground.

The marching music started, and the winners paraded by. Rose waved to me as she passed. I saw Jeff walking proudly near the back of the line, his gold coins jangling around his neck.

After the ceremony, I hurried back to the room and climbed into bed. Too many troubling thoughts whirred around in my brain. I wanted to go to sleep and shut them out.

The next morning at breakfast, Rose and Jeff were gone.

22

I searched for Rose and Jeff. And I searched for my brother all morning. I knew he'd be playing hard at one of the sports. But I walked from the soccer field at one end of the camp to the driving range at the other end, and I didn't see him.

Had Elliot disappeared, too?

The frightening thought kept tugging at my mind.

We've got to get out of this camp!

I kept repeating those words to myself as I made my way along the crisscrossing dirt paths.

King Jellyjam, the little purple blob, grinned at me from the signs posted everywhere. Even his cartoon smile gave me the creeps.

Something was terribly wrong at King Jellyjam's Sports Camp. And the more I walked, my eyes searching every face for my brother, the more frightened I became.

Buddy caught up to me after lunch. He led me back to the softball diamond. "Wendy, you can't leave your team," he said sternly. "Forget yesterday. You still have a chance. If you win today, you guys all win King Coins."

I didn't want any King Coins. I wanted to see my parents. I wanted to see my brother. And I wanted to get *out* of there!

I didn't pitch today. I played left field, which gave me plenty of time to think.

I planned our escape.

It won't be that hard, I decided. Elliot and I will sneak out after dinner when everyone is watching the Winners Walk. We'll make our way down the hill, back to the highway. Then we'll walk or hitchhike to the nearest town with a police station.

I knew the police would find Mom and Dad for us easily.

A simple plan, right? Now all I had to do was find Elliot.

Our team lost the game seven to nine.

I grounded out to end the game. The other kids were disappointed that the team lost, but I didn't really care.

I still hadn't won a single King Coin. As we trotted toward our dorms, I saw Buddy watching me. He had a fretful expression on his face.

"Wendy — what's your next sport?" he called to me.

I pretended I didn't hear him and trotted away.

My next sport is running, I thought unhappily. Running away from this horrible place.

The ground began to rumble and shake as I passed the main lodge. This time, I ignored it and kept walking to the dorm.

I didn't find Elliot until after dinner. I saw him heading out the mess-hall door with two buddies. They were laughing, talking loudly, and bumping each other with their chests as they walked.

"Elliot!" I called, chasing after him. "Hey, Elliot — wait up!"

He turned away from his two friends. "Oh. Hi," he said. "How's it going?"

"Did you forget you have a sister?" I demanded angrily.

He narrowed his eyes at me. "Excuse me?"

"Where have you been?" I asked.

A grin spread over his face. "Winning these," he said. He raised the chain around his neck to show off the gold King Coins he was wearing. "I've got five."

"Awesome," I said sarcastically. "Elliot — we've got to get *out* of here!"

"Huh? Get out?" He twisted up his face, confused.

"Yes," I insisted. "We have to get away from this camp — tonight!"

"I can't," Elliot replied. "No way."

Kids pushed past us, on their way to watch the

Winners Walk. I followed Elliot out the mess-hall door. Then I pulled him off the path, onto the grass at the side of the building.

"You can't leave? Why not?" I demanded.

"Not till I win my sixth coin," he said. He jangled the coin necklace in my face.

"Elliot — this place is dangerous!" I cried. "And Mom and Dad must be — "

"You're just jealous," he interrupted. He jangled the coins again. "You haven't won any — have you!"

I balled my hands into fists. I wanted to strangle him. I really did.

He was such a competitive jerk. He always had to win everything.

I took a deep breath and tried to speak calmly. "Elliot, aren't you at all worried about Mom and Dad?"

He lowered his eyes for a moment. "A little."

"Well, we have to get out of here and find them!" I declared.

"Tomorrow," he replied. "After the track meet in the morning. After I win my sixth coin."

I opened my mouth to argue with him. But what was the point?

I knew how stubborn my brother can be. If he wanted to win that sixth coin, he wouldn't leave till he won it.

I couldn't argue with him. And I couldn't drag him away. "Right after the track meet tomorrow morning," I told him, "we're out of here! Whether you win or lose. Agreed?"

He thought about it. "Okay. Agreed," he said finally. Then he trotted off to find his friends.

Four kids marched in the Winners Walk. As I watched from the sidelines, I thought about the kids I knew who had marched before.

Dierdre. Rose. Jeff . . .

Had they all gone home? Were they picked up by their parents? Were they back home now safe and sound?

Maybe I'm frightening myself for no reason, I thought.

Everyone else in camp seems to be having a great time. Why am I the only worrier?

And then I remembered that I *wasn't* the only worrier.

Alicia's tear-stained face floated into my mind.

What had Alicia seen that had frightened her so much? Why was she desperately trying to warn us to get away?

I'll probably never find out, I told myself.

When the Winners Walk ceremony ended, I didn't feel like going back to the dorm. I knew I couldn't get to sleep. Too many thoughts troubled my mind.

As the other kids made their way to their rooms, I ducked into the deep shadows. Then I sneaked along the path to the sloping hill that led up to the main lodge.

Hiding behind a wide evergreen shrub, I dropped down onto the grass. It was a cool, cloudy night. The air felt heavy and damp.

I raised my eyes to the sky. Clouds covered the stars and the moon. Far in the distance, I could see tiny red lights moving slowly against the blackness. An airplane. I wondered where it was headed.

Crickets began to chirp. The wind rustled my hair.

I gazed up at the starless sky. Trying to relax. Trying to calm myself down.

After a few minutes, I heard voices. Footsteps.

I pulled myself up to my knees and ducked low behind the shrub.

The voices grew louder. A girl laughed.

Carefully, I peered out from between the piney branches. I saw two counselors, walking rapidly along the path that led up the hill.

Behind them, I spotted another group of counselors making their way quickly up the hill. They all seemed to be in a hurry.

I lowered myself behind the shrub and hid in the darkness.

They're heading to the lodge, I decided. Must be some kind of counselors' meeting.

Their white shorts and T-shirts were easy to

see, even on such a dark night. Keeping out of sight, I watched them make their way up the path.

But to my surprise, they didn't go to the lodge. Several yards from the lodge entrance, they turned off the path and ducked into the woods.

Where were they going?

I saw two more groups of counselors make their way into the trees. There must be a hundred counselors at this camp, I realized. And they're all going into the woods tonight.

I waited until I thought all of the counselors had passed by. Then I slowly pulled myself to my feet.

I stared into the woods. But I could see only darkness. Shadows upon shadows.

I ducked back down when I heard two more voices.

Peering through the evergreen branches, I spied Holly and Buddy. They were taking long strides, walking side by side.

I waited till they passed by. Then I jumped up.

Creeping in the deep shadows, I followed them into the woods.

I didn't stop to worry about getting caught. I had to know where the counselors were all going.

Buddy and Holly moved quickly through the woods, pushing tall weeds out of their way, stepping over fallen tree limbs.

To my surprise, a low, white structure came

into view. It appeared to glow dully in the dim light.

The building was built low to the ground. The top was curved.

I squinted at it through the trees. It looks like an igloo, I thought.

What is this strange building? I wondered. Why is it hidden away in the trees?

A dark opening had been cut into the side. Holly ducked into the low entrance. Buddy followed her in.

I waited nearly a minute. Then I stepped up to the opening.

My heart pounded. Such a strange, little building. Round and smooth as ice.

I hesitated. I peered into the entrance, but couldn't see anything inside. I didn't hear any voices.

What should I do? I asked myself.

Should I go in?

Yes.

I took a deep breath and lowered myself into the opening.

23

Three steep steps led down to a dim entryway. A single red light down near the floor gave off the only light.

I stepped into the dark red glow, then stopped and listened.

I could hear voices speaking softly in the next room.

Trailing my hand along the bare, concrete wall, I moved slowly toward the voices. An open doorway came up on my right.

I stopped outside it. Then I slowly, carefully peered in.

I stared into a large, square room. Four torches hanging at the front of the room sent out flickering orange light.

The counselors sat on long wooden benches, facing a low stage. A purple banner hung over the stage. It proclaimed: **ONLY THE BEST.**

It's a little theater, I realized. Some kind of meeting hall.

But why is it hidden away in the woods? And why are the counselors all meeting here to-night?

I didn't have to wait long for my answer.

Buddy stepped on to the small stage. He walked quickly into the flickering orange torchlight. Then he turned to face the audience of counselors.

I crept into the doorway. There were no torches in the back of the hall. It was pitch-black back there.

Walking on tiptoe, I edged my way along the back wall.

The door to a closet of some kind stood open. I ducked into it.

Buddy raised both hands. The counselors instantly stopped talking. They all sat up straight and stared forward at him.

"Time to refresh ourselves," Buddy called out. His voice echoed off the concrete walls.

The counselors sat stiffly. No one moved. No one made a sound.

Buddy pulled a gold coin from his pocket. A King Coin, I figured. It dangled on a long gold chain.

"Time to refresh our minds," Buddy said. "Time to refresh our mission."

He raised the gold coin high. It glowed in the torchlight as he began to swing it. Back and forth. Slowly.

"Clear your minds," he instructed them, speaking softly now. "Clear your minds, as I have cleared mine."

The gleaming gold coin swung slowly back and forth. Back and forth.

"Clear . . . clear . . . clear your minds," Buddy chanted.

He is *hypnotizing* them! I realized.

Buddy is hypnotizing all the counselors. And he's been hypnotized, too!

I took a step forward. I couldn't *believe* what I was seeing and hearing!

"Clear your minds to serve the master!" Buddy declared. "For that is why we are here. To serve the master in all his glory!"

"To serve the master!" the counselors all chanted back together.

Who is the master? I asked myself.

What are they talking about?

Buddy continued chanting out slogans to the crowd of counselors. His eyes were wide. He never blinked.

"We do not think!" he shouted. "We do not feel! We give ourselves up to serve the master!"

And suddenly I had an answer to some of my questions.

Now I knew why Buddy hadn't cried out, hadn't collapsed to the ground when I swung the bat into his chest.

He had hypnotized away all feeling.

He was in some kind of trance. He couldn't feel the bat. He couldn't feel anything.

"Only The Best!" Buddy cried, raising both fists into the air.

"Only The Best!" the counselors all repeated. Their unblinking faces appeared strange, frozen in the flickering orange light.

"Only The Best! Only The Best!"

They all chanted the slogan over and over. Their voices echoed loudly off the walls. Only their mouths moved. Like puppets.

"Only The Best can serve the master!" Buddy shouted.

"Only The Best!" the counselors chanted one more time.

Buddy had been swinging the gold coin over his head during the entire performance. Now he lowered it back into the pocket of his shorts.

The room grew silent.

A heavy silence. An eerie silence.

And then I sneezed.

24

I cupped my hand over my mouth.

Too late.

I sneezed again.

Buddy's mouth opened wide in surprise. He jabbed a finger in the air, pointing at me.

Several counselors jumped to their feet and spun around.

I turned to the door. Could I escape through it before one of them caught me?

No.

No way I could get over there.

My legs were shaking. But I forced myself to move. I backed against the wall.

Why had I stepped so far into the room? Why hadn't I stayed in the safety of the doorway?

"Who's there?" I heard Buddy call. "It's so dark. Who *is* it?"

Good! I thought. He didn't know it was me.

But in seconds, they'd grab me and drag me into the light.

I took another step back. Another.

Darkness fell over me.

I spun around. "Ohh!" I cried out when I saw that I had nearly toppled down a steep stairway.

It wasn't a closet after all.

Black stone steps curved sharply down. Where did they lead?

I couldn't guess. But I had no choice. The steps were my only chance of escape.

I leaned against the wall and plunged down the stairs. My shoes slid on the smooth stones.

I nearly tripped and went sailing head first. But I grabbed the wall and steadied myself as I started to fall.

The stairs curved down. Down.

The air grew hot and sour. I held my breath. The air smelled like sour milk.

A strange, deep moan rumbled up from down below.

I stopped to catch my breath.

Listened hard.

The low moan rolled up the stairway again. A whiff of sour air invaded my nostrils.

I turned back. Was I being followed? Had the counselors seen me escape through the open door?

No. It had been too dark. I didn't hear anyone on the stairs. They weren't following me.

What smelled so bad down below?

I wanted to stop right there. I didn't want to climb down any farther.

But what choice did I have? I knew they'd be searching for me upstairs.

Leaning a hand against the stone wall, I made my way down.

The stairway led into a long, narrow tunnel. I could see pale light at the end of it. Another deep moan rumbled in the distance. The floor shook.

I took a long breath and passed quickly through the tunnel. The air grew hot and damp. My shoes splashed through puddles on the tunnel floor.

Where does this lead? I wondered. Will it take me back outside?

As I neared the end of the tunnel, a whiff of sour air made me choke. I coughed and struggled to stop my stomach from heaving.

What a disgusting smell!

Like decayed meat and rotten eggs. Like garbage left out in the sun for days and days.

I pressed both hands over my mouth. The odor was so strong, I could *taste* it!

I gagged. Once. Twice.

Don't think about the smell! I ordered myself. Think about something else. Think about fresh flowers. Think about sweet-smelling perfume.

Somehow, I calmed my stomach.

Then, pinching two fingers over my nose to

keep the odor out, I stumbled to the end of the tunnel.

I stopped as the tunnel gave way to a huge, brightly lit chamber.

I stopped and stared — at the ugliest, most frightening thing I had ever seen in my life!

25

Squinting into the bright light, I saw dozens of kids with mops, and buckets, and water hoses.

At first, I thought they were cleaning off a giant, purple balloon. Bigger than any balloon in the Thanksgiving Day parade!

But as the water sprayed over it and the mops soaped its sides, the balloon let out a loud groan.

And I realized I wasn't staring at a balloon. It was a creature. And the creature was alive. I was staring at a monster.

I was staring at King Jellyjam.

Not a cute little mascot. But a fat, gross, purple mound of slime, nearly as big as a house. Wearing a gold crown.

Two enormous, watery yellow eyes rolled around in his head. He smacked his fat purple lips and groaned again. Hunks of thick, white goo dripped from his huge, hairy nostrils.

The disgusting odor rolled off his body. Even holding my nose couldn't keep out the sour stench.

He smelled like dead fish, rotting garbage, sour milk, and burning rubber — all at once!

The gold crown bounced on top of his slimy, wet head. His purple stomach heaved, as if an ocean wave was breaking inside him. And he let out a putrid burp that shook the walls.

The kids — dozens of them — worked frantically. They circled the ugly monster. They hosed him down. Scrubbed his body with mops and sponges and brushes.

And as they worked, little round objects rained down on them. *Click. Click. Click.* The little round things clattered to the floor.

Snails!

Snails popping out through King Jellyjam's skin.

I started to gag again when I realized the hideous creature was *sweating snails*!

I staggered back into the tunnel, pressing my hands over my mouth.

How could those kids stand the horrible, sour stench?

Why were they washing him? Why were they working so hard?

I gasped when I recognized some of the kids.

Alicia!

She held a hose with both hands and sprayed King Jellyjam's bulging, heaving stomach. Her red hair was soaked and matted to her forehead. She cried as she worked, bawling loudly.

I saw Jeff. Rubbing a mop up and down on the monster's side.

I opened my mouth to call to Alicia and Jeff. But my breath caught in my throat, and no sound came out.

And then someone came running toward me. Stumbling and staggering. Into the tunnel. Out of the bright light.

Dierdre!

A dripping sponge in one fist. Her streaky blond hair drenched. Her clothes wrinkled and soaked.

"Dierdre!" I managed to choke out.

"Get away from here!" she cried. "Wendy — run!"

"But — but — " I sputtered. "What is happening? Why are you doing this?"

Dierdre uttered a sob. "Only The Best!" she whispered. "Only The Best get to be King Jellyjam's slaves!"

"Huh?" I gaped at her as she trembled in front of me, shivering from the cold water that had drenched her.

"Don't you see?" Dierdre cried. "These are all winners. All six-coin winners. He gets the strongest kids. The best workers."

"But — why?" I demanded.

Snails popped through the creature's skin and clicked as they hit the hard floor. A wave of sour stench blew over us as another rumbling burp escaped his swollen lips.

"Why are you all washing him?" I asked Dierdre.

"He — he has to be washed all the time!" Dierdre exclaimed with a sob. "He has to be kept wet. And he can't stand his own smell. So he gets the strongest kids down here. And makes us wash him night and day."

"But, Dierdre — " I started.

"If we stop washing," she continued. "If we try to take a rest, he — he'll *eat* us!" Her entire body shook. "He — he ate three kids today!"

"No!" I cried, gasping in horror.

"He's so disgusting!" Dierdre wailed. "Those horrible snails popping out of his body . . . that putrid smell."

She grabbed my arm. Her hand was wet and cold. "The counselors are all hypnotized," she whispered. "King Jellyjam has total control over them."

"I — I know," I told her.

"Get out of here! Hurry!" Dierdre pleaded, squeezing my arm. "Get help, Wendy. Please — "

An angry roar made us both jump.

"Oh, no!" Dierdre wailed. "He's seen us! It's too late!"

26

The monster let out another roar.

Dierdre loosened her grip on my arm. We both turned toward him, shaking with fright.

He was bellowing at the ceiling, roaring just to keep everyone terrified. His watery yellow eyes were shut. He hadn't seen Dierdre and me — yet.

"Get help!" Dierdre whispered to me. Then she raised the sponge and ran back to her place at King Jellyjam's side.

I froze for a moment. Froze in horror. In disbelief.

Another rumbling burp jolted me from my thoughts and sent me scurrying through the tunnel. At least now I knew why the camp ground shook so often!

The sour stench followed me through the tunnel and back up the curving, stone steps. I wondered if I could ever get rid of it. I wondered if I could ever breathe freely again.

How can I help those kids? I asked myself. What can I do?

I was too terrified to think clearly.

As I ran through the darkness, I could picture King Jellyjam smacking his gross purple lips. I could see him rolling his yellow eyes. And the ugly black snails squeezing out through his skin.

I felt sick as I reached the top of the stairs. But I knew I didn't have time to worry about myself. I had to save the kids who had been forced to be the monster's slaves. And I had to save the rest of the kids in camp — before they became slaves, too.

I poked my head out of the closet door. The four torches still burned at the front of the small theater. But the room was empty.

Where were the counselors? Out searching for me?

Probably.

Where can I go? I asked myself. I can't spend the night in this closet. I have to breathe some fresh air. I have to go somewhere where I can think.

Carefully, I made my way out of the low igloo. Into the starless night. Hiding behind a wide tree trunk, my eyes searched the woods.

Narrow beams of white light from flashlights darted through the trees, over the ground.

Yes, I told myself. The counselors are searching for me.

I backed up, away from the crisscrossing lights. Trying not to make a sound, I crept between the trees and tall weeds, toward the path that led to the lodge.

Can I get to the dorms and warn everyone? I wondered. Will *anyone* believe me? Will there be counselors guarding the dorms? Waiting for me to show up?

I heard voices on the path. I ducked behind a tree and let two counselors pass. Their flashlights made wide circles over the sloping hill.

As soon as they were out of sight, I darted out from the trees. I ran down the hill. Keeping in deep shadows, I made my way past the swimming pool. Past the tennis courts. All dark and silent now.

A clump of tall hedges beside the track would hide me from all sides, I realized. I ducked behind the hedges, gasping for breath. Dropping to my knees, I crawled into their shelter.

I settled myself on the prickly pine needles beneath the hedges. And peered out. Only darkness now.

I took a deep breath. Then another. Such sweet-smelling air.

I've got to think, I told myself. Got to think . . .

Shouting voices startled me awake.

When had I fallen asleep? Where was I?

I blinked several times. Sat up and stretched.

My body felt stiff. My back ached. Every muscle ached.

I gazed around. Discovered I was still hidden inside the hedges. A gray, cloudy morning. The sun trying to burn through the high clouds.

And the voices?

Cheers?

I raised myself up and peered through the hedges.

The track competition! It had just begun. I saw six boys in shorts and T-shirts, leaning forward as they ran around the track. A crowd of kids and counselors cheering them on.

And in the lead?

Elliot!

"No!" I cried hoarsely, my voice still choked with sleep.

I stepped out from the hedges. Made my way across the grass toward the track.

I knew I had to stop him. I couldn't let him win the race. I couldn't let him win his sixth coin. If he did, they'd make Elliot a slave, too!

He ran hard. He pulled far out in front of the other five.

What could I do? *What?*

In my panic, I remembered our signal.

My two-fingered whistle. My signal for Elliot to take it easy.

He'll hear the whistle and slow down, I told myself.

I raised two fingers to my mouth.

I blew.

No sound came out. My mouth was too dry.

My heart thudded in my chest. I tried again.

No. No whistle.

Elliot turned into the last lap. There was no way to stop him from winning now.

27

No way to stop him — unless I beat him there!

With a desperate cry, I plunged forward and started to run to the track.

My shoes pounded the grass. I kept my eyes on Elliot and the finishing line as I ran. Faster. Faster.

If only I could fly!

Loud cheers rang out as Elliot neared the finish. The other five boys were miles behind!

My shoes thudded onto the asphalt track. My chest felt about to burst. It hurt to breathe. My breath came in loud wheezes.

Faster. Faster.

I heard cries of surprise as I raced over the track. I plunged up behind Elliot, reached out both hands — and tackled him from behind.

We both toppled in a heap, rolling over the hard track, onto the grass. The other boys raced past us to the finish line.

"Wendy, you jerk!" Elliot screamed, jumping to his feet.

"I — can't explain now!" I shouted back, struggling to breathe, struggling to stop the aching in my chest.

I scrambled to my feet and pulled Elliot up. He angrily tried to jerk free. "Why'd you do that, Wendy? Why?"

I saw three counselors running toward me.

"Hurry — !" I ordered my brother. I pulled him away. "Just hurry!"

I think he saw the terror in my eyes. I think he realized that tackling him was a *desperate* act. I think he saw how serious I was.

Elliot stopped protesting and started to run.

I led him over the grass. Up the sloping hill by the lodge. Into the woods.

"Where are we going?" he called breathlessly. "Tell me what's happening!"

"You'll see in a minute!" I called back. "Get ready for a really bad smell!"

"Huh? Wendy — have you totally lost it?"

I didn't answer. I kept running. I led the way into the woods. To the igloo-shaped building.

At the low entrance, I turned back to see if we were being followed. I didn't see anyone.

Elliot followed me into the theater. The torches weren't lit. It was pitch-black inside.

Feeling my way along the back wall, I found

the closet door. I pulled it open and led the way down the curving stairs.

Halfway down, the sour odor floated up to greet us. Elliot cried out and cupped both hands over his nose and mouth. "It stinks!" His cry was muffled by his hands.

"It gets worse," I told him. "Try not to think about it."

We jogged side by side through the long tunnel. I wished I had time to warn Elliot. I wished I could tell him what he was about to see.

But I was desperate to save Dierdre, Alicia, and the others.

Gasping from the smell, I burst into King Jellyjam's brightly lit chamber. Water from a dozen hoses splashed over the monster's purple body. Kids scrubbed furiously as he sighed and groaned.

I saw the startled horror on my brother's face. But I couldn't worry about Elliot now.

"Hit the floor!" I screamed at the top of my lungs, cupping my hands into a megaphone. "EVERYBODY — HIT THE FLOOR! NOW!"

I had a plan.

Would it work?

28

The monster's watery yellow eyes grew wide with surprise. His bloated lips parted. I could see two pink tongues dart and coil inside his mouth.

A few of the kids dropped their hoses and mops and flattened themselves on the floor. Others turned to stare at me.

"Stop washing him!" I cried. "Put down your hoses and brushes! Stop working! And hit the floor!"

Beside me, Elliot uttered gasping sounds. I glimpsed him struggling to keep the sick smell from overpowering him.

King Jellyjam let out a furious roar as the rest of the kids obeyed my instructions. Thick, white slime dripped from his nose. His two tongues flicked out between his purple lips.

"Get flat!" I screamed to the kids. "Stay down!"

And then I saw the monster raise a fat purple arm. With a disgusting groan, he leaned over. His slimy flesh rippled all over his body as he reached out.

Reached out to grab Alicia!

"Help! He's going to eat me!" Alicia shrieked. She started to get up.

"No!" I shrieked. "Stay down! Stay flat!"

With a terrified cry, Alicia dropped back to the floor.

King Jellyjam swung his fat hand down. Fumbled it over her. Tried to lift the little girl up. Tried again. Again.

But I had figured right! The monster's fingers were too big, too clumsy to pick up anyone who lay flat on the floor.

King Jellyjam tilted his head back and uttered a roar of disgust.

I cupped my hand over my nose as the disgusting odor grew more intense. Snails pop-pop-popped out of his skin. Rolled down his slimy body. Bounced noisily onto the floor.

The monster flailed his arms. He leaned down again and struggled to pick up some other kids.

But they pressed themselves flat on the floor. He couldn't lift them.

He roared again, weaker this time. His eyes rolled wildly in his enormous head.

The smell burned my eyes. It swirled around me, surrounded me in its sour stench.

King Jellyjam grabbed for a hose. Couldn't pick

it up. He slammed his hand into a bucket. Struggled frantically to splash water on himself.

I stood trembling. Watching every move.

My plan was working. I knew it would work. It *had* to work!

The stench grew even stronger. I could taste it. I could smell it on my skin.

King Jellyjam flailed both arms. Frantically, he struggled to wash himself.

His roars became groans. His body began to shake.

I gasped as he narrowed his eyes at me. He raised a swollen purple finger and pointed. Accusing me!

He leaned forward. Reached out.

Swiped out his enormous hand.

I couldn't move. I was too stunned.

I shuddered.

His hand slid over me. And before I could struggle, he began to tighten his slimy, stinking fingers around my body.

29

"Ohhh." I uttered a horrified moan.

The fat, wet fingers tightened. Waves of odor rose up around me.

I held my breath. But the smell was *everywhere*.

The fingers wrapped themselves tighter.

The monster began to lift me off the ground. Raise me toward his gaping mouth. The two tongues darted and flicked.

And then the tongues drooped over his purple lips.

The fingers loosened their grip.

I slid free as King Jellyjam groaned and fell forward. Kids rolled quickly out of the way. King Jellyjam toppled over headfirst.

The gold crown bounced away. The monster's body made a loud *splat* as it spread over the floor.

"*Yes!*" I choked out happily. I was still shaking, still trying to forget the slimy feel of his fingers against my skin. "*Yes!*"

My plan had worked perfectly.

The kids stopped washing — and King Jellyjam suffocated from his own foul smell!

"Are you okay?" Elliot asked in a trembling voice.

I nodded. "Yes. I think I'm going to be fine."

Elliot held his nose. "I'll never complain about Dad's garden fertilizer again!" he declared.

Cheering and shouting, the other kids climbed to their feet.

"Thank you!" Alicia cried, wrapping me in a hug. The others rushed forward to thank me, too.

There were lots of hugs, lots of tears as we made our way up to the theater and then out into the woods.

"We are *out* of here!" I cried happily to Elliot.

But we all stopped at the edge of the woods when we saw the counselors.

They all stood in front of us, dozens of them, side by side in their white shirts and shorts. They had formed a line along the path.

And I could see from the hard expressions set on their faces that they had not come to welcome everyone back.

As I stared from face to face, Buddy stepped forward. He gave a signal to the other counselors. "Don't let them get away!" he cried.

30

The counselors stepped forward, moving in a line. Their expressions remained hard and threatening. They kept their arms at their sides.

They moved stiffly. Like robots. In a trance.

They took two more steps.

Then a shrill whistle broke the silence.

"Stop right there! Everybody freeze!" a man's voice boomed.

I heard another shrill whistle.

I turned to see several blue-uniformed police officers running up the hill.

The counselors shook their heads, blinked, uttered soft cries. They made no attempt to run.

"Where *are* we?" I heard Holly mutter.

"What's happening?" another counselor asked.

They all appeared dazed and confused. The police whistles seemed to have broken the trance that held them.

The other kids and I all cheered happily as the officers swarmed up the hill.

"How did you know we needed help?" I called.

"We didn't," an officer replied. "A horrible smell floated into town. We wanted to find out what was causing it. We followed it here!"

I had to laugh. The same smell that had killed the monster had actually saved us kids.

"We didn't know there was a problem at this camp," an officer announced. "We'll contact your parents as soon as we can."

Elliot and I led the way down the hill. We were so eager to see Mom and Dad!

The counselors muttered to themselves, gazing around, trying to figure out what had happened.

I turned to Buddy as Elliot and I walked past him. "Are you feeling better?" I asked.

He narrowed his blue eyes at me and squinted hard. He didn't seem to be able to focus. "Only The Best," he murmured. "Only The Best."

Elliot and I were never so glad to be home!

"What took you so long to find us?" Elliot demanded.

Mom and Dad shook their heads. "The police checked everywhere, trying to find you two," Dad replied. "They called the camp several times. The counselor who answered the phone told the police that you weren't there."

"We were so worried," Mom said, biting her bottom lip. "So terribly worried. When we found the trailer empty, we didn't know what to think!"

"Well, we're home safe and sound now," I replied with a grin.

"Maybe you two would like to go away to a *real* camp next summer," Dad said.

"Uh . . . no way!" Elliot and I answered together.

Two weeks later, we had a surprise visitor.

I opened the door to find Buddy on the front stoop. His blond hair was neatly brushed. He wore chinos, a blue-and-white-striped sportshirt, and a dark blue tie.

"I'm so sorry about what happened at camp," Buddy said.

I was still too shocked at seeing him to reply. I just held on to the door and gaped at him.

"Is Elliot home?" Buddy asked.

"Hi." Elliot stepped up beside me. "Buddy! What's up?"

"I brought you this," Buddy replied. He reached into his pants pocket and pulled out a gold coin.

"It's a King Coin," he told Elliot. "You earned it, remember? You actually won the race."

Elliot reached out for it. Then stopped. His hand hung in midair.

I knew what my brother was thinking. This would be his sixth King Coin.

Should he take it?

Finally, he grabbed it. "Thanks, Buddy," Elliot said.

Buddy said good-bye and gave us a wave. Elliot and I watched him get into a car and drive away. Then we closed the door behind us.

"Are you sure you should've taken that?" I asked Elliot.

"Why not?" he replied. "That purple monster is dead — right? What could happen?"

Five minutes later, we both smelled the horrible odor at the same time.

"Yuck!" Elliot groaned. He swallowed hard. "Wendy, wh-what's that smell?" he stammered.

"I — I don't know," I replied in a shaky voice.

I heard Mom laugh behind us. We turned to see her standing in the doorway to the kitchen. "What's wrong?" she asked. "I have a pot of brussels sprouts boiling on the stove!"

Ghost Camp

GOOSEBUMPS #45

1

"You know I get bus sick, Harry," Alex groaned.

"Alex, give me a break." I shoved my brother against the window. "We're almost there. Don't start thinking about getting bus sick now!"

The bus rumbled over the narrow road. I held onto the seat in front of me. I gazed out the window.

Nothing but pine trees. They whirred past in a blur of green. Sunlight bounced off the dusty glass of the window.

We're almost to Camp Spirit Moon, I thought happily.

I couldn't wait to get off the bus. My brother, Alex, and I were the only passengers. It was kind of creepy.

The driver was hidden in front of a green curtain. I had glimpsed him as Alex and I climbed on board. He had a nice smile, a great suntan, curly blond hair, and a silver earring in one ear.

"Welcome, dudes!" he greeted us.

Once the long bus ride began, we didn't see him or hear from him again. Creepy.

Luckily, Alex and I get along okay. He's a year younger than me. He's eleven. But he's as tall as I am. Some people call us the Altman twins, even though we're not twins.

We both have straight black hair, dark brown eyes, and serious faces. Our parents are always telling us to cheer up — even when we're in really good moods!

"I feel a little bus sick, Harry," Alex complained.

I turned away from the window. Alex suddenly looked very yellow. His chin trembled. A bad sign.

"Alex, pretend you're not on a bus," I told him. "Pretend you're in a car."

"But I get carsick, too," he groaned.

"Forget the car," I said. Bad idea. Alex can get carsick when Mom backs down the driveway!

It's really a bad-news habit of his. His face turns a sick yellow. He starts to shake. And then it gets kind of messy.

"You've got to hold on," I told him. "We'll be at camp soon. And then you'll be fine."

He swallowed hard.

The bus bounced over a deep hole in the road. Alex and I bounced with it.

"I really feel sick," Alex moaned.

"I know!" I cried. "Sing a song. That always

cures you. Sing a song, Alex. Sing it really loud.
No one will hear. We're the only ones on the bus."

Alex loves to sing. He has a beautiful voice.

The music teacher at school says that Alex has
perfect pitch. I'm not sure what that means. But
I know it's a good thing.

Alex is serious about his singing. He's in the
chorus at school. Dad says he's going to find a
voice teacher for Alex this fall.

I stared at my brother as the bus bounced again.
His face was about as yellow as a banana skin.
Not a good sign.

"Go ahead — sing," I urged him.

Alex's chin trembled. He cleared his throat.
Then he began to sing a Beatles song we both
really like.

His voice bounced every time the bus bumped.
But he started to look better as soon as he started
to sing.

Pretty smart idea, Harry, I congratulated myself.

I watched the pine trees whir past in the sunlight and listened to Alex's song. He really does
have an awesome voice.

Am I jealous?

Maybe a little.

But he can't hit a tennis ball the way I can. And
I can beat him in a swim race every time. So it
evens out.

Alex stopped singing. He shook his head unhappily. "I wish Mom and Dad signed me up for the music camp." He sighed.

"Alex, the summer is half over," I reminded him. "How many times do we have to go over this? Mom and Dad waited too long. It was too late."

"I know," Alex said, frowning. "But I wish — "

"Camp Spirit Moon was the only camp we could get into this late in the summer," I said. "Hey, look — !"

I spotted two deer outside the window, a tall one and a little baby one. They were just standing there, staring at the bus as it sped by.

"Yeah. Cool. Deer," Alex muttered. He rolled his eyes.

"Hey — lighten up," I told him. My brother is so moody. Sometimes I just want to shake him. "Camp Spirit Moon may be the coolest camp on earth," I said.

"Or it may be a dump," Alex replied. He picked at some stuffing that poked up from a hole in the bus seat.

"The music camp is so great." He sighed. "They put on *two* musicals each summer. That would have been so awesome!"

"Alex, forget about it," I told him. "Let's enjoy Camp Spirit Moon. We only have a few weeks."

The bus suddenly screeched to a stop.

Startled, I bounced forward, then back. I

turned to the window, expecting to see a camp out there. But all I could see were pine trees. And more pine trees.

"Camp Spirit Moon! Everybody out!" the driver called.

Everybody? It was just Alex and me!

The driver poked his blond head out from behind the curtain. He grinned at us. "How was the ride, dudes?" he asked.

"Great," I replied, stepping into the aisle. Alex didn't say anything.

The driver climbed out. We followed him around to the side of the bus. Bright sunlight made the tall grass sparkle all around us.

He leaned into a compartment and pulled out our bags and sleeping bags. He set everything down on the grass.

"Uh . . . where's the camp?" Alex asked.

I shielded my eyes with my hand and searched around. The narrow road curved through a forest of pine trees as far as I could see.

"Right through there, dudes," the driver said. He pointed to a dirt path that cut through the trees. "It's a real short walk. You can't miss it."

The driver shut the baggage compartment. He climbed back onto the bus. "Have a great time!" he called.

The door shut. The bus roared away.

Alex and I squinted through the bright sunlight at the dirt path. I swung my duffel bag over my shoulder. Then I tucked my sleeping bag under one arm.

"Shouldn't the camp send someone out here to greet us?" Alex asked.

I shrugged. "You heard the driver. He said it's a very short walk."

"But still," Alex argued. "Shouldn't they send a counselor to meet us out here on the road?"

"It's not the first day of camp," I reminded him. "It's the middle of the summer. Stop complaining about everything, Alex. Pick up your stuff, and let's get going. It's hot out here!"

Sometimes I just have to be the big brother and order him around. Otherwise, we won't get anywhere!

He picked up his stuff, and I led the way to the path. Our sneakers crunched over the dry red dirt as we made our way through the trees.

The driver hadn't lied. We'd walked only two or three minutes when we came to a small, grassy clearing. A wooden sign with red painted letters proclaimed CAMP SPIRIT MOON. An arrow pointed to the right.

"See? We're here!" I declared cheerfully.

We followed a short path up a low, sloping hill. Two brown rabbits scurried past, nearly in front of our feet. Red and yellow wildflowers swayed along the side of the hill.

When we reached the top, we could see the camp.

"It looks like a real camp!" I exclaimed.

I could see rows of little white cabins stretching in front of a round blue lake. Several canoes were tied to a wooden dock that stuck out into the lake.

A large stone building stood off to the side. Probably the mess hall or the meeting lodge. A round dirt area near the woods had benches around it. For campfires, I guessed.

"Hey, Harry — they have a baseball diamond *and* a soccer field," Alex said, pointing.

"Excellent!" I cried.

I saw a row of round red-and-white targets at the edge of the trees. "Wow! They have archery, too," I told Alex. I love archery. I'm pretty good at it.

I shifted the heavy duffel bag on my shoulder. We started down the hill to the camp.

We both stopped halfway down the hill. And stared at each other.

"Do you notice anything weird?" Alex asked.

I nodded. "Yeah. I do."

I noticed something *very* weird. Something that made my throat tighten and my stomach suddenly feel heavy with dread.

The camp was empty.

No one there.

2

"Where *is* everyone?" I asked, moving my eyes from cabin to cabin. No one in sight.

I squinted at the lake behind the cabins. Two small, dark birds glided low over the sparkling water. No one swimming there.

I turned to the woods that surrounded the camp. The afternoon sun had begun to lower itself over the pine trees. No sign of any campers in the woods.

"Maybe we're in the wrong place," Alex said softly.

"Huh? Wrong place?" I pointed to the sign. "How can we be in the wrong place? It says Camp Spirit Moon — doesn't it?"

"Maybe they all went on a field trip or something," Alex suggested.

I rolled my eyes. "Don't you know anything about camp?" I snapped. "You don't go on field trips. There's nowhere to go!"

"You don't have to *shout*!" Alex whined.

"Then stop saying such stupid things!" I replied angrily. "We're all alone in the woods in an empty camp. We've got to think clearly."

"Maybe they're all in that big stone building over there," Alex suggested. "Let's go check it out."

I didn't see any signs of life there. Nothing moved. The whole camp was as still as a photograph.

"Yeah. Come on," I told Alex. "We might as well check it out."

We were still about halfway down the hill, following the path through the tangles of pine trees — when a loud cry made us both stop and gasp in surprise.

"Yo! Hey! Wait up!"

A red-haired boy, in white tennis shorts and a white T-shirt, appeared beside us. I guessed he was sixteen or seventeen.

"Hey — where did you come from?" I cried. He really startled me. One second Alex and I were alone. The next second this red-haired guy was standing there, grinning at us.

He pointed to the woods. "I was gathering firewood," he explained. "I lost track of the time."

"Are you a counselor?" I asked.

He wiped sweat off his forehead with the front of his T-shirt. "Yes. My name is Chris. You're Harry and you're Alex — right?"

Alex and I nodded.

"I'm sorry I'm late," Chris apologized. "You weren't worried, were you?"

"Of course not," I replied quickly.

"Harry was a little scared. But I wasn't," Alex said. Sometimes Alex can really be a pain.

"Where is everyone?" I asked Chris. "We didn't see any campers, or counselors, or anyone."

"They all left," Chris replied. He shook his head sadly. When he turned back to Alex and me, I saw the frightened expression on his face.

"The three of us — we're all alone out here," he said in a trembling voice.

3

"Huh? They *left*?" Alex cried shrilly. "But — but — where did they go?"

"We *can't* be all alone!" I cried. "The woods — "

A smile spread over Chris's freckled face. Then he burst out laughing. "Sorry, guys. I can't keep a straight face." He put his arms around our shoulders and led us toward the camp. "I'm just joking."

"Excuse me? That was a joke?" I demanded. I was feeling very confused.

"It's a Camp Spirit Moon joke," Chris explained, still grinning. "We play it on all the new campers. Everyone hides in the woods when the new campers arrive at camp. Then a counselor tells them that the campers all ran away. That they're all alone."

"Ha-ha. Very funny joke," I said sarcastically.

"You always try to *scare* the new campers?" Alex asked.

Chris nodded. "Yeah. It's a Camp Spirit Moon

tradition. We have a lot of great traditions here. You'll see. Tonight at the campfire — "

He stopped when a big black-haired man — also dressed in white — came lumbering across the grass toward us. "Yo!" the man called in a booming, deep voice.

"This is Uncle Marv," Chris whispered. "He runs the camp."

"Yo!" Uncle Marv repeated as he stepped up to us. "Harry, what's up?" He slapped me a high five that nearly knocked me into the trees.

Uncle Marv grinned down at Alex and me. He was so *huge* — he reminded me of a big grizzly bear at the zoo back home.

He had long, greasy black hair that fell wildly over his face. Tiny, round blue eyes — like marbles — under bushy black eyebrows.

His arms bulged out from under his T-shirt. Powerful arms like a wrestler's. His neck was as wide as a tree trunk!

He reached down and shook Alex's hand. I heard a loud *crunch* and saw Alex gasp in pain.

"Good firm handshake, son," Uncle Marv told Alex. He turned to me. "Did Chris play our little 'Alone in the Woods' joke on you guys?" His voice boomed so loud, I wanted to cover my ears.

Does Uncle Marv ever whisper? I wondered.

"Yeah. He fooled us," I confessed. "I really thought there was no one here."

Uncle Marv's tiny blue eyes sparkled. "It's one

of our oldest traditions," he said, grinning. What a grin! It looked to me as if he had at least *six rows* of teeth!

"Before I take you to your cabin, I want to teach you the Camp Spirit Moon greeting," Uncle Marv said. "Chris and I will show it to you."

They stood facing each other.

"Yohhhhhhhh, Spirits!" Uncle Marv bellowed.

"Yohhhhhhhh, Spirits!" Chris boomed back.

Then they gave each other a left-handed salute, placing the hand on the nose, then swinging it straight out in the air.

"That's how Camp Spirit Moon campers greet each other," Uncle Marv told us. He pushed Alex and me together. "You two try it."

I don't know about you, but this kind of thing embarrasses me. I don't like funny greetings and salutes. It makes me feel like a jerk.

But I had just arrived at camp. And I didn't want Uncle Marv to think I was a bad sport. So I stood in front of my brother. "Yohhhhhhhh, Spirits!" I shouted. And I gave Alex a sharp nose salute.

"Yohhhhhhhh, Spirits!" Alex showed a lot more enthusiasm than I did. He likes this kind of thing. He flashed me a sharp salute.

Uncle Marv tossed back his head in a loud, bellowing laugh. "Very good, guys! I think you're both going to be great Camp Spirit Moon campers."

He winked at Chris. "Of course, the campfire tonight is the *real* test."

Chris nodded, grinning.

"The campfire tonight?" I asked. "A test?"

Uncle Marv patted my shoulder. "Don't worry about it, Harry."

Something about the way he said that made me worry a *lot*.

"All new campers come to a Welcoming Campfire," Chris explained. "It's a chance to learn our Camp Spirit Moon traditions."

"Don't tell them any more about it," Uncle Marv told Chris sharply. "We want them to be surprised — don't we?"

"Surprised — ?" I choked out.

Why did I suddenly have such a bad feeling? Why did my throat tighten up again? Why did I have a fluttering feeling in my chest?

"Do we sing camp songs at the Welcoming Campfire?" Alex asked. "I'm really into singing. I take voice lessons back home and — "

"Don't worry. You'll sing. Plenty," Uncle Marv interrupted in a low, almost menacing voice.

I caught the cold look in his tiny eyes — cold as blue ice. And I felt a shiver roll down my back.

He's trying to scare us, I thought. It's all a joke. He's having fun with us. He always tries to scare new campers. It's a Camp Spirit Moon tradition.

"I think you boys will enjoy the campfire tonight," Uncle Marv boomed. "If you survive it!"

He and Chris shared a laugh.

"Catch you later," Chris said. He gave Alex and me a nose salute and vanished into the woods.

"This will be your bunk," Uncle Marv announced. He pulled open the screen door of a tiny white cabin. "Whoa!" He nearly pulled the door off its hinges.

Alex and I dragged our duffels and sleeping bags into the cabin. I saw bunk beds against three of the walls. Narrow wooden chests of drawers. Cubbyholes for storing things.

The walls were white. A light dangling from the ceiling cast a bright glow. The afternoon sun sent orange rays through a small window above one of the bunk beds.

Not bad, I thought.

"That bunk is free," Uncle Marv told us, pointing to the bed against the window. "You can decide who gets the top and who gets the bottom."

"I need the bottom," Alex said quickly. "I toss and turn a lot at night."

"And he sings in his sleep," I told Uncle Marv. "Do you believe it? Alex is so into singing, he doesn't even stop when he's sleeping!"

"You will have to try out for the talent show," Uncle Marv told Alex. And then he repeated in a low voice, "If you survive tonight." He laughed.

Why did he keep saying that?

He's kidding, I reminded myself. Uncle Marv is just *kidding*.

"The boys' cabins are on the left," Uncle Marv told us. "And the girls' cabins are on the right. We all use the lodge and mess hall. It's that big stone building near the woods."

"Should we unpack now?" Alex asked.

Uncle Marv pushed back his greasy black hair. "Yes. Use any cubbies that are empty. You'd better hurry, guys. The rest of the campers will be back from the woods soon with firewood. It will be time for our campfire."

He gave us a "Yohhhhhhhh, Spirits!" and a sharp nose salute.

Then he turned and lumbered away. The screen door slammed hard behind him.

"Fun guy," I muttered.

"He's kind of scary," Alex admitted.

"He's just joking," I said. "All summer camps try to terrify the new campers. I think." I dragged my duffel bag over to the bed.

"But it's all in fun. There's nothing to be scared about, Alex," I told my brother. "Nothing at all."

I tossed my sleeping bag into the corner. Then I started toward the low dresser to see if I could find an empty drawer.

"Whoa — !" I cried out as my sneaker stuck on something.

I peered down.

A blue puddle.

My sneaker had landed in a sticky blue puddle.

"Hey — " I tugged my sneaker out. The blue

liquid was thick. It stuck to the bottom and sides of my shoe.

I glanced around the room.

And saw more blue puddles. A sticky blue puddle in front of every bed.

"What's going *on* here? What *is* this stuff?" I cried.

4

Alex had his bag open and was pulling stuff out and spreading it on the bottom bed. "What's your problem, Harry?" he called without turning around.

"It's some kind of blue slime," I replied. "Check it out. There are puddles all over the floor."

"Big deal," Alex muttered. He turned and glanced at the blue liquid stuck to my sneaker. "It's probably a camp tradition," he joked.

I didn't think it was funny. "Yuck!" I exclaimed. I reached down and poked my finger into the tiny, round puddle.

So cold!

The blue slime felt freezing cold.

Startled, I pulled my hand away. The cold swept up my arm. I shook my hand hard. Then I rubbed it, trying to warm it.

"Weird," I muttered.

Of course, everything got a lot weirder. In a hurry.

"Campfire time!"

Uncle Marv's cry through the screen door shook our cabin.

Alex and I spun to face the door. It had taken us forever to unpack our stuff. To my surprise, the sun had lowered. The sky outside the door was evening gray.

"Everyone is waiting," Uncle Marv announced. A gleeful smile spread over his face. His tiny eyes practically disappeared in the smile. "We all *love* the Welcoming Campfire."

Alex and I followed him outside. I took a deep breath. The air smelled fresh and piney.

"Wow!" Alex cried out.

The campfire was already blazing. Orange and yellow flames leaped up to the gray sky.

We followed Uncle Marv to the round clearing where the fire had been built. And saw the other campers and counselors for the first time.

They sat around the fire, all facing us. Watching us.

"They're all dressed alike!" I exclaimed.

"The camp uniform," Uncle Marv said. "I'll get you and Alex your camp uniforms tonight after the campfire."

As Alex and I neared the circle, the campers and counselors rose to their feet. A deafening "YOHHHHHHHHHH, SPIRITS!" shook the trees. Then a hundred left-handed nose salutes greeted us.

Alex and I returned the greeting.

Chris, the red-haired counselor, appeared beside us. "Welcome, guys," he said. "We're going to roast hot dogs on the fire before the campfire activities begin. So grab a stick and a hot dog, and join in."

The other kids were lining up in front of a long food table. I saw a huge platter of raw hot dogs in the center of the table.

As I hurried to get in line, several kids said hi to me.

"You're in my cabin," a tall boy with curly blond hair said. "It's the best cabin!"

"Cabin number seven rules!" a girl shouted.

"This is an awesome camp," the kid in front of me turned to say. "You're going to have a great time, Harry."

They seemed to be really nice kids. Up ahead, a boy and a girl were having a playful shoving match, trying to knock each other out of line. Other kids began cheering them on.

The fire crackled behind me. The orange light from its flames danced over everyone's white shorts and shirts.

I felt a little weird, not being dressed in white.

I was wearing an olive-green T-shirt and faded denim cutoffs. I wondered if Alex felt weird, too.

I turned and searched for him in the line. He was behind me, talking excitedly to a short blond boy. I felt glad that Alex had found a friend so fast.

Two counselors handed out the hot dogs. I suddenly realized I was *starving*. Mom had packed sandwiches for Alex and me to eat on the bus. But we were too excited and nervous to eat them.

I took the hot dog and turned to the crackling fire. Several kids were already huddled around the fire, poking their hot dogs on long sticks into the flames.

Where do I get a stick? I asked myself, glancing around.

"The sticks are over there," a girl's voice called from behind me — as if she had read my mind.

I turned and saw a girl about my age, dressed in white, of course. She was very pretty, with dark eyes and shiny black hair, pulled back in a ponytail that fell down her back. Her skin was so pale, her dark eyes appeared to glow.

She smiled at me. "New kids never know where to find the sticks," she said. She led the way to a pile of sticks leaning against a tall pine tree. She picked up two of them and handed one to me.

"Your name is Harry, right?" she asked. She had a deep, husky voice for a girl. Like she was whispering all the time.

"Yeah. Harry Altman," I told her.

I suddenly felt very shy. I don't know why. I turned away from her and shoved the hot dog onto the end of the stick.

"My name is Lucy," she said, making her way to the circle of kids around the fire.

I followed her. The kids' faces were all flickering orange and yellow in the firelight. The aroma of roasting hot dogs made me feel even hungrier.

Four girls were huddled together, laughing about something. I saw a boy eating his roasted hot dog right off the stick.

"Gross," Lucy said, making a disgusted face. "Let's go over here."

She led me to the other side of the campfire. Something popped in the fire. It sounded like a firecracker exploding. We both jumped. Lucy laughed.

We sat down on the grass, raised the long sticks, and poked our hot dogs into the flames. The fire was roaring now. I could feel its heat on my face.

"I like mine really black," Lucy said. She turned her stick and pushed it deeper into the flames. "I just love that burnt taste. How about you?"

I opened my mouth to answer her — but my

hot dog fell off the stick. "Oh no!" I cried. I watched it fall into the sizzling, red-hot blanket of flames.

I turned to Lucy. And to my surprise — to my *horror* — she leaned forward.

Stuck her hand deep into the fire.

Grabbed my hot dog from the burning embers and lifted it out.

5

I jumped to my feet. "Your hand!" I shrieked.

Yellow flames leaped over her hand and up her arm.

She handed me the hot dog. "Here," she said calmly.

"But your hand!" I cried again, gaping in horror.

The flames slowly burned low on her skin. She glanced down at her hand. Confused. As if she didn't know why I was in such a panic.

"Oh! Hey — !" she finally cried. Her dark eyes grew wide. "Ow! That was hot!" she exclaimed.

She shook her hand hard. Shook it until the flames went out.

Then she laughed. "At least I rescued your poor hot dog. Hope you like yours burned!"

"But — but — but — " I sputtered. I stared at her hand and arm. The flames had spread all over her skin. But I couldn't see any burns. Not a mark.

"The buns are over there," she said. "You want some potato chips?"

I kept staring at her hand. "Should we find the nurse?" I asked.

She rubbed her arm and wrist. "No. I'm fine. Really." She wiggled her fingers. "See?"

"But the fire — "

"Come on, Harry." She pulled me back to the food table. "It's almost time for the campfire activities to start."

I ran into Alex at the food table. He was still hanging out with the short blond boy.

"I made a friend already," Alex told me. He had a mouthful of potato chips. "His name is Elvis. Do you believe it? Elvis McGraw. He's in our cabin."

"Cool," I muttered. I was still thinking about the flames rolling up and down Lucy's arm.

"This is a great camp," Alex declared. "Elvis and I are going to try out for the talent show *and* the musical."

"Cool," I repeated.

I grabbed a hot dog bun and tossed some potato chips on my plate. Then I searched for Lucy. I saw her talking to a group of girls by the fire.

"Yohhhhhhhh, Spirits!" a deep voice bellowed. No way anyone could mistake that cry. It had to be Uncle Marv.

"Places around the council fire, everyone!" he ordered. "Hurry — places, everyone!"

Holding plates and cans of soda, everyone scurried to form a circle around the fire. The girls all sat together and the boys all sat together. I guessed each cabin had its own place.

Uncle Marv led Alex and me to a spot in the middle.

"Yohhhhhhhh, Spirits!" he cried again, so loud the fire trembled!

Everyone repeated the cry and gave the salute.

"We'll begin by singing our camp song," Uncle Marv announced.

Everyone stood up. Uncle Marv started singing, and everyone joined in.

I tried to sing along. But of course I didn't know the words. Or the tune.

The song kept repeating the line, "We have the spirit — and the spirit has us."

I didn't really understand it. But I thought it was pretty cool.

It was a long song. It had a lot of verses. And it always came back to: "We have the spirit — and the spirit has us."

Alex was singing at the top of his lungs. What a show-off! He didn't know the words, either. But he was faking it. And singing as loud as he could.

Alex is so crazy about his beautiful singing voice and his perfect pitch. He has to show it off whenever he can.

I gazed past my brother. His new friend, Elvis,

had his head tossed back and his mouth wide open. He was singing at the top of his lungs, too.

I think Alex and Elvis were having some kind of contest. Seeing who could sing the leaves off the trees!

The only problem? Elvis was a *terrible* singer!

He had a high, whiny voice. And his notes were all coming out sour.

As my dad would say, "He couldn't carry a tune in a wheelbarrow!"

I wanted to cover my ears. But I was trying to sing along, too.

It wasn't easy with the two of them beside me. Alex sang so loud, I could see the veins in his neck pulsing. Elvis tried to drown him out with his sour, off-key wails.

My face felt hot.

At first, I thought it was the heat from the blazing campfire. But then I realized I was blushing.

I felt so embarrassed by Alex. Showing off like that on his first night at camp.

Uncle Marv wasn't watching. He had wandered over to the girls' side of the fire, singing as he walked.

I slipped back, away from the fire.

I felt too embarrassed to stay there. I'll sneak back into place as soon as the song is over, I decided.

I just couldn't sit there and watch my brother act like a total jerk.

The camp song continued. "We have the spirit — and the spirit has us," everyone sang.

Doesn't the song ever end? I wondered. I backed away, into the trees. It felt a lot cooler as soon as I moved away from the fire.

Even back here, I could hear Alex singing his heart out.

I've got to talk to him, I told myself. I've got to tell him it isn't cool to show off like that.

"Ohh!" I let out a sharp cry as I felt a tap on my shoulder.

Someone grabbed me from behind.

"Hey — !" I spun around to face the trees. Squinted into the darkness.

"Lucy! What are *you* doing back here?" I gasped.

"Help me, Harry," she pleaded in a whisper. "You've got to help me."

6

A chill ran down my back. "Lucy — what's wrong?" I whispered.

She opened her mouth to reply. But Uncle Marv's booming voice interrupted.

"Hey, you two!" the camp director shouted. "Harry! Lucy! No sneaking off into the woods!"

The campers all burst out laughing. I could feel my face turning hot again. I'm one of those kids who blushes very easily. I hate it — but what can I do?

Everyone stared at Lucy and me as we made our way back to the fire. Alex and Elvis were slapping high fives and laughing at us.

Uncle Marv kept his eyes on me as I trudged back. "I'm glad you make friends so easily, Harry," he boomed. And all the campers started laughing at Lucy and me again.

I felt so embarrassed, I wanted to shrivel up and disappear.

But I was also worried about Lucy.

Had she followed me to the woods? Why? Why did she ask me to help her?

I sat down between Lucy and Elvis. "Lucy — what's wrong?" I whispered.

She just shook her head. She didn't look at me.

"Now I'm going to tell the two ghost stories," Uncle Marv announced.

To my surprise, some kids gasped. Everyone suddenly became silent.

The crackling of the fire seemed to get louder. Behind the pop and crack of the darting flames, I heard the steady whisper of wind through the pine trees.

I felt a chill on the back of my neck.

Just a cool breeze, I told myself.

Why did everyone suddenly look so solemn? So frightened?

"The two ghost stories of Camp Spirit Moon have been told from generation to generation," Uncle Marv began. "They are tales that will be told for all time, for as long as dark legends are told."

Across the fire, I saw a couple of kids shiver.

Everyone stared into the fire. Their faces were set. Grim. Frightened.

It's only a ghost story, I told myself. Why is everyone acting so weird?

The campers must have heard these ghost stories already this summer. So why do they look so terrified?

I snickered.

How can *anyone* be afraid of a silly camp ghost story?

I turned to Lucy. "What's up with these kids?" I asked.

She narrowed her dark eyes at me. "Aren't you afraid of ghosts?" she whispered.

"Ghosts?" I snickered again. "Alex and I don't believe in ghosts," I told her. "And ghost stories never scare us. Never!"

She leaned close to me. And whispered in my ear: "You might change your mind — after tonight."

7

The flames flickered, crackling up to the dark, starry sky. Uncle Marv leaned into the orange firelight. His tiny, round eyes sparkled.

The woods suddenly became quiet. Even the wind stopped whispering.

The air felt cold on my back. I scooted closer to the campfire. I saw others move closer, too. No one talked. All eyes were on Uncle Marv's smiling face.

Then, in a low voice, he told the first ghost story. . . .

A group of campers went into the woods for an overnight. They carried tents and sleeping bags. They walked single file along a narrow dirt path that twisted through the trees.

Their counselor's name was John. He led them deeper and deeper into the woods.

Dark clouds floated overhead. When the clouds covered the full moon, the darkness swept over the campers. They walked close together, trying to see the curving path.

Sometimes the clouds moved away, and the moonlight poured down on them. The trees glowed, silvery and cold, like ghosts standing in the forest.

They sang songs at first. But as they moved deeper into the woods, their voices became tiny and shrill, muffled by the trees.

They stopped singing and listened to the scrape of their footsteps and the soft rustlings of night animals scampering through the weeds.

"When are we going to stop and set up camp?" a girl asked John.

"We have to go deeper into the woods," John replied.

They kept walking. The air became colder. The trees bent and shivered around them in a swirling breeze.

"Can we set up camp now, John?" a boy asked.

"No. Deeper," John replied. "Deeper into the forest."

The path ended. The campers had to make their way through the trees, around thorny bushes, over a deep carpet of crackling dead leaves.

Owls hooted overhead. The campers heard the flutter of bat wings. Creatures scratched and slithered around their feet.

"We're really tired, John," a boy complained. "Can we stop and set up the tents?"

"Deeper into the woods," John insisted. "An overnight is no fun unless you are deep, deep in the woods."

So they kept walking. Listening to the low hoots and moans of the night animals. Watching the old trees bend and sway all around them.

Finally they stepped out into a smooth, wide clearing.

"Can we set up camp now, John?" the campers begged.

"Yes," John agreed. "We are deep in the woods now. This is the perfect place."

The campers dropped all the bags and supplies in the middle of the clearing. Silvery moonlight spilled all around them, making the smooth ground shimmer.

They pulled out the tents and started to unfold them.

But a strange sound made them all stop their work.

Ka-thump ka-thump.

"What was that?" a camper cried.

John shook his head. "Probably just the wind."

They went back to the tents. They pushed tent poles into the soft, smooth ground. They started to unfold the tents.

But the strange sound made them stop again.

Ka-thump ka-thump.

A chill of fear swept over the campers.

"What *is* that sound?" they asked.

"Maybe it's some kind of animal," John replied.

Ka-thump ka-thump.

"But it sounds so close!" a boy cried.

"It's coming from right above us," another boy said. "Or maybe beneath us!"

"It's just a noise," John told them. "Don't worry about it."

So they set up the tents. And they spread sleeping bags inside the tents.

Ka-thump ka-thump.

They tried to ignore the sound. But it was so close. So close.

And such a strange — but familiar — sound.

What could it be? the campers wondered. What on earth makes a sound like that?

Ka-thump ka-thump.

The campers couldn't sleep. The noise was too loud, too frightening — too near.

Ka-thump ka-thump.

They burrowed deep into their sleeping bags. They zipped themselves in tight. They covered their ears.

Ka-thump ka-thump.

It didn't help. They couldn't escape the sound.

"John, we can't sleep," they complained.

"I can't sleep, either," John replied.

Ka-thump ka-thump.

"What should we do?" the campers asked the counselor.

John didn't get a chance to answer.

They heard another *Ka-thump ka-thump*.

And then a deep voice growled: *"WHY ARE YOU STANDING ON MY HEART?"*

The ground shook.

The campers suddenly realized what the frightening sound was. And as the ground rose up, they realized — too late — they had camped on the smooth skin of a hideous monster.

"I guess we went *too deep* into the woods!" John cried.

His last words.

Ka-thump ka-thump.

The monster's heartbeat.

And then its huge, hairy head lifted up. Its mouth pulled open. And it swallowed John and the campers without even chewing.

And as they slid down the monster's throat, the sound of the heartbeat grew louder and louder.

Ka-thump ka-thump. Ka-thump ka-thump. Ka-THUMP!

Uncle Marv shouted the last *Ka-thump* at the top of his lungs.

Some campers screamed. Some gazed at Uncle Marv in silence, their faces tight with fear. Beside me, Lucy hugged herself, biting her bottom lip.

Uncle Marv smiled, his face flickering in the dancing orange flames.

Laughing, I turned to Elvis. "That's a funny story!" I exclaimed.

Elvis narrowed his eyes at me. "Huh? Funny?"

"Yeah. It's a very funny story," I repeated.

Elvis stared hard at me. "But it's *true!*" he said softly.

8

I laughed. "Yeah. For sure," I said, rolling my eyes.

I expected Elvis to laugh. But he didn't. The firelight flickered in his pale blue eyes as he stared at me. Then he turned to talk to my brother.

A chill ran down my back. Why was he acting so weird?

Did he really think I'd believe a crazy story like that was true?

I'm twelve years old. I stopped believing in things like the Easter Bunny and the Tooth Fairy a long time ago.

I turned to Lucy. She was still hugging herself, staring intently into the fire.

"Do you believe him?" I asked, motioning to Elvis. "Is he weird or what?"

Lucy stared straight ahead. She seemed so deep in thought, I don't think she heard me.

Finally she raised her head. She blinked. "What?"

"My brother's new friend," I said, pointing to Elvis again. "He said that Uncle Marv's story was true."

Lucy nodded, but didn't reply.

"I thought it was a funny story," I said.

She picked up a twig and tossed it on the fire. I waited for her to say something. But she seemed lost in thought again.

The flames of the campfire had died down. Sparkling red embers and chunks of burning wood spread over the ground. Chris and another counselor carried fresh logs into the meeting circle.

I watched them rebuild the fire. They piled armfuls of twigs and sticks onto the burning embers. When the sticks burst into flames, the two counselors lowered logs over them.

Then they stepped back, and Uncle Marv took his place in front of the fire. He stood with his hands in the pockets of his white shorts. The full moon floated behind his head, making his long black hair shine.

He smiled. "And now I will tell the second traditional story of Camp Spirit Moon," he announced.

Once again, the circle of campers grew silent. I leaned back, trying to get my brother's attention. But Alex was staring across the fire at Uncle Marv.

Alex probably thought the first ghost story was

kind of dumb, I knew. He hates ghost stories even more than I do. He thinks they're silly baby stuff. And so do I.

So what was Elvis's problem?

Was he goofing? Just teasing me? Or was he trying to scare me?

Uncle Marv's booming voice interrupted my thoughts. "This is a story we tell every year at Camp Spirit Moon," he said. "It's the story of the Ghost Camp."

He lowered his deep voice nearly to a whisper, so that we all had to lean closer to hear him. And in hushed tones, he told us the story of the Ghost Camp.

The story takes place at a camp very much like Camp Spirit Moon. On a warm summer night, the campers and counselors met around a blazing council fire.

They roasted hot dogs and toasted marshmallows. They sang the camp songs. One of the counselors played a guitar, and he led them in singing song after song.

When they were tired of singing, the counselors took turns telling ghost stories. And telling the legends of the camp, legends that had been passed on from camper to camper for nearly a hundred years.

The evening grew late. The campfire had died

low. The moon floated high in the sky, a pale full moon.

The camp director stepped forward to end the council meeting.

Suddenly, darkness swept over the circle of campers.

They all looked up — and saw that the moon had been covered by a heavy blanket of black clouds.

And swirls of fog came drifting over the camp. A cold, wet fog. Cloudy gray at first. Then darkening.

And thickening.

Until the fog swept over the camp, billowing like black smoke.

Tumbling and swirling, the cold wet fog rolled over the dying campfire. Rolled over the campers and counselors. Over the cabins and the lake and the trees.

A choking fog, so thick and dark the campers couldn't see each other. Couldn't see the fire. Or the ground. Or the moon in the sky.

The fog lingered for a short while, swirling and tossing, low over the ground. Wet, so wet and silent.

It moved on just as silently.

Like smoke blown away.

The moonlight shone through. The grass sparkled as if a heavy dew had settled.

The fire was out. Dark purple embers sizzled over the ground.

The fog swirled away. Swept over the trees. And vanished.

And the campers sat around the dead campfire. Their eyes blank. Their arms limp at their sides.

Not moving. Not moving. Not moving.

Because they were no longer alive.

The fog had left a ghost camp in its wake.

The campers, the counselors, the camp director — they were all ghosts now.

All spirits. All ghosts. Every last one of them.

They climbed to their feet. And returned to their bunks.

They knew the ghost camp was their home now — *forever!*

With a smile, Uncle Marv stepped back from the fire.

I glanced around the circle. The faces were so solemn. No one smiled or laughed.

It's a pretty good story, I thought. Kind of scary.

But it doesn't have much of an ending.

I turned to see what Alex thought.

And gasped when I saw the terrified expression on his face. "Alex — what?" I cried, my voice cutting through the silence of the circle. "What's wrong?"

He didn't reply. His eyes were raised to the sky. He pointed up.

I gazed up too — and let out a cry of horror.

As a black, swirling fog came sweeping over the camp.

9

My mouth dropped open as I watched the fog roll closer. It darkened the ground as it moved steadily toward us.

Darkened the trees. Darkened the sky.

This is *crazy*, I told myself.

This is *impossible*!

I scooted next to Alex. "It's just a coincidence," I told him.

He didn't seem to hear me. He jumped to his feet. His whole body trembled.

I stood up beside him. "It's only fog," I said, trying to sound calm. "It gets foggy out here in the woods all the time."

"Really?" Alex asked in a tiny voice.

The black smoky fog swirled over us.

"Of course," I replied. "Hey — we don't believe in ghosts, remember? We don't think ghost stories are scary."

"But — but — " Alex stuttered. "Why is everyone staring at us?" he finally choked out.

I turned and squinted through the thick fog.

Alex was right. All around the circle, the other campers had their eyes on Alex and me. Their faces appeared to dim behind the curtain of dark mist.

"I — I don't know why they're watching us," I whispered to my brother.

Fog billowed around us. I shivered. It felt cold against my skin.

"Harry — I don't like this," Alex whispered.

The fog was so thick now, I could barely see him, even though he stood close beside me.

"I know we don't believe in ghosts," Alex said. "But I don't like this. It — it's too creepy."

From the other side of the circle, Uncle Marv's voice broke the silence. "It's a beautiful fog tonight," he said. "Let's all stand up and sing the Camp Spirit Moon song."

Alex and I were already standing. The other campers and counselors obediently climbed to their feet.

Their pale faces shimmered in and out of the fog.

I rubbed my arms. Cold and wet. I dried my face with the front of my T-shirt.

The fog grew even heavier and darker as Uncle Marv began to sing. Everyone joined in. Beside me, Alex began to sing, quieter this time.

Our voices were muffled by the heavy mist. Even Uncle Marv's booming voice sounded smaller and far away.

I tried to sing too. But I didn't know the words. And my own voice came out choked and small.

As I stared into the swirling fog, the voices faded. Everyone sang, but the sound sank into the fog.

The voices vanished. All of them. All except for Alex's.

He seemed to be the only one still singing, his voice pure and soft beside me in the dark mist.

And then Alex stopped singing, too.

The fog swept on. The darkness lifted.

Silvery moonlight washed down on us once again.

Alex and I gazed around in surprise.

No one else remained.

Alex and I were all alone. All alone in front of the dying fire.

10

I blinked. And blinked again.

I don't know what I expected. Did I think they would all appear again?

Alex and I gazed across the circle in stunned silence.

They had vanished with the fog. The campers. The counselors. Uncle Marv.

A chill ran down my back. My skin still felt damp and cold from the heavy mist.

"Wh-where — ?" Alex choked out.

I swallowed hard.

A burned log crumbled into the purple embers. The soft thud startled me.

I jumped.

And then I started to laugh.

Alex squinted at me, studying me. "Harry — ?"

"Don't you see?" I told him. "It's a joke."

He squinted at me harder. "Huh?"

"It's a camp joke," I explained. "It's a joke they probably always play on new campers here."

Alex twisted up his whole face. He was thinking about it. But I don't think he believed me.

"They all ran off into the woods," I told him. "They hid behind the fog and ran away. They were all in on the joke. I'll bet they do it to every new kid."

"But — the fog — " Alex choked out.

"I'll bet the fog was a fake!" I exclaimed. "They probably have some kind of smoke machine. To help them with the joke."

Alex rubbed his chin. I could still see the fear in his eyes.

"They probably do this all the time," I assured him. "Uncle Marv tells the story. Then somebody turns on the smoke machine. The black smoke rolls over the campfire circle. And everyone runs and hides."

Alex turned and stared into the woods. "I don't see anyone hiding back there," he said softly. "I don't see anyone watching us."

"I'll bet they're all back at the cabins," I told him. "I'll bet they're waiting for us. Waiting to see the looks on our faces."

"Waiting to laugh at us for falling for their dumb joke," Alex added.

"Let's go!" I cried. I slapped him on the shoulder. Then I started running across the wet grass toward the row of cabins.

Alex ran close behind. The moon sent a silvery path across the grass in front of us.

Sure enough — as we came near the cabins, the campers all came running out. They were laughing and hooting. Slapping each other high fives.

Enjoying their joke. A joke they play on new campers when the fog rolls in, they told us.

I saw Lucy laughing along with a bunch of girls.

Elvis grabbed Alex and wrestled him playfully to the ground.

Everyone teased us and told us how scared we looked.

"We weren't scared even for a second," I lied. "Alex and I figured it out before the fog cleared."

That made everyone start laughing and cheering all over again.

"*Owoooooooh!*"

Some of the kids cupped their hands around their mouths and made ghost howls.

"*Owoooooooh!*"

That led to more laughing and joking.

I didn't mind the teasing. Not a bit.

I felt so relieved. My heart was still pounding like crazy. And my knees felt kind of weak.

But I felt so happy that it was all a joke.

Every summer camp has its jokes, I told myself. And this is a pretty good one.

But it didn't fool me. Not for long, anyway.

"Lights Out in five minutes," Uncle Marv's booming command stopped the fun. "Lights Out, campers!"

The kids all turned and scurried to their bunks.

I stared down the row of cabins, suddenly confused. Which one was ours?

"This way, Harry," Alex said. He tugged me toward the third cabin down the path. Alex has a better memory than I do for things like that.

Elvis and two other guys were already in the cabin when Alex and I came in. They were getting changed for bed. The other guys introduced themselves. Sam and Joey.

I made my way to the bunk bed and started to undress.

"Owooooooooh!" A ghostly howl made me jump.

I spun around and saw Joey grinning at me.

Everyone laughed. Me, too.

I like camp jokes, I thought. They're mean. But they're kind of fun.

I felt something soft and gooey under my bare foot. Yuck! I glanced down.

And saw that I had stepped in a fresh puddle of blue slime.

The cabin lights went out. But before they did, I saw blue puddles — fresh blue puddles — all over the floor.

The cold blue stuff stuck to the bottom of my foot. I stumbled through the dark cabin and found a towel to wipe it off.

What *are* these blue puddles? I asked myself as I climbed up to my top bunk.

I glimpsed Joey and Sam in the bunk against the wall.

I gasped.

They stared back at me, their eyes shining like flashlights!

What is going on here? I wondered.

What are the sticky blue puddles all over the floor?

And why do Sam and Joey's eyes glow like that in the dark?

I turned my face to the wall. I tried not to think about anything.

I had almost drifted to sleep — when I felt a cold, slimy hand sliding down my arm.

11

"Huh?"

I shot straight up. Still feeling the cold, wet touch on my skin.

I stared at my brother. "Alex — you scared me to death!" I whispered. "What do you want?"

He stood on his mattress, his dark eyes staring at me. "I can't sleep," he moaned.

"Keep trying," I told him sharply. "Why are your hands so cold?"

"I don't know," he replied. "It's cold in here, I guess."

"You'll get used to it," I said. "You always have trouble sleeping in new places."

I yawned. I waited for him to drop back onto the bottom bunk. But he didn't move.

"Harry, you don't believe in ghosts — do you?" he whispered.

"Of course not," I told him. "Don't let a couple of silly stories creep you out."

"Yeah. Right," he agreed. "Good night."

I said good night. He disappeared back to his bed. I heard him tossing around down there. He had a very squeaky mattress.

Poor guy, I thought. That dumb Ghost Camp joke with the fog really messed him up.

He'll be fine in the morning, I decided.

I turned and gazed across the dark cabin toward Joey and Sam's bunk. Were their eyes still glowing so strangely?

No.

Darkness there.

I started to turn away — then stopped.

And stared hard.

"Oh no!" I murmured out loud.

In the dim light, I could see Joey. Stretched out. Asleep.

Floating two feet above his mattress!

12

I scrambled to climb out of bed. My legs tangled in the blanket, and I nearly fell on my head!

"Hey — what's up?" I heard Alex whisper below me.

I ignored him. I swung myself around, and leaped to the floor.

"Ow!" I landed hard, twisting my ankle.

Pain shot up my leg. But I ignored it and hobbled to the door. I remembered the light switch was somewhere over there.

I had to turn on the light.

I had to see for sure that I was right. That Joey slept floating in the air above his bed.

"Harry — what's wrong?" Alex called after me.

"What's up? What time is it?" I heard Elvis groan sleepily from the bunk against the other wall.

I pulled myself across the cabin. My hand fumbled against the wall until I found the light switch.

I pushed it up.

The overhead light flashed on, flooding the tiny cabin in white light.

I raised my eyes to Joey's bunk.

He lifted his head from the pillow and squinted down at me. "Harry — what's your problem?" he asked. He was sprawled on his stomach, on top of his blanket.

Not floating in the air. Not floating.

Resting his head in his hands, yawning and staring down at me.

"Turn off the light!" Sam barked. "If Uncle Marv catches us with the light on . . ."

"But — but — " I sputtered.

"Turn it *off*!" Elvis and Sam both insisted.

I clicked off the light.

"Sorry," I muttered. "I thought I saw something."

I felt like a jerk. Why did I think I saw Joey floating in the air?

I must be as creeped out as Alex, I decided. Now I'm *seeing* things!

I scolded myself and told myself to calm down.

You're just nervous because it's your first day in a new camp, I decided.

I started slowly across the cabin to my bed. Halfway there, I stepped in a cold, sticky puddle of goo.

The next morning, Alex and I found our white Camp Spirit Moon uniforms — white shorts and

T-shirts — waiting for us at the foot of our beds.

Now we won't stand out like sore thumbs, I thought happily.

Now we can really be part of Camp Spirit Moon.

I quickly forgot about my fears from the night before. I couldn't wait for the camp day to get started.

That afternoon, Alex tried out for the Camp Spirit Moon talent show.

I had to be at the soccer field. A bunch of us were supposed to practice putting up tents. We were getting ready for an overnight in the woods.

But I stopped in front of the outdoor stage at the side of the lodge to listen to Alex sing.

A counselor named Veronica, with long, copper-colored hair all the way down her back, was in charge of the tryouts. I leaned against a tree and watched.

A lot of kids were trying out. I saw two guitar players, a boy with a harmonica, a tap dancer, and two baton twirlers.

Veronica played a small upright piano at the front of the stage. She called Alex up and asked him what song he wanted to sing.

He picked a Beatles song he likes. My brother doesn't listen to any new groups. He likes the Beatles and the Beach Boys — all the groups from the sixties.

He's the only eleven-year-old I know who

listens to the oldies station. I feel kind of sorry for him. It's like he was born in the wrong time or something.

Veronica played a few notes on the piano, and Alex started to sing.

What a voice!

The other kids had all been laughing and talking and messing around. But after Alex sang for a few seconds, they got real quiet. They huddled close to the stage and listened.

He really sounded like a pro! I mean, he could probably sing with a band and make a CD.

Even Veronica was amazed. I could see her lips form the word "Wow!" as she played the piano for Alex.

When Alex finished singing, the kids all clapped and cheered. Elvis slapped Alex a high five as he hopped off the small stage.

Veronica called Elvis up next. He told her he wanted to sing an Elvis song, since he was named after Elvis Presley.

He cleared his throat and started to sing a song called "Heartbreak Hotel."

Well . . . it really *was* a heartbreak — because Elvis couldn't sing a single note on key!

Veronica tried to play along with him. But I could see that she was having trouble. I think she probably wanted to stop playing the piano and cover her ears!

Elvis had a high, scratchy voice. And the notes

came out really sour. Sour enough to make your whole face pucker up.

The kids around the stage started grumbling and walking away.

Elvis had his eyes shut. He was so wrapped up in his song, he didn't even see them!

Doesn't he know how bad he is? I wondered. Why does he want to enter a talent show when he sounds like a squealing dog?

Elvis started to repeat the chorus. I decided I had to get away from there before my eardrums popped.

I flashed Alex a thumbs-up and hurried to the soccer field.

Sam, Joey, and a bunch of other kids were already unfolding tents, getting ready for tent-raising practice. Chris, the counselor, was in charge.

He waved to me. "Harry — unroll that tent over there," he instructed. "Let's see how fast you can put it up."

I picked up the tent. It was bundled tightly, no bigger than a backpack. I turned it over in my hands. I'd never set up a tent before. I wasn't even sure how to unwrap it.

Chris saw me puzzling over it and walked over. "It's easy," he said.

He pulled two straps, and the nylon tent started to unfold. "See? Here are the poles. Just stretch it out and prop it up."

He handed the bundle back to me.

"Yeah. Easy," I repeated.

"What's that noise?" Joey asked, looking up from his tent.

I listened hard. "It's Elvis singing," I told them.

The sour notes floated over the soccer field from the stage.

Sam shook his head. "It sounds like an animal caught in a trap," he said.

We all laughed.

Joey and Sam took off their sneakers and went barefoot. I took mine off, too. The warm grass felt good under my feet.

I unfolded the tent and spread it out on the grass. I piled the tent poles to the side.

The sun felt hot on the back of my neck. I slapped a mosquito on my arm.

I heard a shout and glanced up to see Sam and Joey wrestling around. They weren't fighting. They were just goofing.

They both picked up tent poles and started dueling with them, having a wild sword fight. They were laughing and having fun.

But then Sam tripped over a tent.

He lost his balance. Stumbled forward. Fell hard.

I let out a scream as the tent pole went right through his foot.

13

My stomach lurched. I felt sick.

The pointed pole had pierced the top of Sam's foot, nailing his foot to the ground.

Joey gaped, openmouthed, his eyes wide with surprise.

With a gasp, I searched for Chris. I knew Sam needed help.

Where had Chris wandered off to?

"Sam — " I choked out. "I'll get help. I'll — "

But Sam didn't cry out. He didn't react at all. Didn't even grimace.

He calmly reached down with both hands — and pulled the pole from his foot.

I let out a groan. *My* foot ached! In sympathy, I guess.

Sam tossed the pole aside.

I stared down at his foot. No cut. No blood.

It wasn't bleeding!

"Sam!" I cried. "Your foot. It's not bleeding!"

He turned and shrugged. "It missed my toes," he explained.

He dropped onto his knees and started propping up the tent.

I swallowed hard, waiting for my stomach to stop churning.

Missed his toes? I thought. Missed his *toes*?

I saw the pole sink right into his foot!

Or was I seeing things again?

For the rest of the afternoon, I tried not to think about it. I worked on the tent. Once I got it spread out, it was easy to set up.

Chris had us fold and unfold them a few times. Then we had a race to see who could set up a tent the fastest.

I won easily.

Sam said it was beginner's luck.

Chris said I was definitely ready for the overnight.

"Where do we go for the overnight?" I asked.

"Deep, deep into the woods," Chris replied. He winked at Sam and Joey.

I felt a chill, thinking about Uncle Marv's ghost story.

I shook the chill away. *No way* I was going to let myself get scared by a silly camp story.

We had instructional swim at the waterfront. The lake was clear and cold. I'm up to Junior

Lifesaver. Joey and I took turns rescuing each other.

I didn't think about Sam driving the pole through his foot. I forced it from my mind.

After the swim, I returned to the bunk to get changed for dinner. There were fresh puddles of blue goo on the cabin floor.

Nobody made a big deal about them. I didn't want to, either. So I tried hard not to think about them.

Alex came in, very excited. "I'm going to be the first act in the talent show!" he announced. "And Veronica liked my singing so much, she wants me to star in the camp musical."

"Way to go!" I cried. I slapped him a high five. Then I asked, "What about Elvis?"

"He's going to be in the show, too," Alex replied. "He's going to be stage manager."

I pulled on my white Camp Spirit Moon shorts and T-shirt and headed to the mess hall for dinner.

I saw a group of girls come out of the cabins on the other side. I searched for Lucy, but didn't see her.

I was feeling pretty good.

Not thinking about the strange things I'd seen.

Not thinking about the blue puddles of slime. The mysterious black fog.

Not thinking about the ghost story that Elvis said was true.

338

Not thinking about Lucy sticking her hand into the fire and pulling out my flaming hot dog.

Not thinking about Joey floating above his bed. Or Sam jamming a thick pole through his foot.

And not bleeding. Not crying out.

So totally calm about it. As if he couldn't feel it, couldn't feel any pain.

I was starving. Looking forward to dinner. Not thinking about any of these puzzling things.

Feeling really good.

But then Joey ruined my good mood at dinner. And forced all the scary thoughts back into my mind.

The food had just been served. Chicken in some kind of creamy sauce, spinach, and lumpy mashed potatoes.

I didn't care *what* it was. I was so hungry, I could eat anything!

But before I had a chance to eat, Joey called out to me from across the table. "Hey, Harry — look!"

I glanced up from my plate.

He picked up his fork — and jammed it deep into his neck!

14

"Ohhh." I let out a groan. My fork fell from my hand and clattered to the floor.

Joey grinned at me. The fork bobbed up and down, stuck in his neck.

I felt sick. My heart started to pound.

He pulled the fork out with a hard tug. His grin didn't fade. "*You* try it!" he called.

"Joey — stop it!" Elvis cried from across the table.

"Yeah. Give us a break," Sam agreed.

I stared at Joey's neck. No cut. No fork marks. No blood.

"How — how did you *do* that?" I finally stammered.

Joey's grin grew wider. "It's just a trick," he replied.

I glimpsed Alex at the end of the table. Had he seen Joey's "trick"?

Yes. Alex looked green. His mouth had dropped open in horror.

"Here. I'll show you how to do it," Joey offered.

He raised the fork again — but stopped when he saw Uncle Marv leaning over his shoulder.

"What's going on, Joey?" Uncle Marv demanded sharply.

Joey lowered the fork to the table. "Just kidding around," he replied, avoiding the camp director's hard stare.

"Well, let's eat our dinner, guys," Uncle Marv said sternly. "Without kidding around." His stubby fingers tightened over Joey's shoulders. "We have a night soccer game, you know. Boys against the girls."

Uncle Marv loosened his grip on Joey's shoulders and moved on to the next table. A food fight had broken out there. And the mashed potatoes were flying.

Joey mumbled something under his breath. I couldn't hear him over all the noise.

I turned to see how Alex was doing at the end of the table. He had his fork in his hand, but he wasn't eating. He was staring hard at Joey. My brother had a very thoughtful expression on his face.

I knew he was wondering exactly the same thing I was.

What is going on here?

Joey said the fork-stabbing was just a trick. But how did he do it? Why didn't it hurt? Why didn't he bleed?

"Night soccer games are cool!" Elvis declared. He was stuffing chicken into his mouth. The cream sauce ran down his chin.

"Especially boys against the girls," Sam agreed. "We'll *kill* them! They're pitiful."

I glanced at the girls' table across the room. They were chattering noisily. Probably about the soccer game.

I saw Lucy in the shadows near the wall. She didn't seem to be talking to anyone. She had a solemn expression on her face.

Did she keep looking over at me?

I couldn't really tell.

I ate my dinner. But my appetite had disappeared.

"How did you do that fork thing?" I asked Joey.

"I told you. It's just a trick," he replied. He turned away from me to talk to Sam.

Dessert was little squares of red, yellow, and green Jell-O. It was okay. But it needed some whipped cream.

As I was finishing my dessert, I heard some squeals from the front of the big room. I turned toward the cries — and saw a bat swooping wildly back and forth over the mess hall.

Some of the younger kids were screaming. But everyone stayed calm at my table.

The bat fluttered noisily, swooping and diving, darting from one end of the hall to the other.

Uncle Marv followed it with a broom. And after

only a minute or two, he gently pinned the bat to the wall with the straw broom head.

Then he lifted the bat off the wall, carrying it in one hand.

It was so tiny! No bigger than a mouse.

He carried it out the door and let it go.

Everyone cheered.

"That happens all the time," Sam said to me. "It's because there aren't any screens on the mess hall doors."

"And the woods are full of bats," Joey added. "Killer bats that land in your hair and suck the blood out of your head."

Sam laughed. "Yeah. Right." He grinned at me. "That's what happened to Joey. That's why he acts so weird now."

I laughed along with everyone else.

But I wondered if Sam was really joking.

I mean, Joey *did* act weird.

"Soccer field, everyone!" Uncle Marv boomed from the mess hall door. "Check with the sports counselors. Alissa and Mark will set up the teams."

Chairs scraped over the stone floor as everyone jumped up.

I saw Lucy waving to me. But Sam and Joey pulled me away.

Into a cool, cloudy night. The full moon hidden behind low clouds. The grass already wet with a heavy dew.

The counselors divided up the teams. Alex and I were on the second team. That meant we didn't play the first period. Our job was to stand on the sidelines and cheer on the boys' first team.

Two floodlights on tall poles sent down wide triangles of white light over the field. It wasn't really enough light. Long shadows spread over the field.

But that was part of the fun.

Alex stood close beside me as the game began. The girls' team scored a goal in less than a minute.

Girls on the sidelines went wild.

The players on the boys' team stood around, scratching their heads and muttering unhappily.

"Lucky break! Lucky break!" yelled Mark, a tall, lanky boys' counselor. "Go get them, guys!"

The game started up again.

The light from the floodlights appeared to dim. I raised my eyes to the sky — and saw fog rolling in.

Another swirling fog.

Mark jogged past us, looking like a big stork. "Going to be another foggy night," he said to Alex and me. "Night games are more fun in the fog." He shouted instructions to the boys' team.

The thick fog swept over us quickly, driven by a gusting wind.

Alex huddled close to me. I turned and caught his worried expression.

"Did you see what Joey did at dinner?" he asked softly.

I nodded. "He said it was a trick."

Alex thought about that for a moment. "Harry," he said, keeping his eyes on the game. "Don't you think some of these kids are a little weird?"

"Yeah. A little," I replied. I thought about the tent pole going through Sam's foot.

"Something happened at the waterfront," Alex continued. "I can't stop thinking about it."

I watched the game, squinting into the drifting fog. It was getting hard to see the players.

Cheers rang out from the girls' side. I guessed they had scored another goal. Layers of heavy fog blocked my view.

I shivered. "What happened?" I asked my brother.

"I had free swim. After tryouts for the show," he said. "There was my group and a couple of girls' groups. Younger girls, mostly."

"The lake is nice," I commented. "It's so clear and clean. And not too cold."

"Yeah. It's good," Alex agreed. He frowned. "But something strange happened. I mean — I *think* it was strange."

He took a deep breath. I could see he was really upset.

"Let's go, guys! Go, go, go!" Mark shouted to the team.

The glow from the floodlights twisted and bent in the fog, sending strange shadows over the playing field. The fog was so thick now, I had trouble telling the players from the shadows.

"I was floating on top of the water," Alex continued, wrapping his arms around his chest. "Sort of taking it easy. Moving slowly. Stroke . . . stroke . . . very slow.

"It was free swim. So we could do what we wanted. Some of the guys were having a back-floating race near the shore. But I floated out by myself.

"The water was so clear. I put my face in the water, and I stared down to the bottom. And — and I saw something down there."

He swallowed hard.

"What was it? What did you see?" I asked.

"A girl," Alex replied with a shudder. "One of the girls from the younger group. I don't know her name. She has short, curly black hair."

"She was under the water?" I demanded. "You mean, swimming underwater?"

"No." Alex shook his head. "She wasn't swimming. She wasn't moving. She was *way* underwater. I mean, near the bottom of the lake."

"She dove down?" I asked.

Alex shrugged. "I got so scared!" he cried over the shouts of the two teams. "She wasn't moving. I didn't think she was breathing. Her arms floated up and down. And her eyes — her eyes stared out blankly into the water."

"She *drowned*?" I cried.

"That's what I thought," Alex said. "I panicked. I mean, I didn't know what to do. I couldn't think. I *didn't* think. I just dove down."

"You dove down to the bottom to get her?" I asked.

"Yeah. I didn't really know if I was too late. Or if I should get a counselor. Or what," Alex said, shuddering again.

"I swam down. I grabbed her arms. Then I gripped her under the shoulders. I pulled her up. She floated up easily. Like she was weightless or something.

"I pulled her up to the surface. Then I started to drag her to the shore. I was gasping for breath. Mostly from panic, I think. My chest felt about to burst. I was so scared.

"And then I heard laughing. She laughed at me. I was still holding her under the shoulders. She turned — and spit water in my face!"

"Oh, wow!" I gasped. "Wow, Alex. You mean she was okay?"

"Yeah," Alex replied, shaking his head. "She was perfectly okay. She was laughing at me. She thought it was really funny.

"I just stared at her. I couldn't believe it. I mean, she had been way down at the bottom. For a long, long time.

"I let go of her. She floated away from me, still laughing.

"I said, 'How did you do that?' That's what I asked her. I asked, 'How long can you hold your breath?'

"And that made her laugh even harder. 'How long?' I asked.

"And she said, 'A long, long time.'

"And then she swam back to the other girls."

"And what did *you* do?" I asked Alex.

"I had to get out of the water," he replied. "I was shaking all over. I couldn't stop shaking. I — I thought . . ." His voice trailed off.

"At least she was okay," he murmured after a while. "But don't you think that was weird, Harry? And then at dinner, when Joey stuck that fork in his neck — "

"It's weird, Alex," I said softly. "But it may just be jokes."

"Jokes?" he asked. His dark eyes stared hard into mine.

"Kids always play jokes on new campers," I told him. "It's a camp tradition. You know. Terrify the new kids. It's probably just jokes. That's all."

He chewed his bottom lip, thinking about it. Even though he was standing so close to me, the swirling black fog made him appear far away.

I turned back to the game. The boys were moving across the grass toward the goal. Passing the ball, kicking it from player to player. They looked unreal, moving in and out of the swirling shadows.

Jokes, I thought.

All jokes.

I squinted into the fog. And saw something that *couldn't* be a joke.

A boy kicked the ball to the net. The girls' goalie moved to block the shot.

She wasn't fast enough. Or she stumbled.

The ball hit her smack in the forehead.

It made a sickening *thud*.

The ball bounced onto the ground.

And her head bounced beside it.

15

I gasped. And started to run.

Through the thick wisps of black fog.

The swirling, dark mist seemed to float up from the ground and sweep down from the trees. It felt cold and wet on my face as I hurtled toward the girl.

Squinting into the heavy darkness, I could see her sprawled on her stomach on the ground.

And her head . . .

Her head . . .

I bent down and grabbed it. I don't know what I was thinking.

Did I plan to plop it back on her shoulders?

In a total panic, trembling with horror, I bent into the swirling mist — and picked up the head with both hands.

It felt surprisingly hard. *Inhumanly* hard.

I raised it. Raised it close to my face.

And saw that I held a soccer ball.

Not a head. Not a girl's head.

I heard a groan. And gazed down to see the girl climb to her knees. She muttered something under her breath and shook her head.

Her head. The head on her shoulders.

She stood and frowned at me.

I stared at her face, her head. My whole body was still shaking.

"Your head — " I choked out.

She tossed back her straight blond hair. Brushed dirt off her white shorts. Then she reached for the ball.

"Harry — you're not on the first team!" I heard a boy call.

"Get off the field!" another boy demanded.

I turned and saw that the players had all gathered around.

"But I saw her head fall off!" I blurted out.

I instantly regretted it. I *knew* I shouldn't have said it.

Everyone laughed. They tossed back their heads and laughed at me. Someone slapped me on the back.

Their grinning, laughing faces floated all around me. For a moment, it looked to me as if *all* their heads had come off. I was surrounded by laughing heads, bobbing in the eerie, shadowy light from the floodlights.

The girl raised her hands to the sides of her head and tugged up. "See, Harry?" she cried. "See? It's still glued on!"

"Someone better check Harry's head!" a boy cried.

Everyone laughed some more.

A kid came up, grabbed my head, and tugged it.

"Ow!" I screamed.

More wild laughter.

I tossed the goalie the soccer ball. Then I slunk off the field.

What is *wrong* with me? I wondered. Why am I so messed up?

Why do I keep seeing things?

Am I just nervous because I'm in a new camp? Or am I totally losing it?

I trudged to the sidelines and kept walking. I didn't know where I was going. I just knew I wanted to get away from the laughing kids, away from the soccer game.

The heavy fog had settled over the field. I glanced back. I could hear the players' shouts and cheers. But I could barely see them.

I turned and started toward the row of cabins. The dew on the tall grass tickled my legs as I walked.

I was halfway to the cabins when I realized I was being followed.

16

I spun around.

A face floated out of the darkness.

"Alex!" I cried. In all the excitement over the soccer ball and the goalie's head, I had forgotten all about him.

He stepped close to me, so close I could see beads of sweat on his upper lip. "I saw it, too," Alex whispered.

"Huh?" I gasped. I didn't understand. "You saw *what?*"

"The girl's head," Alex said sharply. He turned back to the soccer field. To see if anyone had followed him, I guess.

Then he turned back to me and tugged my T-shirt sleeve. "I saw her head fall off, too. I saw it bounce on the ground."

I swallowed hard. "You did? Really?"

He nodded. "I thought I was going to puke. It — it was so gross."

"But — it didn't fall off!" I cried. "Didn't you

see? When I ran onto the field? I picked up the ball. Not her head."

"But I *saw* it, Harry," Alex insisted. "At first I thought it was just the fog. You know. My eyes playing tricks on me because of the heavy fog. But — "

"It had to be the fog," I replied quietly. "That girl — she was perfectly okay."

"But if we both saw it . . ." Alex started. He stopped and sighed. "This camp — it's so weird."

"That's for sure," I agreed.

Alex shoved his hands into the pockets of his shorts. He shook his head unhappily. "Elvis says the ghost stories are true," he said.

I put my hands on Alex's shoulders. I could feel him trembling. We don't believe in ghosts — remember?" I told him. "Remember?"

He nodded slowly.

The first howl made us both jump.

I turned to the woods. Another eerie howl rose up from the same spot.

Not an animal howl. Not an animal cry at all.

A long, mournful howl. A *human* howl.

"*Owwoooooooooooooooo.*"

Another deeper cry made me gasp.

Alex grabbed my arm. His hand felt cold as ice.

"What *is* that?" he choked out.

I opened my mouth to reply — but another mournful howl interrupted.

"*Owwooooooooooooo.*"

I heard two creatures howling. Maybe three. Maybe more.

The eerie wails floated up from behind the trees. Until it sounded as if the whole woods were howling.

Inhuman howls. *Ghostly* howls.

"We're surrounded, Harry," Alex whispered, still gripping my arm. "Whatever it is, it's got us surrounded."

17

"*Owwooooooo.*"

The frightening wails rose up from the trees.

"Run!" I whispered to Alex. "To the main lodge. Maybe we can find Uncle Marv. Maybe — "

Heading into the fog, we started running toward the lodge.

But the howls followed us. And grew louder.

I heard the heavy thud of footsteps behind us, tromping over the grass.

We can't escape, I realized.

Alex and I both turned at the same time.

And saw Elvis, Sam, and Joey — grinning as they ran after us.

Sam cupped his hands around his mouth and let out a long, ghostly howl. Laughing, Elvis and Joey tossed back their heads and howled too.

"You jerks!" I screamed, swinging a fist at them.

I could feel the blood rushing to my face.

I felt ready to explode. I wanted to punch those three clowns. And kick them. And pound their grinning faces.

"Gotcha!" Elvis cried. "Gotcha!" He turned to Sam and Joey. "Look at them! They're shaking! Oh, wow! They're shaking!"

Sam and Joey laughed gleefully. "Did you think there were wolves in the woods?" Sam asked.

"Or ghosts? Did you think we were ghosts?" Joey demanded.

"Shut up," I replied.

Alex didn't say a word. He lowered his eyes to the ground. I could see that he was as embarrassed as I was.

"Owwoooooo!" Elvis uttered another high-pitched howl. He threw his arms around my brother's waist and wrestled him to the ground.

"Get off! Get off!" Alex cried angrily.

The two of them wrestled around in the wet grass.

"Did I scare you?" Elvis demanded breathlessly. "Admit it, Alex. You thought it was a ghost, right? Right?"

Alex refused to reply. He let out a groan and heaved Elvis off him. They wrestled some more.

Sam and Joey stepped up beside me, grinning. Very pleased with themselves.

"You guys aren't funny," I grumbled. "That was so babyish. Really."

Joey slapped Sam a high five. "Babyish?" he cried. "If it was so babyish, why did you fall for it?"

I opened my mouth to reply — but only a choking sound came out.

Why *did* I fall for it? I asked myself.

Why did I let myself get scared by three guys standing behind trees and making howling sounds?

Normally, I would have laughed at such a dumb joke.

As the five of us walked to the cabin, I thought hard about it. The campers and counselors had all been trying to scare Alex and me since we arrived, I realized. Even Uncle Marv had tried to scare us with his creepy stories.

They must have a tradition of trying to scare new campers at Camp Spirit Moon, I decided.

And it works. It really has scared Alex and me. It has made us tense. Jumpy. Ready to leap out of our skins at the slightest noise.

We stepped into the cabin. I clicked the light on.

Elvis, Sam, and Joey were still laughing, still enjoying their joke.

Alex and I have got to get it together, I decided.

We've got to shove all the stupid stuff about ghosts out of our heads.

We don't believe in ghosts, I told myself.

We don't believe in ghosts. We don't believe in ghosts.

I repeated that sentence over and over. Like a chant.

Alex and I don't believe in ghosts. We've never believed in ghosts.

Never. Never.

One night later . . . after a short hike through the woods — I *did* believe in ghosts!

18

Alex and I took a lot of teasing the next day.

Coming out of the mess hall after breakfast, someone tossed a soccer ball at me and screamed, "My head! Give me back my head!"

We had instructional swim in the morning. Joey and Sam and some of the other guys started howling like ghosts. Everyone thought it was a riot.

I saw Lucy hanging out on the shore with some girls from her cabin. The other girls were laughing at the ghostly howls. Lucy was the only one who didn't laugh.

In fact, she had a solemn expression on her face. A thoughtful expression.

Several times, I caught her staring at me.

She's probably thinking about what a total baby I am, I told myself unhappily. I'll bet she feels sorry for me. Because I acted like such a jerk in front of everyone on the soccer field last night.

After instructional swim, I dried myself off.

Then I wrapped the towel around myself and walked over to Lucy at the little boat dock.

The other girls had wandered away. Lucy stood in her white shorts and T-shirt. She had one foot on a plastic canoe, making it bob up and down in the shallow water.

"Hi," I said. I suddenly realized I didn't know what to say.

"Hi," she replied.

She didn't smile. Her dark eyes locked on mine.

To my surprise, she turned quickly — and ran off.

"Hey — !" I called. I started to run after her. But stopped when my legs got tangled in my towel. "Hey — what's your problem?"

She vanished behind the Arts and Crafts cabin. She never looked back.

I *know* what her problem is, I told myself sadly. She doesn't want to be seen talking to a total nutcase. To someone who thinks that a girl's head can roll off. And who thinks there are howling ghosts lurking in the woods.

I wrapped the towel around me. Sam and Joey and some other guys were staring at me from the shore. I could see by the grins on their faces that they had seen Lucy run away from me.

"Maybe it's your breath!' Joey teased.

They all fell on the ground, howling.

*　　*　　*

After lunch, we had letter-writing time. The counselors made sure we all stayed in our bunks and wrote letters home to our parents.

It was a camp rule that we had to write home once a week. "So your parents won't worry about you," Uncle Marv announced at lunch. "We want them to know that you're having the best summer of your lives — right?"

"Yohhhhhhhhhh, Spirits!" everyone cheered.

I wasn't exactly having the best summer of my life.

In fact, so far, this was one of the worst.

But I decided not to write that in my letter home.

I climbed up to my top bunk and started to think about my letter to Mom and Dad.

Please come and get me, I thought I might write.

Everyone is weird here. Alex and I are both scared out of our wits.

No. No way. I couldn't write that.

I leaned over the side of the mattress and peered down at my brother. He was sitting on his bunk, crouched over his letter. I could see him scribbling away.

"What are you writing?" I called down.

"I'm telling them about the Camp Spirit Moon talent show," he replied. "How I'm going to be the star. And how I'm going to be in the musical next week."

"Nice," I muttered.

I decided I'd tell my parents only good things, too. Why worry them? Why make them think that I'm losing it?

If Alex isn't writing about all the weird things, I won't either, I decided.

I leaned over my sheet of paper and started my letter:

Dear Mom and Dad,

Camp Spirit Moon is a lot more exciting than I ever dreamed. . . .

"Tonight's after-dinner activity is a night hike," Uncle Marv announced.

A cheer shook the wooden rafters of the huge mess hall.

"Where are we going to hike?" someone called out.

Uncle Marv grinned. "Deep, deep into the woods."

Of course, that answer reminded everyone of Uncle Marv's ghost story. Some kids cheered. Others laughed.

Alex and I exchanged glances.

But the hike turned out to be fun. A full moon made the woods glow. We followed a path that curved around the lake.

Everyone seemed in a good mood. We sang the camp song so many times, I almost learned the words!

About halfway around the lake, two deer stepped out onto the path. A mother and her doe.

The little one was so cute. It looked just like Bambi.

The two deer stared at us. They turned up their noses, as if to say, "What are *you* doing in *our* woods?"

Then they calmly loped into the trees.

The path headed through a small, round clearing. As we stepped out of the trees, the ground appeared to light up. The moonlight poured down so brightly, I felt as if I could see every bush, every weed, every blade of grass.

It was really awesome.

I started to relax. Sam, Joey, and I walked along singing, making up funny words to songs we knew. We sang "On Top of Spaghetti" about twenty times — until kids *begged* us to stop singing it!

Why have I been so crazy? I asked myself.

I've made some cool new friends here at Camp Spirit Moon. I'm having an excellent time.

I felt great until we returned to camp.

The black fog had started to roll in. It greeted us, wrapping its cold, wet mists around us, darkening the sky, the ground, the whole camp.

"Lights Out in ten minutes," Uncle Marv announced.

Kids scampered to their cabins.

But two strong arms held me from behind. Held me back.

"Hey — !" I cried out. I felt myself being pulled into the trees.

"Ssshhhhh," someone whispered in my ear.

I spun around to find Lucy holding onto me. "What are you doing?" I whispered. "We have to go to our bunks. We have to get ready for — "

"Ssshhhhhh," she hissed again in my ear.

Her dark eyes searched my face. Were those tears staining her pale cheeks?

Clouds of fog rolled around us.

She loosened her grip on my arms. But her eyes stayed on mine. "Harry, you've got to help me," she whispered.

I swallowed hard. "Lucy, what's wrong?"

"I think you know," she said softly. "It's all true. What you think. It's true."

I didn't understand. I stared back at her with my mouth open.

"We're ghosts, Harry," Lucy told me. "We're all ghosts at this camp."

"But, Lucy — " I started.

"Yes." She nodded sadly. "Yes. Yes. Yes. I'm a ghost too."

19

The trees disappeared behind the fog. The moonlight made Lucy's eyes sparkle like dark jewels. But the light faded from her eyes as the fog covered the moon.

I didn't blink. I didn't move. I suddenly felt as wooden as the trees hiding behind the swirling fog.

"You — you're joking, right?" I stammered. "This is one of those great Camp Spirit Moon jokes?"

But I knew the answer.

I could read the answer in her dark eyes. In her trembling mouth. In her pale, pale skin.

"I'm a ghost," she repeated sadly. "The stories — they're true, Harry."

But I don't believe in ghosts!

That's what I almost blurted out.

But how could I not believe in ghosts when one stood right in front of me, staring into my face?

How could I not believe in Lucy?

"I believe you," I whispered.

She sighed. She turned her face away.

"How did it happen?" I asked.

"Just as Uncle Marv told in the story," she replied. "We were sitting around the campfire. All of us. Just like the other night. The fog rolled in. Such a dark, heavy fog."

She sighed again. Even in the darkness, I could see the tears glistening in her eyes.

"When the fog finally floated away," Lucy continued, "we were all dead. All ghosts. We've been out here ever since. I can't explain any more. I don't know any more."

"But — when did it happen?" I demanded. "How long . . . how long have you been a ghost, Lucy?"

She shrugged. "I don't know. I've lost track of time. There *is* no time when you're a ghost. There's just one day and then the next. And then the next. Forever, I guess."

I stared at her without speaking.

Chill after chill swept down my back. My whole body was shaking. I didn't even try to stop it.

I reached out and grabbed her hand.

I guess I wanted to see if she was real or not. One last test to see if she was pulling a joke.

"Oh!" I dropped her hand as its icy cold shot through me. So cold. Her hand — as cold as the black fog.

"You believe me now?" she asked softly. Once again her dark eyes studied my face.

I nodded. "I — I believe you," I stammered. "I believe you, Lucy."

She didn't reply.

I could still feel the cold of her hand on my fingers.

"The blue puddles," I murmured. "The sticky blue puddles on the cabin floor. Do you know what they are?"

"Yes," she replied. "Those puddles are drops of protoplasm."

"Huh? Protoplasm?"

She nodded. "The puddles are made when we materialize. When we make ourselves visible."

She twisted her face into a sorrowful frown. "It takes so much strength to make ourselves visible. So much energy. The protoplasm puddles are made when we use that energy."

I didn't really understand.

But I knew when I stepped in them that the slimy blue puddles were something strange. Something inhuman.

Traces of ghosts.

"And the things Alex and I saw?" I demanded. "Kids floating above their bunks? Their eyes glowing like spotlights? Kids stabbing themselves and not bleeding? Not crying out in pain?"

"Some of the kids tried to scare you," Lucy confessed. "They only wanted a little fun, Harry.

It isn't fun being a ghost. Believe me. It isn't fun spending day after day after day out here, knowing you aren't real anymore. Knowing you will never grow. Knowing you will never change." She uttered a loud sob from deep in her chest. "Knowing you will never have a *life*!"

"I — I'm so sorry," I stammered.

Her expression changed.

Her eyes narrowed. Her mouth twisted into an unpleasant sneer.

I took a step back, suddenly afraid.

"Help me, Harry," Lucy whispered. "I can't stand it anymore. You've got to help me get away from here."

"Get away?" I cried, taking another step back. "How?"

"You've got to let me possess your mind," Lucy insisted. "You've got to let me take over your body!"

20

"No!" I gasped.

Panic shot through my body. I felt every muscle tense. The blood throbbed at my temples.

"I need to take over your mind, Harry," Lucy repeated, stepping toward me. "Please. Please help me."

"No!" I uttered again.

I wanted to turn and run. But I couldn't move. My legs felt like Jell-O. My whole body shook.

I don't believe in ghosts.

That thought flashed into my mind.

But it wasn't true anymore.

I stood at the edge of the woods — staring at Lucy. Staring at Lucy's ghost.

The fog swept around us.

Again, I tried to run. But my legs wouldn't cooperate.

"Wh-what do you want to do to me?" I finally choked out. "Why do you have to take over my mind?"

"It's my only way to escape," Lucy replied. Her eyes locked on mine. "My only way."

"Why don't you just run away?" I demanded.

She sighed. "If I try to leave the camp by myself, I'll disappear. If I try to leave the others, I'll fade away. I'll join the mist, be part of the fog."

"I — I don't understand," I stammered.

I took a step back. The fog seemed to tighten around me, cold and wet.

Lucy stood two feet in front of me. But I could barely see her. She seemed to shimmer in and out with the fog.

"I need help." Her voice floated softly. I had to struggle to hear her. "The only way a ghost can escape is to take over the mind of a living person."

"But — that's *impossible!*" I screeched.

What a dumb thing to say, I scolded myself. *Seeing a ghost* is impossible! *Everything* happening to me is impossible.

But it's happening.

"I need to possess the mind and body of a living boy or girl," Lucy explained. "I need to take over your body, Harry. I need you to take me away from here."

"No!" I screamed again. "I can't! I mean . . ." My heart thudded so hard, I could barely speak.

"I can't let you take over my mind," I finally managed to say. "If you do that, I won't be *me* anymore."

I started to back away.

I have to get to the cabin, I decided. I have to get Alex. We have to run away from this camp. As fast as we can.

"Don't be scared," Lucy pleaded. She followed me. The fog circled us, as if holding us inside.

"Don't be scared," Lucy said. "As soon as we are far away from here, I'll get out. I'll leave your mind. I'll leave your body. I promise, Harry. As soon as we escape this camp, I'll go away. You will be yourself again. You will be perfectly okay."

I stopped backing up. My whole body trembled. The fog washed its cold mist over me.

"Please, Harry," Lucy begged. "Please. I promise you'll be okay. I promise."

I squinted at her through the rising mists.

Should I do it?

Should I let Lucy take over my mind?

Will she give it back?

Can I believe her?

21

Lucy floated in front of me. Her dark eyes pleaded with me. "Please," she whispered.

"No. I'm sorry. I can't." The words escaped my lips almost before I thought them. "I can't, Lucy."

She shut her eyes. I could see the muscles in her jaw tighten as she gritted her teeth.

"I'm sorry," I repeated, backing up.

"I'm sorry too," she said coldly. Her eyes narrowed. Her lips formed a sneer. "I'm really sorry, Harry. But you don't have a choice. You *have* to help me!"

"No! No way!"

I turned and tried to run.

But something held me back. The fog. It tightened around me.

The thick, wet mist. A choking mist. It drew around me, pushing me, holding me in place.

I tried to scream for help. But the fog muffled my cry.

Lucy vanished behind the black fog.

And then I felt something cold on the top of my head.

My hair tingled.

I reached up with both hands. And felt ice. As if a frost had settled over my hair.

"No!" I screamed. "Lucy — no!"

The cold sank down. My scalp itched. My face froze.

I rubbed my cheeks.

Numb.

Cold and numb.

"Lucy — please!" I begged.

I could feel her — so light, so cold — settling into my body. Sinking into my brain.

I could feel her. And I could feel myself slipping away.

Slipping . . . slipping . . .

As if drifting into a deep sleep.

The cold spreading over me. Sweeping down my neck. Down my chest.

"Nooooo!" I uttered a long howl of protest.

I shut my eyes tight. I knew I had to concentrate. I had to think hard. I had to keep awake. I couldn't let myself fade away.

I couldn't let her take over.

I couldn't let her shove my mind aside. And take control. Take control of my body.

I set my jaw hard. And kept my eyes shut. And tightened every muscle.

No! I thought. *No — you can't do this to me, Lucy!*

You can't take my mind!

You can't take over. You can't — because I won't let you!

The cold settled over me. My skin tingled. I felt numb all over.

And so sleepy . . . so sleepy . . .

22

"Nooooo!" I tossed back my head in another long howl.

If I can keep screaming, I can keep awake, I told myself.

And I can fight Lucy off. I can force her away.

"Noooooooo!" I wailed into the spinning, whirling fog.

"Noooooooo!"

And I felt the cold start to lift.

"Noooooo!"

I squeezed my arms. Rubbed my cheeks. And knew the feeling was returning.

"Nooooooo!"

I suddenly felt lighter. And totally alert.

I did it! I realized. I fought her off!

But how long did I have before she tried to take over again?

I took a deep breath. Then another.

I'm breathing, I told myself. I'm me — and I'm breathing.

I felt stronger now. I lowered my head and darted into the fog.

My sneakers pounded the ground. I made my way to the cabin.

The lights were out. The other guys were in their bunks.

I burst inside and let the screen door slam behind me.

"What's up?" Sam demanded.

I didn't answer him. I ran across the room. Grabbed my brother. Shook him hard. "Come on. Hurry," I ordered.

"Huh?" Alex squinted up at me sleepily.

I didn't say another word. I tossed him his shorts and his sneakers.

I heard the other guys stirring. Joey sat up in his bed. "Harry — where *were* you?" he asked.

"Lights Out was ten minutes ago," Sam said. "You're going to get us all in trouble."

I ignored them. "Alex — hurry!" I whispered.

As soon as he had his sneakers tied, I grabbed his arm and tugged him to the door. "Harry — what's wrong?" he asked.

"Where are you two going?" I heard Joey call.

I pulled Alex outside. The screen door slammed behind us.

"Run!" I cried. "I'll explain later. We have to get out of here — now!"

"But, Harry — "

I pulled Alex over the grass. The fog had parted

enough to let a trail of moonlight slip through. We followed the trail to the woods.

Our sneakers slipped and slid over the wet grass. The only other sound was the chirp of crickets and the rush of wind rattling the pine trees.

After a minute or two, Alex wanted to stop to catch his breath.

"No," I insisted. "Keep moving. They'll follow us. They'll find us."

"Where are we going?" Alex demanded.

"Deep into the woods," I told him. "As far away from that camp as we can."

"But I can't keep running, Harry," Alex cried. "My side hurts and — "

"They're all ghosts!" I blurted out. "Alex — I know you won't believe me — but you've got to try. The kids. The counselors. Uncle Marv. They're all ghosts!"

Alex's expression grew solemn. "I know," he replied in a tiny voice.

"Huh? How do you know?" I demanded.

We squeezed between two tangled tree trunks. Over the chirp of crickets, I could hear the lake washing over the shore just beyond some tall shrubs.

We're still too close to the camp, I told myself.

I pulled my brother in the other direction. Away from the lake. Pushing aside tall weeds and shrubs, we made our own path, deeper into the woods.

"Alex — how do you know?" I repeated.

"Elvis told me," he replied, wiping sweat off his forehead with his arm.

We ducked under a tall thorn bush. Thorns scraped the top of my head. I ignored the pain and kept moving.

"Elvis said the ghost story about the fog was true," Alex continued. "I thought he was just trying to scare me. But then he — he — " Alex's voice trailed off.

We ran into a small clearing. Moonlight made the grass glow like silver. My eyes flashed in one direction, then the other. I couldn't decide which way to run.

I swatted a mosquito off my arm. "What did Elvis do?" I asked Alex.

Alex raked back his dark hair. "He tried to take over my mind," he told me in a trembling voice. "He floated into the fog. And then I started to feel really cold."

Twigs snapped. Dry leaves crackled.

Footsteps?

I shoved Alex back into the trees. Out of the clearing.

We pressed against a wide tree trunk and listened.

Silence now.

"Maybe it was a squirrel, or a chipmunk, or something," Alex whispered.

"Maybe," I replied, listening hard.

Moonlight trickled through the treetops. It made shadows dance over the smooth clearing.

"We have to keep going," I said. "We're still too close to the camp. If the ghosts follow us . . ."

I didn't finish my thought. I didn't want to *think* about what would happen if the ghosts followed us. If they caught us . . .

"Which way is the highway?" Alex asked, his eyes searching the trees. "It isn't too far from the camp — right? If we can get to the highway, someone will give us a ride."

"Good idea," I said. Why hadn't I thought of that?

Now here we were, in the middle of the woods. Far from the highway.

I didn't even know which direction to go to find it.

"It must be back that way," Alex suggested, pointing.

"No. That's the way back to the camp," I argued.

Alex started to reply — but a loud thumping sound made him stop. "Did you hear that?" he whispered.

I did.

And then I heard it again.

A loud thump. Very close by.

"Is it an animal?" I cried softly.

"I — I don't think so," Alex stammered.

KA-THUMP.

Louder.

Is it a ghost? I wondered.

Has one of them found us?

"Quick — this way!" I urged. I grabbed Alex by the wrist and tugged him hard.

We had to get away from whatever was making that frightening noise.

KA-THUMP.

Louder.

"We're going the wrong way!" I cried.

We spun around and darted back into the clearing.

KA-THUMP.

"Which way?" Alex screeched. "Which way? It — it's *everywhere!*"

KA-THUMP.

And then — from somewhere just ahead of us — a deep, booming voice growled, *"WHY ARE YOU STANDING ON MY HEART?"*

23

The ground tumbled and shook.

Alex and I both let out terrified cries.

But our cries were drowned out by a rumbling sound that quickly rose to a roar.

The ground gave way beneath us.

We both raised our arms high as we toppled over.

I landed on my hands and knees. Alex fell onto his back. The ground trembled and tossed, tumbling us around.

"It — it's the *monster*!" Alex shrieked.

But that's impossible! I thought, struggling to my feet.

That monster is from a story. A dumb camp ghost story.

It can't be here in the woods.

I helped pull Alex up. But the ground shook again, and we both fell to our knees.

KA-THUMP. KA-THUMP.

"It can't be real!" I cried. "It can't — "

My mouth dropped open in horror as a huge, hairy head raised itself in front of us. Its eyes glowed as red as flames — round, terrifying, glowing eyes set deep in an ugly, growling face. The creature glared furiously at us.

"Th-the monster!" Alex stuttered.

We were both on our knees, bouncing helplessly on the rolling, tossing ground.

Was it the ground? Or the monster's chest?

The creature opened an enormous cavern of a mouth. It flashed rows and rows of jagged yellow teeth.

Slowly it raised its head, moving closer. Closer.

Opening its hairy jaws wide. Preparing to swallow us as we frantically struggled to scramble away.

"Harry — ! Harry — !" Alex shrieked my name. "It's going to eat us! It's going to swallow us whole!"

And then — in a flash — I had an idea.

24

The huge monster uttered a low growl.

Its hairy mouth opened wider. An enormous purple tongue rolled out. I gasped when I saw that the tongue was covered in prickly burrs.

"Look out, Alex!" I cried.

Too late.

The ground tossed, bouncing us both into the air. We landed with a hard *plop* on the tongue.

"Owwww!" we both howled. It felt like a cactus!

Slowly, the prickly purple tongue began to slide, carrying us into the creature's open mouth.

"We don't believe in monsters," I told Alex.

I had to shout over the bellowing of the hungry monster. The tongue carried us closer. Closer to the rows of jagged yellow teeth.

"We don't believe in this monster!" I shouted. "It is just made up. Part of a story. If we don't believe in it, it can't exist!"

Alex's whole body shook. He hunched over,

making himself into a tight ball. "It looks pretty real!" he choked out.

The tongue dragged us closer. I could smell the monster's foul breath. I could see black stains on its jagged teeth.

"Concentrate," I instructed my brother. "We don't believe in you. We don't believe in you."

Alex and I began chanting those words, over and over.

"We don't believe in you. We don't believe in you."

The purple tongue carried us into the huge mouth. I tried to grab onto the teeth. But they were too slippery.

My hands slid off. I felt myself being swallowed.

Down, down. Into sour darkness.

"We don't believe in you. We don't believe in you." Alex and I continued to chant.

But our voices were muffled as we slid down the creature's throbbing throat.

"Harry — it *swallowed* us!" Alex wailed.

"Keep chanting," I ordered him. "If we don't believe in it, it *can't* exist!"

"We don't believe in you. We don't believe in you."

A glob of thick saliva rolled over me. I gagged as it clung to my clothes, my skin — hot and sticky.

The walls of the throat throbbed harder.

Pulling us down. Down.

Down into the vast, churning gurgling pit of a stomach below.

"Ohhhh." Alex let out a long, defeated sigh. He sank to his knees. He was covered in thick saliva too.

"Keep chanting! It's got to work! It's got to!" I screamed.

"We don't believe in you. We don't believe in you."

"We don't believe in you!"

Alex and I both opened our mouths in screams of horror as we began to fall.

Falling, falling, into the churning stomach below.

25

I shut my eyes.

And waited for the splash. Waited for the crash.
Waited to hit the stomach floor.

Waited.

When I opened my eyes, I was standing on
the ground. Standing next to Alex in a grassy
clearing.

The pine trees shivered in the breeze. A full
moon poked out from behind wispy clouds.

"Hey — !" I cried. I was so happy to hear my
own voice!

So happy to see the sky. The ground. So happy
to breathe the cool air.

Alex started spinning. Spinning like a top.
Laughing at the top of his lungs. "We didn't believe in you!" he cried gleefully. "We didn't believe
in you — and it *worked*!"

We were both so thrilled. So excited that the
monster had vanished.

Poof! A puff of imagination.

I started to spin with Alex. Spinning and laughing.

We stopped when we realized we were no longer alone.

I let out a startled cry when I saw the faces all around us. The pale, pale faces with their glowing eyes.

I recognized Sam, and Joe, and Lucy, and Elvis.

I moved close to Alex as the campers — the ghost campers — moved to form a circle around us. To trap us.

Uncle Marv moved into the circle. His tiny eyes glowed red as fire. He narrowed them angrily at Alex and me.

"Capture them!" he bellowed. "Take them back to camp. No one ever escapes Camp Spirit Moon."

Several counselors moved quickly to grab us.

We couldn't move. There was nowhere to run.

"What are you going to *do* to us?" I cried.

26

"We need living kids," Uncle Marv boomed. "We cannot allow living kids to escape. Unless they carry one of us with them."

"Noooo!" Alex wailed. "You can't take over my mind! You can't! I won't let you!"

The ghostly circle tightened. The ghost campers moved in on us.

I tried to stop my legs from shaking. Tried to slow my pounding heart.

"Alex — we don't believe in *them*, either," I whispered.

He stared at me, confused for a moment. Then he understood.

We made the monster vanish by not believing in him. We could do the same thing to the ghost campers.

"Grab them. Take them back to camp," Uncle Marv ordered the counselors.

"We don't believe in you. We don't believe in you," Alex and I started to chant.

"We don't believe in you. We don't believe in you."

I stared hard at the circle of ghostly faces. Waited for them to disappear.

I chanted with my brother. Chanted faster. Chanted louder.

"We don't believe in you. We don't believe in you."

I shut my eyes. Shut them tight.

And when I opened them . . .

The ghosts were still there.

"You can't make us disappear, Harry," Lucy said, stepping into the circle. She narrowed her eyes at me. They glittered cold and silvery in the moonlight.

"You made the monster disappear because it wasn't real, just one of our ghost tricks," Lucy explained. "We made you see it. But we're all real! All of us! And we're not going to vanish in a puff of smoke."

"We're not going away," Elvis added, moving close to my brother. "In fact, we're coming closer. A lot closer."

"I'm taking over your mind," Lucy whispered to me. "I'm going to escape Camp Spirit Moon inside your mind and body."

"Nooo! No — please!" I protested.

I tried to back up. But the other ghost campers had me trapped.

"You can't! I won't let you!" I shrieked to Lucy, frozen in terror.

"Go away!" Alex shouted at Elvis.

The woods darkened as clouds swept over the moon. All around me, the ghostly eyes appeared to glow brighter.

I saw Elvis reach for my brother.

And then my view was blocked by Lucy. She floated up. Up off the ground. Up over me.

"No! Stay away! Stay away!" I screamed.

But I felt my hair tingle.

I felt the cold sweep down over me. Down, down.

I felt Lucy's ghostly cold. Felt her slipping into my mind.

Slipping down, down. Taking over.

And I knew I couldn't escape.

27

"Get away, Lucy. I'm going first!" I heard a voice shout.

"No way!" a boy cried. "Move out of the way. Uncle Marv said I could be first!"

I could feel the cold sweep up from my body. I opened my eyes — and saw Lucy back on the ground.

Other kids tugged her away.

"Let go of me!" Lucy screamed, pulling back. "I saw him first!"

"Finders keepers!" another ghostly girl cried.

They are fighting over me, I realized.

They pulled Lucy away. And now they're fighting to see who will take over my mind.

"Hey — let go!" I heard a ghostly girl cry. I saw her wrestling with another girl.

The ghosts were wrestling and fighting, shoving and clawing at each other. I saw the counselors join the fight.

"Stop this! Stop this!" Uncle Marv bellowed.

He tried to pull the fighting campers apart.

But they ignored him and continued to battle.

And as I stared in horror, they began to spin around me. Faster and faster. A ghostly circle of wrestling, fighting, shrieking campers. Boys and girls, counselors and Uncle Marv, spinning, struggling, clawing.

Faster. Faster.

They spun around and around my brother and me.

Until they became a swirl of white light.

And then the light faded. Faded to gray smoke.

Wisps of smoke that floated to the trees. And disappeared in the trembling branches.

Alex and I stood watching until the last wisp of smoke had floated away.

"They're gone," I choked out. "They fought each other. And they're gone. All of them."

I shook my head. I drew in a deep breath of fresh air.

My heart was still pounding. My whole body trembled.

But I was okay. Alex and I were okay.

"Are they really gone?" Alex asked in a tiny voice.

"Yes. Let's go," I said, taking his arm. "Come on. Hurry. Let's get away from here."

He followed me eagerly. "Where are we going?"

"To the highway," I said. "We'll walk past the camp to the highway. And we'll stop the first car that comes by. We'll get to a phone. We'll call Mom and Dad."

I slapped my brother on the back. "We'll be okay, Alex!" I cried happily. "We'll be home before you know it!"

We walked quickly through the woods. Pushing bushes and weeds out of the way. Making our own path.

As we made our way to the highway, Alex started to hum a song to himself.

"Whoa!" I cried. "Alex, what's wrong?"

"Huh?" He stared at me in surprise.

I stopped and held him in place. "Sing that again," I ordered.

He sang a little more.

Horrible! His singing was horrible. Totally off-key and sour.

I stared hard into my brother's eyes. "Elvis — is that *you* in there?" I cried.

Elvis's voice came out of Alex's mouth. "Please, Harry, don't tell," he begged. "I *swear* I'll never sing again — if you promise not to tell!"